WHIRLWIND

Also by Michael Grant Jaffe

DANCE REAL SLOW

SKATEAWAY

WHIRLWIND

A Novel

Michael Grant Jaffe

W. W. Norton & Company

New York   London

For information about permission to reproduce selections from this book, write to
Permissions, W. W. Norton & Company, Inc., 500 Fifth Avenue, New York, NY 10110

Manufacturing by The Courier Companies, Inc.
Book design by Blue Shoe Studio
Production manager: Amanda Morrison

Library of Congress Cataloging-in-Publication Data

Jaffe, Michael Grant.
Whirlwind : a novel / Michael Grant Jaffe.— 1st ed.
p. cm.
ISBN 0-393-05961-8
1. Meteorologists–Fiction. 2. North Carolina–Fiction. 3. Divorced
men–Fiction. 4. Celebrities–Fiction. 5. Hurricanes–Fiction.
6. Survival–Fiction. 1. Title.
PS3560.A3134W48 2004
813'.54—dc22
2004012202

W. W. Norton & Company, Inc., 500 Fifth Avenue, New York, N.Y. 10110
www.wwnorton.com

W. W. Norton & Company Ltd., Castle House, 75/76 Wells Street, London W1T 3QT

1 2 3 4 5 6 7 8 9 0

For Scout, for Esmé

Special thanks to Georges Borchardt, Jill Bialosky, my parents, Robert & Margo Roth, Karen, Jennifer, Jane and the rest of my family . . .

Also, a sincere thanks to Peter Henkel, Wally Naymon, Steve Rushin, Sherrie Wyatt, David Bauer, Jim Courier, the Roches, Dave Eggers, Rebecca Kurson, Jeff Cole, DeAnna Heindel, Richard Gildenmeister, Joshua Skoff, Peter Scott, Gabe Miller, Bertis Downs, Mike Mills, Michael Stipe, Peter Buck, Sarah Petit, Alex Greenberg, Jack McCallum, David Sabino, Ed Markey, Mary Neagoy, Alan Richman, Michael Ruhlman, Eric & Scott Hamilton, Hank Hersch, Stefanie Krasnow, Roger Krulak, Albert Kim, Helen Moise, Paul Leslie, Bruce Newman, Greg Kelly and Mark Nolan . . .

WHIRLWIND

Fame, if not double-faced,
        Is double-mouthed,
And with contrary blast
        Proclaims most deeds;
On both his wings, one
        Black, the other white,
Bears greatest names in
        His wild airy flight.
—JOHN MILTON, *Paradise Lost*

First they made me the king then they made me pope
Then they brought the rope.
—BRUCE SPRINGSTEEN, "Local Hero"

THE IMAGE ARRIVES BY SATELLITE. Slow, choppy. A thousand miles of clouds sucked through a cone of frothy darkness. It twirls across the television with the sleepy drawl of a carnival ride. Or a vanilla malted caught in a blender's undertow. I watch from bed. My left eye burns so badly I'm convinced there's something wedged beneath its lid. Maybe a cinder, a fingernail clipping. But I'm too exhausted to rise and check the damn thing in my bathroom—a place with accessories for disengaging foreign objects kissed against eyeballs: tweezers; cotton swabs; an illuminated mirror with enough magnification power to burst blackheads from pores.

Still, I can't move.

I take a deep breath. Then another. The stacked blue dashes on my digital clock read 11:28. Discounting illness, I haven't slept this late since college. I squeeze my eyes closed, hoping to swallow away the discomfort. My clothes from last night lay snarled on a chair across the room. They smell of liquor and bar food.

I roll my right knee over my left leg in a stretch to release the tension on the throbbing disc in my lower back. I hit the TV remote, flipping past the predictable fare of Sunday morning programming—cartoonish preachers, infomercials, football pregame shows—in favor of the Weather Channel. Standing beside a map of the Atlantic Ocean is a guy named Brad Bell, whom I met a couple years ago at a meteorology conference in Syracuse.

"This mass is spinning counterclockwise," he says, waving his hand above an enormous inkblot of clouds in a manner reminiscent of someone applying wax to a car door. "And because the winds near the water's surface have increased to about sixty miles per hour, we can now categorize this as a tropical *storm* instead of a tropical depression."

Brad has mistakenly chosen to wear a gingham-patterned shirt. Whenever he moves, the shirt leaves a staticky blur across the screen.

"But we're going to watch the storm very closely," he says, changing graphics in favor of an isolated close-up of the spidery cloud mass. "If the winds gain a little more speed, about fifteen miles per hour, it will become a hurricane."

And a hurricane is exactly what Brad and our meteorological brethren want—though they'd never admit it. Big-time storms are ratings bonanzas for weathercasters. They're our version of sweeps. Viewers can't seem to get enough weather when the threat of something severe is looming. Everybody wants to be informed—they long to be the first to call their Aunt Wilma or Cousin Nick with reports of impending disaster.

I wander into the kitchen and start a pot of coffee. I pick at the final pair of brown-sugar-frosted Pop-Tarts. I've had a couple of pissy days. Listening to Brad Bell's voice from the bedroom, I consider how quickly I'd swap his drama for my absurdity. On Friday, I delivered my weathercast from Bentleyville's annual Boat Show. Held in an old warehouse on the western edge of town, it took my cameraman, Trip, and me about ninety minutes to set up the shoot. The plan was for me to stand on a scaffolding stretched across a giant swimming pool and, interspersed throughout the broadcast, ask probing questions of Chan the Waterskiing Squirrel's owner. It would have been fine—*fine* for a remote weathercast in coastal North Carolina—had Chan's owner not inadvertently elbowed the joystick guiding the squirrel's tiny speedboat.

In the time it took me to mumble *Oh, shit* on live television, the boat began yanking the squirrel in a series of rapid figure eights. As Chan's owner fiddled madly with buttons and knobs on the remote, centrifugal force overpowered the squirrel. Finally, horrifically, Chan capsized.

"Goodness . . ." I heard one of the anchors moan into my earpiece.

The speedboat continued pulling the submerged squirrel in ever-widening parabolas. With Trip's camera still trained on the ugliness—should we be *showing* this? do people *really* want to watch a furry little animal dragged to its death during the dinner hour?—Chan's owner dove into the water and rescued the rodent. On the scaffolding, he performed a fingertip version of CPR. When the squirrel began to twitch, scrambling waterlogged into his owner's arms, I could hear our anchors applauding in my earpiece.

"Nicely done," said Trip sarcastically, slapping me on the back as we broke for commercial.

The memory still fresh in my head, I move across the

kitchen and pour myself some coffee. On the side of the cup, it reads, WYIP CHANNEL 7: LET US GIVE YOU THE YIPS IN BENTLEYVILLE, N.C. I dribble creamer onto the counter. I scratch a flaky scab of psoriasis on the back of my arm.

My life is filled with countless examples of the weatherman as carnival barker, court jester. Yesterday I honored a commitment made by our station's general manager to send one of WYIP's on-air personalities to the grand opening of the newest Shockley's Audio & Television Superstore. As I waited to be introduced—my duties included engaging in pleasing conversation, scribbling my signature across eight-by-ten photographs depicting a dim-eyed version of me, and drawing raffle cards from a disemboweled TV set—I munched on a greasy chicken leg.

"Name Ebert C. Shockley," said, presumably, Ebert C. Shockley, who approached me with his arm outstretched.

I wiped my fingers clean on the thigh of my trousers.

"A big ol' thank you for comin' down here today," he said, motioning over a Superstore employee wearing a badge that read HELLO, MY NAME IS . . . WALTER on his left breast. "Make sure Mr. Prouty gets one of them new remote control radios before he leaves."

Ebert C. Shockley called it a *ree*-mote control.

He was wearing an expensive-looking dress shirt with cufflinks the size of griddle cakes. His bulky torso was bisected by a yellow necktie and two-inch-wide suspenders embroidered with tiny floating birthday cakes. When he lifted his arm to flick a bud of perspiration from his nose, he nearly concussed himself with a large gold wristwatch.

I spent the next hour sitting behind a collapsible banquet table, drinking discount soda and making small talk with Shockley's customers. Some of them wanted me to personalize a photograph from the optimistically high stack at my side—*To Mary, To Bob Jr., To Slick Rick.* Others felt the need to criticize the station's business practices—"You don't devote enough time to weather," "You devote too *much* time to weather," and, my favorite, "The colors on your set make me want to puke." I had mangled the cap on the Sharpie pen in my right hand.

When it was over, I taped a promotional spot for the six o'clock news standing between a bouquet of metallic helium balloons and Bentleyville High's marching band. During playback, though, we discovered that two trombone players were flipping us the bird. To make it work, we'd have to crop the band out of the picture—thereby defeating the entire purpose of the promo.

Before we departed, Trip and I watched a college football game—Georgia versus Tennessee—on forty simultaneous screens in the superstore's showroom.

THOUGH I'M *TECHNICALLY* NOT WORKING today, Trip and I must retape our failed promotional spots. We drive silently to the station. Since the end of summer a few weeks ago, there has been a steady decline in the town's population. Shop owners have tacked large signs to their windows announcing sales on a surplus of inventory: beach chairs, Styrofoam coolers, sand toys, charcoal grills; great tonnage of food: crates of soda, hot dogs, snack chips, frozen hamburger pucks. We double-park in front of the hardware store so Trip can buy duct tape to seal a loose compartment on his camera. Two doors down, a teenager with spiky orange hair is sweeping the entrance to a record store called Wax Teeth. Not long ago, one of Channel 7's reporters, Lindsey Ott, shot a piece on a series of complaints filed by other neighborhood merchants who were upset with the music being played from a loudspeaker above the store's front door. Someone has covered the offending speaker with a partially transparent red circle with a diagonal line running through it.

In season, khaki-uniformed students are hired by city hall to trawl the sidewalks with long, chalk-tipped sticks and mark the tires of parked cars. When a car sits for more than forty-five minutes—a period of time that's so widely publicized it appears each day in a boxed reminder on the front page of the local newspaper—the students slide a ticket (eight dollars if paid within seventy-two hours; sixteen dollars thereafter) beneath the windshield wipers.

"Do you want anything from Prahti's?" asks Trip, appearing suddenly in the van's window.

Prahti's is near the end of the block. It's a bakery that is regionally famous for making hand-dipped sour cream donuts.

"No, I'm good."

On the wall behind Prahti's cash register is a collection of newspaper and magazine stories, yellowed by sun, praising the "down-home wonders" of the shop's baked goods. Trip climbs into the van with half a donut hanging from his mouth, resembling a badly swollen lip.

"Aren't you supposed to be dieting?"

He shrugs.

I want to encourage him to lose the thirty-pound belly that's presently squished against the lower moon of the steering wheel. But I don't have the strength. We pull from the curb, bearing right as Patterson curls around the post office. At a stoplight, two kids on their bicycles ease to a halt beside the van. One of them motions for me to lower my window.

"Look at the sky," he says, pointing above the craggly treetops. "Those are *rain* clouds."

I nod.

"We had a soccer game last night. Under the lights. You said it wasn't going to rain until today."

I shrug.

"Weather *wonk*," he says.

"Asshole," says the other boy as they ride away, splashing through a puddle for emphasis.

"Gosh, that's sweet," says Trip. "Isn't it wonderful to be appreciated for your work?"

The insults twitter against the sides of my head—one for each ear—like a tight ballcap. We wait for a train to pass through the intersection. As the breeze shifts, we can smell the peppery-sweet stink of smoked sausage coming from a nearby factory that produces canned meats. Suspended above the plant's gate by inch-thick cables screwed into slabs of concrete is a comic-book youth in denim overalls. A spear of hay pokes rigidly from his mouth. The statue, doubtlessly Billy of Billy's Pure Foods, is considered a holy grail for drunken college students headed south on spring break. One year, the state troopers found Billy waist-deep—he's fourteen feet tall—in a swimming pool at a Super 8 Motel in Daytona Beach, Florida. It seemed some fraternity brothers from Virginia, armed with cable cutters and harnesses and pulley-type things, had loaded the figurine onto a boat trailer. They'd hid it beneath a protective tarpaulin for the rest of their drive.

Dangling from a canopy of trees, rogue branches claw against the roof of our van. We're zagging through a gauntlet of similar-looking houses with similarly manicured lawns. We listen to the radio. When I was a teenager growing up in Mill Valley, Michigan, I spent several summers busing tables and making pizzas at a small Italian restaurant. My first responsibility each morning was prepping for the day's meals: I'd grind mozzarella into rubbery threads for topping pizza; I'd stir oregano and other predetermined spices into pots of tomato sauce; I'd make dough, in a huge mixer, and cleave ham-size lumps for large and small pies. The restaurant was managed by a guy named Jimmy Lucci, who once played third base in the Red Sox organization. Before I was employed at the restaurant, I don't remember paying much attention to popular music. But Mr. Lucci would keep a portable radio, on a shelf above the sink, tuned to a local oldies station. Only a few bars into nearly every song he would announce the artist, title and, occasionally, if he was feeling particularly spirited, the date the record was first released. During the final weeks of each of the three summers I worked for Mr. Lucci, he would quiz me.

"Okay, Lucas," he'd say, shaving a wafer of parmesano reggiano from a block and placing it against his tongue. "Who's singing this one?"

Usually he'd begin with something easy: "Get a job" by The Silhouettes or "Shimmy, Shimmy, Ko-Ko-Bop" by Little

Anthony and The Imperials or "Sherry" by Frankie Valli. (Disturbingly, Mr. Lucci believed there had been a music-industry conspiracy against Valli. He was certain various record executives never wanted Valli to become another Sinatra and they sabotaged his career.) Often, in the long hours of a busy Saturday night, Mr. Lucci—and WIXY 1260 AM—would uncork something difficult, like "Close Your Eyes" by The Five Keys. When, invariably, I'd fail to identify either the song or the artist, responding instead with a slow shrug, Mr. Lucci would tap me on the head with a stick of uncut pepperoni and announce the correct answer.

The kinds of things Mr. Lucci taught me are the kinds of things you don't realize you're learning until years later. In college, I once helped a girlfriend's sorority make a pasta dinner for a hundred people. (You can't know how many pounds of spaghetti it takes to feed that many mouths without having had some experience.) And whenever I find myself listening to oldies music, like this morning, I can usually name six or seven songs out of ten. To me, the most impressive thing about the parlor trick is that these aren't songs from my childhood—I'm thirty-six—but songs from my *parents'* childhood.

"You're a freak," says Trip, in the moments after I successfully identify the titles and performers of three consecutive songs. "I promise I'm going to have the radio removed from this van."

A COUPLE HOURS AND A DOZEN PAINFUL takes later, I'm back home. Dressed in blue jeans and a white button-down shirt, I stand before the bathroom mirror. I squirt a transparent, steroid-based solution through my hair and massage it into my itchy scalp. From the bedroom, I can still hear the folks at the Weather Channel prattling on about the possibility of a hurricane. They want action, they want anything other than "partly cloudy" and "pleasant."

Last February, forecasters in Manhattan interrupted prime-time programming with near-constant crawls across the bottoms of TV screens promising a nor'easter would dump a foot of snow by morning. A few stations even abandoned their regular schedules to seesaw from studio to remote—a reporter dressed in puffy parka standing amid the bustle of Times Square interviewing passersby about their preparations for the Storm of the Decade. The networks were hoping to show footage of traditionally skeptical New Yorkers sprinting down the aisles of grocery stores to stockpile essentials. During one shot, a reporter pleaded with a shopper to describe the contents of his basket—imported olives, chèvre, French bread, Tobblerone chocolate and a pricey bottle of merlot. When the reporter arched his eyebrows disapprovingly, the shopper, confused, looked into the lens of the camera and deadpanned, "What storm?"

A fat sheaf of computer printouts rests on my nightstand. They're daily maps prepared by the U.S. Department of Commerce. Virtually every credible weatherperson in America consults them. Forecasting is based on models: What type of conditions have occurred in the past when a particular region has encountered a similar set of weather patterns? There's an old joke: Gather ten meteorologists in a room and they'll give you eleven different predictions.

 · In addition to the printouts, I review our Doppler radar.

Lots of stations have gimmicky names for their radar–Storm Center, Storm Tracker or something equally dramatic. But it's all Doppler: a huge globe perched on a tower that reads weather systems through the frequency of radio waves. Instead of "seeing" weather fronts as plodding, nebulous blobs, like the old style of radar, Doppler is so sensitive it can detect wind patterns and raindrops and, sometimes, even clouds of insects.

The prep work is boring, predictable. And however absurd the (botched) location shoot with Chan the Waterskiing Squirrel or the promos from Shockley's Superstore, they still serve to rattle the monotony of the day.

I use a small, battery-powered device to trim my nose hair. Its business end is roughly the size and shape of a cigarette filter, with shrunken blades that rotate beneath a protective lip. Usually, when I'm finished, the sink looks as though it's coated in fine steel dust.

The anchors at the station where I work, WYIP Channel 7, have a team of writers and researchers to help them prepare their broadcast scripts. But my material is all self-generated. I rarely use notes. Mostly, the weather graphics serve as my guide. There isn't much I say that's not eventually displayed across our viewers' TVs. Occasionally I'll announce a low temperature in Duluth or explain the counterclockwise whirl of a warm front. There are times when the remote control fails to advance the screen and I'm forced to improvise. About a year ago, a photograph of a local high school cheerleading squad fleetingly replaced a satellite shot of the toothy North Carolina coast. It was so unexpected that I fell agonizingly silent. "Well, Lucas," said anchorwoman Wendy after seven seconds had elapsed. "It appears you've got one of ours. The Kennedy High School cheerleaders!" (The girls had finished third at a national competition in Little Rock, Arkansas.)

In the parking lot beside my condominium complex, I touch thumbs to the small of my back and lean skyward. It's a stretching exercise I learned from an orthopedic surgeon. The stiffness in my spine is caused by two herniated discs. The pain is sharpest when I'm seated for long periods of time. On airplanes, behind my desk.

I've made concessions to the discomfort: firm mattress, proper-posture chair, a regimen of stretching exercises on those mornings when I can hardly move. There's even the car I'm preparing to board. Instead of something sporty and sleek, I drive a full-size Crown Victoria, provided gratis by a local dealership in exchange for my image and voice on a series of shlocky commercials. I'm told the Crown Vic is the vehicle of choice by more of the country's police departments than any other automobile. This explains why I get so many dirty looks when I'm driving my car, white with beige interior, along the roadways of North Carolina. I'm often greeted by illuminated brake lights as the Crown Vic appears in the rearview mirrors of fellow motorists. Once I pass, though, the drivers can be counted on to crunch their faces in disgust, as if they're saying, "You're not a *cop*."

Backing out of the lot, I hear several halftime football scores on the radio. I'm reminded of our station's lunkhead sportscaster, Wes Nichols. Or, more precisely, I'm thinking about an incident from last Thursday between Nichols's son and me. Walking from the restroom to my desk, I was considering two neckties—draped across my arm like a waiter's towel—for the night's newscast. As with nearly every sizable television station, we have a chroma-key wall: the electric-blue scrim I stand beside, and on which graphics—local and national maps, swirling three-dimensional weather models—are superimposed during the forecast.

I almost missed the boy completely. He was near the chroma-key, gripping the remote control I press to convert from screen to screen. With each squeeze of his thumb, he peered at the monitor to his right and made spastic swings with his arms. He was poking fun at me (or *someone*) as he offered his own rendition of the day's weather.

"Lots of rain," he said, opening and closing the fingers of his free hand as though he were casting a spell. "Just look out your windows, dummies."

When the image on the wall switched to a colorful map of the nation with conveniently stenciled borders, the boy raised his arms in front of his body. He resembled a blind person feeling for furniture. Soon he made grunting noises. He was pretending to be some kind of monster, stomping recklessly through the cookie-cutter collection of states. "Aaaargh!" he shouted, planting a haymaker, appropriately enough, into hay capital Kansas. As he clawed down through Idaho and Nevada, one of his fingernails caught against the fabric of the blue scrim and opened a small tear.

"Hey!" I said, startling the boy.

He stood motionless as I made my way to his side, crouching to better examine the damage.

"Shit," I said.

As I attempted to push the scored material together with my fingertips, the boy took a step backward. From behind my left shoulder came a familiar voice.

"What's up?"

It was Wes Nichols.

"You having a problem there, Prouty?"

He likes to call everyone by their last name, as though the whole world is part of some ridiculous sports team.

"He ripped a hole in the chroma-key," I said, turning to the boy.

"This is my son." Nichols wrestled the boy into a playful headlock. "Christ, Prouty. I hope you're not scaring the kid."

Wes Nichols is a jackass.

"He's five years old," he added.

In fact, *everyone* thinks he's a jackass.

The boy buried his face behind his father's leg.

"This has to be repaired in time for the ten o'clock news."

Nichols moved his nose to within a few inches of the fissure.

"Here's an idea, Prouty. Pretend it's the goddam Grand Canyon."

"Look at the monitor," I said, gesturing. "Do you even know what state he ripped? It's Nevada. The Grand Canyon's *not* in Nevada; it's in Arizona."

"Puh-*leeze*," said Nichols, leading his son by the shoulder. "Do you think anyone gives a hooey?" They walked down the hall in tandem and I heard Nichols say, "Nevada, Arizona; Arizona, Nevada. Sheesh."

Even the memory of our exchange causes me to grow

agitated. Weaving the Crown Vic through Bentleyville's back-streets, I squeeze the steering wheel with a febrile strength. I do feel badly about frightening his son. I drive for a few minutes and pull to the curb in a familiar place. The playground to my right is crowded with children. There are swings and monkey bars and cement animal sculptures for them to climb. Every couple weeks I'll pack a lunch and sit behind the wheel of my car, watching the kids through my windshield.

When one of the older boys scales the face of the slide—arms aloft like he's riding a surfboard—a smaller boy tries to follow. But he loses his footing after a couple steps, skidding backward as though he's on an escalator that has suddenly changed directions.

A few months ago while I was nibbling on a sandwich, a patrol car stopped beside me in this very spot. I was told a "concerned citizen" had called in a complaint.

I admitted I didn't have a legitimate reason to be here—other than I enjoyed watching the children play. Reaching into my wallet, I removed a tiny hospital bracelet that had been pressed flat over time. "This is probably more information than you want," I said. Trying to keep emotion from creeping into my voice, I explained how during my brief, unsuccessful marriage my wife gave birth to a dead baby—a stillborn, they call it—and if the infant had lived she would now be about the same age as the little boy in the purple and orange shirt sitting in the sandbox.

Since that awful morning, there have been a great many occurences in my life for which I don't have a suitable explanation—failed friendships, disturbing behavioral patterns, curious career moves. Witness my applying for (and accepting) the meteorologist post at Channel 7 because Bentleyville's located in a part of the country where I didn't know a soul.

The officer removed his hat, running his fingers through his crooked bangs. He sighed, started to speak and sighed again. Clearly, the police academy hadn't taught him how to handle brooding, pathetic almost-fathers.

"Next time I'll try to be more discreet," I said.

"Right," he responded, shifting his car into gear. "That would be good."

Before returning the bracelet to my wallet, I placed it on the dashboard. My eyes shifted focus from the small laminated strap to the playground and back to the strap. The quick change in perspective reminded me of a film director's cheap camera stunt: the blurred hospital band of a dead newborn in the foreground, a group of rollicking children in the distance.

We had a girl's name, my ex-wife and I. After winnowing down our list of prospects—Lily, Frances, Isabella—we chose Flynn for the simple reason that we both liked the way it sounded.

"Flynn," I said after the squad car had rounded the corner. "*Flynn . . .*"

There are moments when I find myself talking to her aloud—or maybe to the *idea* of her. The other night I was fixing myself some rye toast. While removing the toaster from the cupboard beneath the sink, I accidentally bumped the darkness-setting lever. "I know, Flynny. I know, I know," I said. A few minutes had passed and I was scraping the burnt part with a knife. "I don't like it this black either."

It was oddly comforting to imagine she was standing beside me in the kitchen, her small hand gripping the loose fabric of my sweatpants. Perhaps if I had a roommate—or if I were still married—I wouldn't think about her so much. But mostly I'm alone. And there's nobody around to tell me it's disturbing to speak her name.

FIVE TRAFFIC LIGHTS SEPARATE CHANNEL 7 from a windowless, two-room restaurant called Stinky's. The place got its name when the prospective owner was walking the grounds with his young son, who, during the tour, exclaimed, "It stinks like sweaty shoes in here." In truth, the sour smell came from the rotting carcasses of two raccoons wedged between the plasterboard walls.

Most days it takes a few minutes for my eyes to grow adjusted to the darkness. I often read the morning newspaper beneath the sepia glow of a neon beer sign or seated beside the jukebox. Suspended inexplicably above the lavatory's twin urinals is a disco-era mirror ball. Once when I was drunk, I walked directly into the twirling globe and cut myself near the eyebrow.

Stinky's is divided into a bar area where people mostly eat and a dining area where they mostly drink. There's a small, dimly lit stage against the restaurant's rear wall; it's compact and out of place, not unlike old high school gymnasiums that doubled as bandbox auditoriums. During luncheon and evening hours, women dance topless for soiled, finger-mashed dollar bills customers press into their G-strings and garter belts. Several times I have been asked by WYIP's station manager, Glenn Fisk, to discontinue patronizing Stinky's. He calls it a "girly club"; he says it's not a suitable environment for a TV personality.

"Like it or not," said Fisk the last time we discussed the matter, "you're a local celebrity. People don't want their weatherman—the very same weatherman they watch over mouthfuls of broiled chicken, mashed potatoes and lima beans—to hang out with naked hoochie-girls. It's not very, er, appetizing."

Appetizing? Two nights earlier, the six o'clock broadcast led with a story about a pair of high school students who were arrested for dismembering neighborhood cats. (The video even showed the animals' husked skins nailed to a tree trunk, suggesting diseased irregularities in the bark.) As a sales associate appeared in Fisk's doorway, I was able to leave before we'd reached any closure.

I find a seat near the end of Stinky's bar. To my right is a bowl of salted nuts, another filled with pretzels shaped like swollen knuckles. Today she's wearing a boy's white undershirt and chinos cinched beneath a wide belt. She says revealing outfits make for better tips. Some afternoons I bring gifts: a ballcap with the station's call letters emblazoned across its crown; tulips pulled from a neighbor's garden; bejeweled vending-machine rings stored in transparent plastic eggs. I visit her a few times a week, helping to make her shifts pass a little quicker. There are evenings when I've had too many drinks and my tongue, bloated and dry, refuses to be lashed to the confines of good taste. I have boldly suggested our relationship move in a more "satisfying" direction.

"Satisfying for whom?" I recall her saying once, arms crossed defiantly against her chest.

She's tending bar while studying for her master's degree in social studies at the University of North Carolina at Wilmington. Though she refuses to dance topless, she doesn't pass judgment on those who do. We first met, Kiki and I, in one of the aisles at Delaney's Drugstore. I remember I had a terrible headache; I was skimming as much information from the labels of analgesic tablets as my bruised brain would process. It was summer and I was wearing flip-flops. With every footstep came a smacking sound that caused my head to erupt.

I finally selected a box, the words *maximum strength* written in yellow cursive below the brand's name. Suddenly I became aware of a liquid, warm and slow, against my left foot. In the fraction of time it took me to look down—my thoughts shifting briefly from medication and migraines—I guessed it might have been a ruptured bottle of mouthwash or, thicker still, maybe cough syrup. But it was reddish and dark, the color—if not the consistency—of a cabernet.

I hadn't realized the woman, Kiki, was standing so near. She was wearing an orange T-shirt and frayed denim shorts; her lemon-colored hair was gathered in a loose ponytail. Wrapped around her right hand was a plaid dish towel. It occurred to me that the smeared streaks of paint, on the towel, on her forearms and cheek, were actually blood.

"Are you okay?" I asked.

She nodded.

As I turned to leave, she dropped a packet of gauze.

"Oh, Jesus," she said. "I'm bleeding all *over* you."

Instinctively, I shook my foot, as though shooing a wasp. Enough blood had pooled across the bridge of my toes that the movement caused it to spray a row of dermatology creams. She crouched down and tried to wipe my instep with the soggy towel. This, of course, only spread the mess.

"I'm sorry," she said, now using the hem of her shirt to clean the blood. "I'm *so* sorry."

I told her it was fine. I grabbed a jar of medicated hemorrhoid wipes and began swabbing the stains—on her wrist, her elbow, her delicate chin. Then I took an Ace bandage and wrapped the wound: a three-inch incision across the palm of her hand. It wasn't until I was sitting beside her in the emergency room, a resident suturing closed the cut, that I learned her name. They used a ridiculously large needle to numb the skin. I was more afraid than Kiki. Though she wouldn't tell them what had happened, she offered, almost nonsensically, that only fighter pilots and "fat redneck sheriffs" should be permitted to wear aviator sunglasses.

They had given her a small sealed envelope with eight pills for the pain. On the drive back to her car, she took three. We stopped at the Dairy Freeze for vanilla milkshakes. We sat on a wooden picnic table, our feet resting on the attached bench. Kiki held her bandaged hand to her face and examined it, turning her arm to the left, then right. Below her ear was a crescent of dried blood that resembled a birthmark.

She started to ramble—about work, school, her sister "the oboe player." When she lay back, staring into the pale blue sky, I wondered whether the medication was making her woozy.

"Those clouds seem fake," she said. "Some painter's notion of the way clouds are *supposed* to look."

"They're called Cumulonimbus."

"Get a load of you." She licked a dribble of milkshake from the corner of her mouth. "Bring on the game shows."

Because she didn't own a television—still doesn't—she had no idea I was a weatherman. She started to talk about a guy with whom she'd gone to high school. It wasn't until she was a few minutes into her story that I realized she intended to make a point. He owned a garage near one of the marinas. Apparently, Kiki had bumped into him a couple weeks earlier at a Bentleyville Bandits baseball game. (The team's a minor-league affiliate for the Atlanta Braves.) During the course of their conversation, he offered to inspect the transmission on her pickup truck; it was making a dull grinding noise whenever she shifted into reverse.

That morning, she was driving down Seaside Lane when she spied the garage—J&R's Service, she remembered—cresting in her windshield. Moments later she was standing in one of the car ports, her thumbs hitched to her belt.

"You look nice," said Jake Esler, the guy from high school.

She thanked him and made her way to the driver's-side door. She asked if she should pop the hood. When he nodded, she leaned across the seat and started fiddling for the small lever beneath the dashboard. Almost instantly she could feel him move closer, his thigh suddenly grazing her arched buttocks.

"What are you doing?" she said.

His mouth spread into a narrow, toothless smile.

"You look *nice*," he said again.

She watched his fingers break apart and begin the painful swim toward her waist.

"It happened so quickly," she told me, her body engulfed by nervous energy. She was sawing the straw of her milkshake through its lid, plastic against squeaky plastic. "I just . . ."

She'd slapped him on the side of his head—a *wallop*—and she could feel the burn in the soft skin of her hand. There was blood across the tip of his nose, above his left eyebrow. But the blood was hers: she had split her palm on the hinge of his sunglasses. The blood was trickling down her fingers to the greasy floor. Her heart was still racing when she climbed back into her truck. They didn't say anything else, neither of them.

After we returned to the drugstore, I followed her to Stinky's. I was trying to decide whether her truck was swerving—she'd had all those painkillers—or it was only my imagination. I thought she should take the night off; I suggested she go home and draw herself a hot bath. It seemed as though we'd known each other for a while, for longer than an afternoon.

She shuffled through the gravel parking lot and leaned on my door, her elbows propped against the open window. A glorious constellation of freckles curled across the bridge of her nose like spattered paint. It was nearly dusk and the faded sunlight made it possible to see the fine hairs along her neck. The pink flesh of her upper lip seemed drawn into a tiny summit, as though she were holding a lozenge against her teeth. For a moment, I considered kissing her. But then I remembered what happened to the guy who made a similar move only a few hours earlier. We thanked each other—why was *I* thanking *her?*—and I promised to come see her later in the week.

THE WALL BEHIND KIKI IS MOSTLY MIRROR. There are three levels of hard spirits and, reflected in the slender necks of green and amber glass, a huge trophy presented to Stinky's for sponsoring the winning softball team in a recreational-league tournament. One of the ballcaps I'd given to her is perched across the great mouth of the cup; the elephant-ear handles are barely visible beneath more of my tokens: a dried daisy chain, a tie-dyed bandanna, a deck of picture postcards.

"See what happens when I watch you?" she says, gesturing toward one of the televisions suspended above the bar.

I know what's coming next.

"Seriously," she says, placing a glass of sweet tea on a square napkin. "What were you hoping to accomplish with that waterskiing squirrel?"

"The weather can be pretty boring." I run the back of my hand down the glass, gathering cold perspiration against my knuckles. "We've got four broadcasts a day—and they're usually all the same. You should be *thanking* me for trying to make it more interesting."

"Then allow me to speak for the general public: We are not *entertained* by horrific accidents involving sweet fuzzy animals and powerboats."

I lean back on my stool and nod.

The cook doesn't arrive for another couple hours, so Kiki

fixes me a plate of fried eggs, grits and rye toast. Down the bar a pair of dancers are flipping through a stack of compact discs. One is wearing a red satin robe, the other's dressed in a blousy football jersey—number sixty-six—and running shorts. Between them is a soft-pack of Camels and a disposable lighter. After a few minutes, a skinny guy with a wispy goatee comes to collect their musical selections for tonight.

Maybe that's the answer, I think. Music and a slight, inoffensive voice-over to team with meteorological graphics. During each newscast I'd feature somebody else—Mendelssohn or Miles or even doo-wop—as the day's graphically enhanced weather report scrolls across the screen. I wouldn't even need to be present. It's going to rain; or not. A few words about, say, something relevent to a particular season: pollen count in spring, snowfall totals in winter. Then the baton is passed to Wes Nichols in sports or one of the caffeinated anchors itching to recount some asinine human-interest story about a woman sharing her house with a hundred cats—a story that will permit viewers to fall asleep with smiles on their faces.

Not long ago, I was returning from the grocery store to my car when a man nearly threatened me with physical violence. He claimed his daughter's birthday party was ruined by a rainstorm; he said his family had spent the week watching my broadcasts and not once did I suggest the possibility of precipitation. I apologized. I explained the suddenness—even to trained professionals—of certain weather fronts. "I was caught by surprise too," I said, sounding slow and pitiful.

It could have been worse. At a meteorological conference in Charlotte, I heard a story about a guy from Oklahoma whose lawn was ruined by an extended drought. He was so upset that he fired three rounds of buckshot into the moving car of his local weatherman. Though the forecaster was only grazed on the side of his head, he wore white gauze and tape, like a turban, during his telecasts in the days that followed. Alarmingly, it seemed to both colleagues and viewers that when he included a longer-than-normal pause in his cadence—maybe while trying to find his place on the weather map—he might be suffering the residual effects of trauma.

Nobody holds newscasters responsible for the substance of a disturbing story. Or sportscasters in contempt when the home team gets hammered. But let the weatherman screw up the arrival of a cold front and viewers want to hang him by his nuts. When it rains on the Fourth of July, I avoid public places. Conversely, an uninterrupted string of gorgeous days means I can expect slaps on the back in restaurants or supermarkets. Even the idiot anchors with whom I work will lead into my forecast for a holiday weekend by suggesting, half seriously, that they're planning a backyard barbecue and I'd better not "rain on [their] parade."

I swear to God, it takes the heart right out of me.

THIS WAS ME IN THIRD GRADE: a shy, doughy kid who would stare for hours out his bedroom window watching storm fronts race across the distant plains of Lake Erie. For my eleventh birthday, my mother bought me a junior-scientist meteorology kit that included a thermometer, which I tacked to our front porch, and devices for measuring the barometric pressure and wind speed. Often, I would take photographs of cloud formations with a Polaroid camera and pin the snapshots to a corkboard beside my desk, labeling each with the appropriate caption: Cirrus, Stratus, Altostratus. I even had a road map of the United States, ironed flat, taped to the back of my door, over which I would practice moving isobars cut by hand from colored construction paper.

As a child, I had the presence to know that my fascination with meteorology was not normal in relation to the types of things that interested others my own age. One afternoon, while playing second base in a neighborhood ball game, I was struck in the chest by a line drive because my attention was focused on a storm climbing the horizon instead of the batter.

Before leaving for school each morning, I would sit in

our breakfast nook opposite my sister and eat cold cereal while watching television through the doorway to the living room. I developed an odd connection to one of the local weathercasters, a train-wreck of a man named Dick Weaver. It's difficult to imagine there existed a less telegenic person in all of broadcasting. His dark hair was wedged into a severe crewcut. He wore loud, plaid sportcoats and neckties with knots the size of a grown man's fist. Curiously, his voice, a steady barritone, would occasionally dip so low that it became nearly impossible to decipher what he was saying. Dick Weaver gave hope to the hopeless: If he could find employment in a world that placed a premium on straight teeth and blemish-free skin, so even could *you*.

More importantly, he took meteorology seriously in a time when most TV weathercasters were only using their posts as springboards to "real" journalistic endeavors. Unlike present-day weathermen, Weaver had little interest in serving as straight man for the news anchors. He didn't engage in witty banter. His was a sobering business, *goddammit!* People *relied* on him.

While I was still in junior high school, I remember an afternoon when my mother was sorting old clothes for the Salvation Army. It was my job to hold open large trash bags so she could neatly insert the clothing. We happened upon a horrendous green and orange blazer that had belonged to my grandfather. I insisted she allow me to keep the sportcoat; it seemed like something Dick Weaver might wear. And in the years that followed, I would dress myself in the oversize jacket and deliver weather reports to my bedroom mirror.

LA VISTA, THE CONDOMINIUM COMPLEX where I live, is situated between a barbershop and a vacant lot. Each unit has a screened back patio with a transparent roof that would offer a terrific window to the heavens if not for a cross-hatching of unkempt maple branches and thick, precariously saggy telephone wires. My couch is positioned in such a way that on warm nights, if I leave the back door open, I can feel a soft breeze while I watch television. Tonight, I ignore most of the newscast until the weather comes on. One of my (numerous) grievances with the news business concerns the kinds of stories that traditionally get played before the anchors toss the show to me. Mostly, they're ridiculously inane pieces—the world's largest bratwurst, a man who's chosen to spend his summer living in a treehouse—that beg some type of clever transitional comment.

Last week, one of the station's anchors, Zane Grobbit, segued into my weathercast with a story about a local auto dealership's newly erected sign featuring a three-story-high rotating ignition key. As I watched the key twirling across my monitor, Zane Grobbit, suitably inspired, managed to perfectly capture the moment for the home audience by errupting with a chesty, "Wow!"

"Hmmm," I responded as the visual switched to a tight shot of me seated in the "weather-well" on Grobbit's left. "Is that a key-chain in your pocket or are you just happy to see me?"

From beyond the camera, I heard several people in the studio gasp. After I'd completed the tease and we'd broken for commercial, Kurt Cadarette, our producer, followed me to a worn red-tape X on the floor beside the chroma-key.

"*Why?*" he asked, allowing his arms to slap against his sides in a display equal parts impatience and disgust.

We'd been through this before.

"I can't help myself," I answered. "If you keep leading into the weather with these pathetic stories, I'm going to keep slugging them over the fence."

After pursing his lips, Cadarette exhaled loudly.

He told me, again, that our sponsors, the people who fund my paychecks, are not amused by cheap allusions to things like hard-ons and, a week earlier, horse feces. "They will kick you out of here on your *ass*," he insisted.

FOLDED INTO THE COUCH, I STIR THE ice cubes in my glass of beer with an index finger. Some evenings while watching myself on tape, I'm nearly appalled by my performance: poor grammar; a reliance on pedestrian verbal crutches such as *like* and *um* and *you know*; and, too often, my right hand fiddling with the device for switching weather screens, or my left hand massaging the top button on my suitcoat. Other times, I'm able to appreciate some of the finer moments of the broadcast: a seamless transition; insight into the unpredictable path of a particular cold front; and a deft turn of phrase.

My shirt is stained from blueberry preserves. Thankfully, I have a big stack of similar T-shirts, white V-necks from

Wylie's Department Store, on a shelf in my bedroom closet. I have become, grotesquely, a creature of habit; I'm swelled by the compulsions to follow the same roads to and from work, eat (nearly) the same foods at the same times and commit to ridiculous routine minutiae such as sanding my finger-nails with an emery board nightly, from left pinkie to right pinkie. I'm single-minded in my pursuit to find the *exact same dish soap.*

Not long ago, I was sitting at my desk preparing for the evening's weathercast when I began watching a story on one of the network magazine shows. The topic was obsessive-compulsive personalities. The narrator focused on a pitiful guy who kept boxes of sandwich bags on his countertops so he could use a fresh baggie to protect his hands from germs each time he touched the handle of a cupboard. I'm not *crazy compulsive* in the sandwich-bag hand-puppet way. But I related to a few of the things I saw. For example, I like a clean work space; I have a very specific way of arranging the items on my desk—pencils, pens and papers form a city planner's wet dream of right angles. I also refuse to re-wear clothing that hasn't been washed; I'll dump a dress shirt into the hamper even if I've only slipped it over my shoulders momentarily to see how it might look with a particular necktie and sportcoat.

There are other things. I get very anxious when the gasoline gauge on my car drifts below half filled. On long road trips I'll exit the highway for refueling twice as often as the average traveler. I have an annoying habit (I'm told) of eating my meals in explicitly defined apportions: I will finish every green bean on my plate before taking a single bite of sweet potato; likewise, I won't start on my chicken until I'm done with the side dishes.

AT NEARLY THE PRECISE MOMENT that I'm watching a videotaped version of myself tell the viewing audience that the leading edge of the tropical storm will hold off until late tomorrow morning, I begin to hear water pattering against the cement floor of my patio. Alas, there's little chance the sound is coming from ruptured plumbing.

I walk outside in bare feet. As the rain grows steadier above the throat-clearing rumble of distant thunderheads, I hear my own nasally voice blathering away from inside my living room. Across the courtyard of the condominium complex comes the urgent call of a woman to her husband; she wants him to rise from bed and assist in retrieving a load of laundry from a wash line strung between two lampposts.

"Everything's getting soaked," she says, in a testy twang that makes the word *soaked* sound like *so*.

Soon the rain's coming so hard I can barely hear the couple arguing about their laundry. I smell cigarette smoke from the young woman who lives next door. I have asked her, on occasion, if she'd mind not smoking on her patio, which is separated from mine only by a porous, board-on-board fence. The wind often leads the smoke through my screen door, it bids her ashes to collect in chalky dunes against the piping of my deck chair. She's only a year out of college; she's training to be a pharmaceutical representative for a huge company that wants her to push a nasal inhaler on allergists. The idea, she once told me, is to get physicians to prescribe the (costly) drug to their allergy-stricken patients. She also told me she's perfectly suited for the job: personable *and* an excellent golfer. She said, "Most of these deals are done right on the golf course." She played on the women's team at Appalachian State. Some afternoons, I watch her pitch balls toward a bucket she places at the opposite end of the courtyard.

Several times the superintendent has warned her about excessive noise coming from her apartment late at night. She's thrown a few parties. Her guests litter the grounds of the complex with beer cans and fast-food wrappers. In fact, I saw a guy skewer a stack of pizza boxes on a fence post. She told me she intends to move into a house when she can save enough money.

"Hilary," I say blindly into the cedar fence. "You there?"

When she doesn't answer I call for her again.

"I'm *inside*, Mr. Prouty," she responds. "My door's only open a tiny bit."

I want to tell her I'm still getting the smell from her cigarettes. But I'm too tired for another protracted discussion on the ills of secondhand smoke. I lay my hands against the high fencing, like a suspect preparing to be frisked. A few minutes pass before I hear the glass door to Hilary's apartment slide open. She takes the three footsteps to where her patio erases into courtyard grass and pokes her head around the wooden divider.

"Hey," she says, shielding her face from the rain with her left hand.

I motion for her to join me beneath the narrow awning.

"Did you call for this weather?" she asks, scooting to my side.

"Yeah." I crack my lower back. "But not for another day."

"Yikes."

Hilary has a compact, athletic build. She has shoulder-length blond hair that's usually kept tied in a tight ponytail. She's lean-waisted and when she walks her hips wink in a not altogether unsexy manner. Nearly unnoticed along the curve of her left elbow is a cat, curled into the shape of a kidney, its head tucked against Hilary's rib cage. The cat is called Remy—named after the liquor.

"I just wanted to ask," Hilary begins, shifting the cat from one arm to the other, "if you happened to see anyone outside my place yesterday."

I shake my head.

"Maybe around dinnertime?"

Again, I shake my head.

"Well, I *know* he was here." Suddenly the cat comes to life and leaps from Hilary's arms. It scurries across the wet patio and disappears beneath the dividing fence. "This guy I was sort of dating—shit, I don't even know if you could call it *dating* because we only went out three or four times. Anyway, I'm almost sure he came here yesterday and stole my charcoal grill."

"That's a strange thing to do."

"Isn't it? I don't understand people anymore . . ."

"Why would he want your grill?"

"Before we broke up—that's what this whole thing's about: I told him I wasn't interested in seeing him again—I said he could have my grill when I bought a new one."

"Something you haven't done yet . . ."

"No," she says, picking random spikes of cat hair from her blouse. "And I wasn't planning on buying a new grill anytime soon. I just tossed the idea out there. To be nice. You know, one of those super-friendly things you say on a date to sound like a better person. 'Next summer we should *definitely* go to Paris together.' Who believes that garbage?"

"He did."

"Oh, he did *not*. He took the fucking thing to be spiteful."

"Or because he needed a place to cook his steaks."

We both smile.

As the rain eases, a feeble whining sound comes from Hilary's side of the fence.

"Ooooh, that's Remy," she says, moving back toward her apartment. "He sometimes gets caught in a wiry hole in our screen door."

"Good luck."

She nods. With her back to me, she gives a tiny, two-finger wave over her shoulder and then she's gone. I hear her talking to the cat in the kind of exaggerated, sugary voice people use with pets. Finally, in midsentence, she slides closed the door. And I'm left with the hard run of rainwater draining down the gutters.

IN THE MORNING, I'M AWAKENED BY THE radio on my nightstand playing an instrumental song filled with lots of brass.

"'Last Night' by The Marquees," I say aloud, groggily, to

myself. And then, if only to hear the rest of the words in their full, impressive truth: "They became the house band for Staxx Records and famously changed their name to . . . Booker T and the MGs."

Standing over the toilet, I listen to the piss erupt from my body like steam. The pain in my back is draining into my left buttock and hip. I remove a few aspirins from the medicine cabinet and muscle them down my throat with a swallow of tap water. I start the coffee; I sit on the couch and eat a bowl of Corn Pops. Using the remote, I skip between WYIP's *Breakfast in Bentleyville* and the Weather Channel.

Some forecasters are keen on including goofy caricatures as harbingers of the week's weather: a grinning sun or scowling storm clouds. My deskmate Rick Fasco, who's Channel 7's morning and weekend meteorologist, is standing beside his illustration of a bulbous-nosed dwarf named Goshen. Since Fasco's arrival at the station nearly two years ago, I have seen Goshen in any number of weather-related ensembles: galoshes, Bermuda shorts, muffler and ski cap. Fasco believes his viewers have come to expect Goshen and, in Fasco's absence—vacations, sick days—I have been asked to include a stock image of the dwarf to maintain morning-show continuity. Nothing's more emasculating than interpreting a dry-air mass with that pumpkin-headed cartoon perched across my left shoulder.

Between sips of grapefruit juice, I watch Fasco—animated, elbowy—talking about the gathering storm in the Atlantic with Goshen, in foul-weather gear, at his side. Once, across a platter of barbecued ribs, Kiki suggested I find my own weather mascot.

A fox or an opossum. Presciently, she'd reached this conclusion before my near-catastrophe with the waterskiing squirrel.

"Not going to happen," I'd said.

I told her about my aversion to small animals, to *rodents*. I shared with her something from my childhood: an evening before my parents separated, before I'd moved with my mother and sister to Michigan. It was late summer and our street was closed to traffic for a block party—though I'm certain we called it something else back then. Because my father thought it would be good for a laugh, he wore an enormous raccoon costume he'd borrowed from a friend at work. As the sun dipped below the ragged treetops, the sky turned a muddy orange. I was shooting a tennis ball into a six-foot-high basketball hoop. My father was sitting on a lawn chair, drinking beers with the other parents. He would occasionally wipe the sweat from his face with the costume's hairy arm. Between his feet was the raccoon's disembodied head, black-eyed and smiling.

I was trying to launch a skyhook like Kareem Abdul-Jabbar; I extended my right arm straight above my head and flicked my wrist. I made it my very first time. I remember turning toward the three boys I'd been playing with, wanting to make sure they'd seen it. I said a few words; and none of them answered. Then I realized they were looking past me at something else. And I knew, instantly, this was going to be bad; I could feel the premonition pass through me like a weak electrical current. I took a step, then another. When I finally made out the jumble of arms and legs and painted fur, I was convinced I was going to lose my lunch. Right there on the makeshift basketball court, in front of the whole neighborhood. My father was throwing punches at a guy I didn't recognize.

"Jeez," said one of the other boys softly. "Your father's beating the crud out of Mr. Arbinali."

It was Mr. Arbinali, without his mustache.

And then, as if it were the first time it had occurred to him, another boy said, "Your father's dressed like a *raccoon*."

I was called home only a few minutes later. I lay in bed and listened to my parents fighting. They were directly beneath me, in the kitchen. A couple times I heard my mother say, "Quiet down or you'll wake the kids." Though I never learned why my father started hitting Mr. Arbinali, I think it had something to do with a debt. Earlier in the summer when we'd passed Mr. Arbinali in our car, my father had called him a "cheap Italian"—he'd pronounced it *eye*-talian—because Mr. Arbinali still owed him money.

I cross my legs against the coffee table. Fasco's necktie wags as he walks from one side of the screen to the other. His mouth is moving the entire time. The weather system has now been upgraded to a tropical storm; they've named it Isabel. Though it's too early for discerning a legitimate path for the storm, Fasco has included a graphic of Goshen beneath an inverted umbrella. A series of tiny dashes imply a strong wind.

IT SEEMS MY SELF-IMAGE OWES A GREAT deal to the arbitrary moods of others. Some days it's enough that I'm forecasting weather at a smallish TV station in North Carolina. I'm still young; I've got plenty of time to move up in the world of meteorology. How many people can say they're (almost) doing what they want to be doing? I truly enjoy tracking the weather. Imagine a job that's part scientist, part journalist and part entertainer.

Other days, though, my outlook is bleak. By now, in my mid-thirties, I should be working in a major market. There's not much satisfaction in glad-handing at the opening of a tire-and-wheel franchise. I feel like a TV pitchman, hawking goods—another sunny day—on an endless string of infomercials. Last week I was called into the station manager's office, again, and told to "quit behaving like a jackass." Seems one of the anchors, Gwen Hawkins, wants me put on probation. (Is there such a thing?) Earlier that day, she'd learned I was the person responsible for leaving a small ribbon of adhesive tape on the side of her door. This angel-of-death indicator notified others when Hawkins was feeling cranky.

I'm providing a service, I said to Glenn Fisk, across his desk. He was not amused.

In my defense, I see many of my ex-wife's traits in Hawkins. My ex-wife's temper was triggered by the smallest things: scratching my scalp, somebody slurping soup, the preparation of oatmeal—which she demanded in the consistency of cookie batter. By the end of our seventeen-month marriage, I'd nearly forgotten I was capable of formulating my own opinions. I had devoted too much energy to avoiding conflict; I was completely focused on saying and doing the "right" things. It was exhausting.

The week before we separated, the two of us sat silently at the dinner table. Every meal was fertile ground for another battle. She *hated* the way I divided my food into little independent courses. This would often part the gates for other topics.

On this night, though, we knew exactly what the other was thinking. These were our final days. She began to weep; and so did I. The strain of the previous few months had taken its toll—this was all too great. We'd hoped to defy the odds and become one of those couples whose damaged relationship actually improves with the birth of a child. But we'd lost our baby girl. And with her our fleeting chance to remain together.

Oddly, the conversation that followed was the most lucid, most pleasant we'd had in weeks. We started to talk about one of our earliest dates—maybe the first of significance, when we saw the gleam of something genuine. We had gone to a Chinese restaurant for dinner. As the waiter arrived to take our order, we noticed smoke seeping from beneath the spring-loaded doors to the kitchen. There was a fire. It was serious enough that the restaurant was evacuated. We stood in the parking lot with small packs of diners and Golden Dragon employees, watching the fire department arrive in two shiny trucks.

We were hungry. Once we'd decided there was nothing more to see—no flames licking out from shattered windows, no high-powered hoses—we began walking to the other end of the strip mall. (We agreed it would've been fantastic, in a dark and unexpected way, if the restaurant had a cache of fireworks.) We passed a cheese store, a deli. But we settled on an old-fashioned candy shop. The walls were lined with enormous glass jars filled with a blinding assortment of penny candy. Behind a long marble bar was a soda fountain and a glass-top freezer, shaped like a coffin, with about a dozen bins of ice cream. The owner was wearing a red-and-white-striped lab coat.

We loaded our brown-paper sacks with licorice twists, jawbreakers, malted milk balls and individually wrapped cubes of caramel.

"You're doing it all wrong," she said. "They charge you by weight. The key is selecting candy that's *large* and *light*."

Between her forefinger and thumb she displayed an orange marshmallow circus peanut.

"Considering our bad luck at the Chinese restaurant," I said, "*and* the fact that technically we're on a date: It's on me."

"In that case . . ." She dumped a scoopful of chocolate-covered raisins into her bag. "Now I'm living dangerously."

We'd promised to eat whatever sweets we purchased in a single sitting. We positioned ourselves on the hood of my car, our heels hitched to the bumper below. We shared a vanilla milkshake and a bottle of water. Between conversation, we could hear the crunching and smacking of gooey candy against our back teeth. When we finished, finally, we both lay back and stared into the black night sky.

"Would you be totally turned off if I threw up?" she asked.

"I won't hold it against *you* if you don't hold it against *me*."

She started taking deep, exaggerated breaths.

"You're not going to believe this," she said. "But I could really go for something salty. Pretzels or a few handfuls of cashews."

On the backseat of my car, I had a half-eaten bag of potato chips from lunch a couple days earlier.

"That hits the spot," she said. "Beats the hell out of Szechuan beef."

It's been a long time since I've had a date like that. Tingling with energy, befogged by promise. I have asked Kiki out—*repeatedly*. But she's made it clear that, at least for now, she's not interested. Though I may be delusional, I take comfort in the fact that her excuses have nothing to do with me. She says she doesn't need any more complications right now. One day, one day when she finishes graduate school she's promised we'll have a night together. The idea that I'm holding her to it, hanging on her very pledge, illustrates the pathetic state of my social life.

Spending such a large portion of my time alone surely isn't helping the cause. Save for my workdays—in a crowded newsroom, shooting remotes with Trip—and my visits to Stinky's, I don't have much interpersonal contact. I can't tell you the last time I had sex—I *can*; yes, I can. It was eight months ago during a weekend trip to Dallas. I was staying in a hotel that was also hosting a Mary Kay Cosmetics convention. Returning from dinner, I nearly became some car's hood ornament in the hotel parking lot. A woman driving a pale pink Cadillac almost plowed into me, stopping short and causing a loud screeching sound with her tires. She was drunk, frisky. And during her apology she invited me to a party in the hospitality suite under the condition that I park her Caddy. ("In case you hadn't noticed," she said in a slurred Southern drawl, "*Ahm* a little tipsy.")

We never made it to the party. Instead, we finished a bottle of vodka in the backseat. Her hair was sprayed high and stiff. The entire time we were screwing, mostly with her on top, I couldn't take my eyes off the big Mary Kay decal in her rear windshield. The company's best saleswomen are *awarded* these cars, I'd remembered reading. Incredibly, given the circumstances, it took me forever to climax because I couldn't get the following thought to leave my head: Were the saleswomen permitted to *remove* the decals? Would they be fired? In the light of my hotel room the next morning, I examined the shirt I'd been wearing the previous night. It was a white button-down draped over the back of a chair. Smeared across its chest were filthy streaks of makeup—crimson lipstick, rouge, an eye shadow of indiscriminate color.

Not counting the weekend in Texas, I'm sure my lack of companionship is partly responsible for my, um, maturity problem. Since my divorce, I have regressed; I no longer have a round-the-clock chaperone to point me in the proper direction. I'm often reprimanded at work. The week before getting busted for leaving masking tape on Gwen Hawkins's doorframe, I asked sportscaster Wes Nichols, *on-air*, if the bandage on his nose was the result of our station manager sitting down while Nichols was "kissing butt." The awkward silence that followed proved to be the *best* part of our exchange: It seemed that earlier in the day Nichols had had a small cancerous lesion removed. The Tourettes-like scolding I received from

Fisk was monumental. He broke new ground, pairing curse words in heretofore undiscovered configurations. *Cock-hag-licker* and *bitchy-jackass-bitch-bitch* were a couple I recalled on the drive home.

"Jesus, Prouty," he'd said, scratching his head, between whiskey-colored hair plugs, with a ballpoint pen. "What's your *problem?*"

A few nights earlier I'd been asked nearly the same question by Gil Vickers, who, among other things, is the owner of WYIP. Seated in a corner booth, *his* booth, at the Maylark Family Restaurant—for if nothing else, Gil Vickers is a family man—we spoke about why I'm so moody.

"What's bugging you, Lou-lou?" he'd asked, pushing a forkful of meatloaf into his mouth. He has all sorts of pet names for people. Depending on the thoughts scuttling through his head in a given moment, he refers to me as either Luke Easter (after a deceased baseball player), Pouty Prouty, the Loop or Lou-lou.

"I haven't yet reached middle age," I said. "So I guess you'd call it a not-quite-midlife crisis."

"Crocodile dung!" There was a speck of brown gravy on Gil's chin, resembling a tiny goatee. "You're not going through any goddam crisis."

Because Gil and I were both raised in the Midwest—Gil in Iowa, me in Michigan—he's felt a certain kinship toward me since nearly the week I began working at the station. Every couple months we have a meal together. And he's always candid. Twice he told me about staffers he intended on having fired in the coming days.

"Does this dinner have anything to do with a pink slip?" I asked.

"Oh, Lou-lou," he said, turning his slab of pecan pie so it faced him like an arrowhead. "You know me better than that. If I was going to have you shit-canned, I'd make Fisk do it."

I don't know when my ambition started to fail me. But nothing has worked out the way I planned. Even in the months after Flynn died, after my divorce and my move to North Carolina, I figured Channel 7 would serve to rebuild my confidence—a place to get back on my feet, establish some distance from my past. Still, I'm miles away from regaining my stride; I'm no closer to landing employment in a top-ten market than I was during any of my previous jobs—three years in Indiana, four in Ohio and now four more in Bentleyville. Last month I participated in a remote from the National Banjo Festival in Rocky Mount. Adding insult to injury, Kurt made me wear a plaid shirt, overalls and a straw hat.

Stabbing at the ice cubes on the oily surface of my cola, I turned to Gil. "I have no idea what this means," I said. "But I've started *ironing* my boxer shorts."

"That's peculiar."

"See this?" I said, removing a tube of salve from my shirt pocket. "I rub this on my face twice a day, mostly near my eyebrows and ears. The doctor says I've got seborrheic dermatitis. It causes my skin to turn all red and flaky."

"Terrific."

"He says it's aggravated by stress."

In the parking lot, Gil stood beside his Lincoln and I could tell he was considering the right words to leave me with.

He was swinging his keys around his index finger, catching them against the dimpled heel of his palm.

SHE'S NO LONGER A TROPICAL STORM. At the break of dawn I receive a phone call from a friend at the National Weather Service. He tells me its winds have surpassed seventy-four miles per hour, classifying Isabel as a hurricane. I decide to leave for work early in order to help Fasco track it. I dig through my drawers for clean underwear—boxers and V-neck. I glance at my reflection in the mirror. My eyes are so doughy and dark they seem for a moment, a fraction of a moment, to belong to somebody else. I take a long, tight-eyed shower. I let the hot water beat against my sore back. I'm deeply, thoroughly tired. It's the kind of total exhaustion that makes me think I'm incapable of performing the simplest tasks: completing coherent sentences, shaving the stubble from my cheeks, finding my way to the station without plowing into a drainage ditch.

Outside, a misty rain seems not so much to be falling as suspended in a gauzy curtain. Along one of the nameless back roads I take is a barbecue shack called the Moonlight Inn. Because they usually serve food until three in the morning, there's still a dying tendril of wood smoke, from split oak and hickory, rising above the backyard. I have been told the man who runs the Moonlight Inn, Adrian Parker, once played offensive tackle for the Washington Redskins. He is physically imposing, larger than most doorframes, and I have been seated at one of the inn's picnic tables, washing down barbecue with sweet tea, when Adrian has "escorted" unruly patrons from the premises.

My car stereo is softly playing. As I turn on the windshield wipers, I bump the radio's scan button. I halt the glowing numbers from somersaulting into infinity. Absentmindedly, I begin nodding my head to a poppy rhythm. Suddenly, secretly, the word *holy* catches my attention. Soon after, I'm struck by *His greatness* followed closely by *How to serve Him.* I reach for the dials so quickly I nearly swerve into a parking meter. Worse than country-and-western music, worse than reggae or heavy metal or worse even than all-night talk radio is Christian rock. It frightens me in its full pepperminty propaganda, blow-darting subliminal—are they considered subliminal?—messages across the wholesome airwaves. Scarier still is the reality that I actually *like* some of the songs. *Does this sound good?* asks a voice in my head. *Is it pleasing? Come, join us here on the dark, wet roadways of North Carolina. Do not be frightened . . .*

I start thinking about Kiki. The other day she was wearing a corrugated tank top and blue jeans. As she made a delicate pirouette, returning a bottle of spirits to its place on the shelf, I'd caught a faint glimpse of her areola behind the layered fabrics of brassiere and undershirt. I squinted. I looked away, quickly, and back again. She reminded me of a Seurat painting: Surely had I been standing farther away—given myself some distance—I would have had a spectacular view of her almond-colored nipples.

The ribbing of the shirt gripped the magnificent dips and bulges in her torso. It was breathtaking to watch her reaction when a customer ordered a drink of sour mash. The shot glasses were lined across a narrow shelf over the bottled liquors. And to reach them Kiki had to stand on tiptoes—a position that turned her buttocks into tight twin fists. In the mirror, I saw the hem of her shirt lift away from the frayed waistband of her jeans. My memory of what came next is unclear. In a blink of time—I was hardly capable of determining fact from fantasy—the smooth skin of her abdomen pulled pleasantly taut. And before me, surrounding a knot of belly-button skin, was a funnel of dainty hairs, tiny and transparent, illuminated by barroom light.

The stir of an erection, slow at first, pushed the head of my penis against my left thigh. In high school I lusted after a girl named Susan Betts. The summer after graduation we both attended a pool party at Martin Keppler's house. I'd had too many cups of beer and I collapsed on a lounge chair; I held my face in my hands to fight past the sickness. By then it was dark, middle of the night. The swimming area was tucked beneath a canopy of leafy trees. Even the twinkling lights from the patio were no longer visible. The pool resembled a pit of crude oil. In between breaths, my head spinning from alcohol and the rubber-cement stink of chlorine, I heard a wet slappy sound. Most of the other kids were entwined against the cascading land around Keppler's house or rummaging through his parents' refrigerator or staggering down the driveway toward their cars.

"Lucas?" said a voice from the water.

Though I wanted to answer, I was preoccupied. My stomach was playing that trick where it chased its contents (warm beer) into the back of my throat, rapidly, before letting the vomit wash down again along the esophagus.

"Lucas?" said the voice again. "It's Susan."

She asked me to hand her a towel. As I struggled to stand, nearly toppling into the asphalt beneath a titanic rush of blood to my head, I watched Susan rise from the water wearing white—goddam phosphorescent!—undergarments. She backed into the towel, pulling the fabric closed around her chest.

"You won't remember this in the morning," she said, inaccurately, curling her arm between her shoulder blades to unfasten her brassiere. She handed me the bra and turned away, a half rotation, before pulling a shirt over her head. "Now close your eyes."

I pretended to obey. But between a tiny fissure in my left eyelid I could see the towel fall gently to her feet as she stepped out of her soggy panties. The darkness hid the best details. Still, I was able to glimpse a shadowy triangle, inverted, balanced atop the seam of her legs.

"Want to see something?" she asked.

I allowed my head to pivot in a silly nod.

We began walking to the front of the house. Midway across the lawn I realized Susan had slipped something in my hand. I looked down, spreading my fingers as though preparing to catch a ball. It took a moment for me to recognize that the object springing to life in my palm was her damp, crumpled underpants. I embarrassedly let my arm drop to my side. Susan continued moving a few paces ahead, pantyless, dressed in a tight T-shirt and short denim skirt.

She wanted to show me her new Toyota Celica—not what I expected—a graduation present from her parents. She shimmied down into the driver's seat, waving me into the car beside her. The hem of her skirt was hiked high, revealing swimsuit-tanned skin, and I massaged the panties between my thumb and forefinger like a talisman. I couldn't stop myself from staring at her glistening thighs or repeating the following phrase in my head: *She's not wearing any underpants.*

We drove around the neighborhoods near Martin Keppler's house. For most of the ride, Susan tried to find a song on her tape player. When she finally let me out, after maybe twenty minutes, we bade each other goodnight without a kiss or caress or even the handshake connection of skin against skin. Probably a hundred times since that night I have fantasized about what *should* have happened between us. Many of the early missteps I've taken in relationships can be directly attributed to my failure to place a hand on Susan Betts's naked thigh. Blunders made during adolescence can swell to outsize proportions; they can retard growth and leave behind a residue of regret. Surely this is part of what fuels my pursuit of Kiki—the thing that keeps me from walking away.

THERE'S AN OLD AXIOM IN NEWSCASTING: *If it bleeds, it leads.* Ratings have long confirmed a spike in viewership whenever there's gore—or even the *threat* of gore. Remember the famous NFL quarterback who had his leg grotesquely fractured by a linebacker? The bones buckled sideways before erupting through his skin. It became nearly impossible to watch TV without seeing the injury replayed, in painful slow motion. The clip became video wallpaper; it filled screens in homes, bars and restaurants on a never-ending loop. We grew so familiar with the ordered images—quarter-back fading for a pass, bracing against the hit, crumpling to the turf and, finally, helpless as the weight of his own body tamped his leg into the number seven—that we were no longer horrified by its violence. Some of us were even *disturbed* that it now failed to *disturb* us.

It's the same with meteorology. The prospect of fierce weather—snowstorms, tornadoes, hurricanes—is usually enough to shackle people to their TVs for hours. They'll watch the same incessant report as often as the forecaster wants to deliver it. As they sit on the edge of their couches, their eyes will tire from reading a ceaseless crawl along the bottom of the screen. For God's sake, they don't want to miss a *thing*!

Earlier this morning I spoke to Fasco. His voice had turned reedy and thin. He blamed it on a nervous condition. "I'll be okay," he'd said, not wanting to miss his chance to locally break a major story. He told me he's been receiving regular updates from the National Weather Service and that they have yet to decide on the two or three most likely paths for Isabel.

Waiting for a traffic light, I suddenly remember a message from my sister. I call her on my cell phone. She lives with her physician husband and two daughters in Lincoln Park, Illinois.

"Is it raining there?" I ask, predictably.

"No," says Jo, sounding annoyed. "I'm grilling cheese sandwiches for the girls' breakfast."

For some time, there's been a strained distance to my

relationship with my sister. She gave birth to her youngest, four-year-old Chloe, not long after we lost Flynn. Jo is careful about what she says to me—maybe that's the problem—and she tries to temper any enthusiasm when discussing her children. Our conversations are best when she lets down her guard, shares the honest moments of their lives. Today she tells me how Chloe has become enamored with all things Peter Pan.

"We bought her a blue nightgown like Wendy's," she says. "It was a monumental mistake."

"How come?"

"Oh, shit—" Jo takes a gaspy breath. She admits to one of the girls, presumably Chloe, that she said a naughty, naughty word. "Mommy should know better than to use language like that. I'm *very* sorry."

"It's potty mouth," says a gentle voice in the background.

"You're absolutely right." I hear the whoosh of liquid being poured into glasses, then she calls them to eat. "Was I telling you about the nightgown?"

"Yes . . ."

"She refuses to take it off."

"That's cute."

"Oh, *please*. It's this horrid thing: polyester and fishnetting from Wal-Mart. She thinks she *is* Wendy, who, you may recall, wears a nightgown throughout the entire movie."

"I don't remember . . ."

Jo's tired. I can tell by the way her consonants break softly when she's completing a sentence, leaving me to wonder if she has finished her thought.

"How's Patrick?"

"Busy," she says, taking a drink. "Most days he leaves for surgery at five-thirty and doesn't come home until the kids are preparing for bed."

She has to hang up. The dog's tail knocked over a glass in the other room and the telephone cord will not reach. Nearing the station, I promise to visit Jo in the coming year. I'll arm myself with gifts for my nieces—costume jewelry, Barbie dolls, pink ballet slippers. The kinds of things I imagine young girls might want.

I PUNCH MY FINGER THROUGH THE DIGITS of the alarm code and gain access into the back of the television studio. The hallway is dimly lit. I pass the dining nook and kitchenette where the chef from *Live at Five* prepares for his weekly segments. The chroma-key has been neatly repaired by someone handy with a needle and thread. From the row of video monitors suspended overhead, I hear Fasco's latest forecast. "We're going to track Isabel over the next eight hours," he says. "For now, the winds continue to increase. This is a full-fledged hurricane."

"A *full-fledged* hurricane," I say, aloud, mocking Fasco's ominous tone.

Across the newsroom, I see anchor Gwen Hawkins tilting her head in an exaggerated fashion toward the lights. She resembles a vacationer straining to milk the final moments of sun before boarding a plane. She remains motionless as Kimmy Wilson hurriedly touches up her makeup. It's a strange juxtaposition, and the irony isn't lost on me: Hawkins insists that her face look *perfect* while, not ten paces away, Fasco is describing the potentially catastrophic force of a major hurricane.

There was a time when I was embarrassed by my line of work. (Consider how many people think weathercasters— TV personalities in general—are complete imbeciles.) When introducing myself to someone for the first time, I would often lie about what I did for a living. Sometimes my make-believe profession was at least in the meteorological field— *I investigate weather disturbances for the Federal Aviation Administration*—and other times I proffered careers seemingly snatched from midair. *I manage a traveling doo-wop show; I own a chain of muffler shops.*

I'm now resigned to the fact that *this* is what I do and, barring a sudden sea change, it will remain my means of employment for the foreseeable future. In truth, I don't know where else I'm qualified to work. On my worst days—during the National Banjo Festival or in the moments after the water-skiing squirrel nearly expired—I openly weigh my options. Perhaps I should send my highlight tape to one of the government's meteorological agencies or, on a whim, to a couple of the networks. But I have tried this before. After the initial surge of adrenaline, hope upon hope, I grow more disheartened with each rejection letter I receive—*many thanks for your interest, blah-blah-blah, we're not presently hiring, blah-blah-blah, we'll keep your application on file.*

Staring into one of the video monitors, I can tell that Fasco's excited about delivering the news of Hurricane Isabel. He looks as though he's going to bust the buttons on his mustard-colored sportcoat. He's grinning his weasly little grin. Instinctively, spitefully, I take a stuffed reproduction of Goshen from our desk and, using a discarded piece of packing twine, tether the stupid figurine to a lamp with a hangman's noose. Fasco has littered the floor around our work space with reams of printouts bearing his scribbles and notations. Beneath the rollers of my ergonomic chair is a map, unfurled, depicting the eastern seaboard of the United States. *For the love of God,* I say to myself, *he's using a* protractor.

When I watch fellow meteorologists on TV, I have an insatiable desire to condemn their performances. No phase of the broadcast is safe: I attack the forecaster's delivery, wardrobe and intellect. Strangely, though, I lose my critical eye when reading the infantile weather page in most news-papers. Even when I *know* a series of twisters is scheduled to land in, say, the Texas Panhandle, having spent the afternoon poring over the national forecast at my desk, I will still scratch my head in a *gee-whiz* way the next morning as I read about the storm damage caused to a local trailer park.

Moments after Fasco's broadcast has ended, he's stand-ing beside me. The phone rings once and, before I can answer it—before I can *think* about answering it—Fasco is engaged in conversation. When I ask him about the protractor, he raises his index finger and turns away. I give serious consideration to socking him on the back of his thick head.

"That was *The Service,*" he says. Fasco has this ridiculous habit of referring to the National Weather Service in a trun-cated, overly dramatic manner. It's the same way that certain cop shows, injecting a pretentious-sounding shorthand, use

The Agency when talking about the CIA. "They just made Isabel a Category Two."

On the Saffir-Simpson scale for rating the destructive potential of hurricanes, the number *one* suggests the prospect for damage is minimal and the number *five* implies a storm of catastrophic proportions.

I want to tell him that the only number two he should be worried about is the crap I'm going to take on his stuff if he doesn't move it. I'm logy, irritable. But I promised Glenn Fisk I would remain on my best behavior. As much as it pains me, I offer a compliment.

"You did a nice job this morning."

It takes him a moment, caught in headlights, to realize I'm serious. He thanks me. Then he provides the details of his phone call. The hurricane, in whorling orbit, is gathering strength. The National Weather Service still has no discernible model of the storm's most likely route. Fasco's speech is pocked with anxious sighs, choppy inhalations. He's a geyser of live-wire histrionics. His intimation, slow to reveal itself, is that the two of us are sharing in something significant, something it will soon be our responsibility to interpret for others.

I have been in this business longer than Fasco. Not only do I fail to share his sense of urgency, but I must now slap him back to sobriety.

"Rick," I say, straightening myself in the chair as though I'm preparing to offer dictation. "I have seen hundreds of these disturbances. *Thousands.* Many of them, like Isabel, ultimately become hurricanes. But the chance of this storm passing anywhere near us is damn slim."

He demurs, quietly running through his list of explanations. He takes several printouts that have been crudely taped together and begins deciphering a collection of colorful, wavy lines. He's *wishing* the storm our way. Grim as it sounds, he's hoping for something—a catastrophe—to break the monotony of his daily life. It wouldn't take much to carry me in his direction.

"You're making sense," I say, spying a pen that belongs to me poking from a booklet of Fasco's papers, marking his place. I remove the pen and hitch it to my left breast pocket. "But you *know* that nothing with these storms is ever logical."

He nods.

Sensing his disappointment—his mouth pitches down near the corners, pulled by mysterious fishhooks, and I swear to God it looks as though he's going to cry—I offer some consolation: Maybe now's the time for our annual spiel on the hazards of severe weather. Imposing statistics, precautionary suggestions.

"I'll do something tonight," I say. "And you can hit them again in the morning."

He is visibly relieved. He collects his materials and departs for the cafeteria—several collapsible tables surrounded by vending machines, a sink, a refrigerator and a microwave oven. I remove a file from the side of the desk and begin paging through my notes. Certain things I copy in longhand onto a legal pad for possible use during my broadcast. *Hurricanes are the only natural disasters we humanize with names. A large hurricane stirs more than a million cubic miles of the atmosphere every second. The width of a typical hurricane is three hundred miles.* And, of course, the kernel of truth even casual weather followers can recite: *The eye of a hurricane is deathly calm.*

It's always difficult for me to distinguish what the average viewer will find useful. I imagine he's lying in bed, fingers laced across his bloated, BVD'd belly. His wife has just marked her page in the latest book-club selection with a dulled emery board. And the two of them are waiting out a commercial break for my forecast. *Everyone* watches the weather.

To be sure, most evenings they only require the bland data for the coming day: temperature (highs and lows), cloud coverage and, on occasion, details of impending inclemency. But their fascination with storm systems, often bordering on preoccupation, always leaves me doubting the information I intend to provide. Should I come at them with both barrels blazing? Or do I appeal to the lowest common denominator? In my notes from a previous hurricane broadcast, I have a graphics-hungry equation. (*Warm ocean water + warm and humid air + weak upper-air currents blowing in the same direction as winds near ocean surface = tropical cyclone.*) Now I can't remember if I actually used it.

These days, near-ubiquitous weather coverage from various media sources leaves me wondering if the improbable threat of a hurricane is reason enough to let flow with a cascade of information. Let our *viewers* pluck what they need from an oversize basket.

I shuffle through more files. The printouts are faint, inkless. I follow the system's serpentine lines; I decode several columns of numbers filled with recent barometric pressure readings. Though the television screen has gone dark, I still see the smoky image of Fasco beside a nonexistent chroma-key map. I turn on a small radio, tuned to the local oldies station, and listen to The Mystics sing "Hushabye." The lyrics chase my mind into a daydream; I imagine Flynn climbing into bed with Annie and me. This isn't the first time I've thought about how it would feel to hear my daughter's gentle footsteps pattering down the hallway on a Sunday morning. Pretending I'm still asleep, I'd watch through squinted eyes as her bright face crested above the edge of the mattress. "Up please, up please," she'd say, raising her hands over her head. I would hoist her by the armpits, her little legs now straddling my rib cage. No matter the season, I always picture her wearing fuzzy footsie pajamas—the one-piece kind that have a zipper down the middle, veering to a halt above the left ankle.

It's difficult to scatter these thoughts, permit something else to enter my brain. As I make my way to the kitchenette for a cup of coffee, I half expect to stumble over Flynn rounding the corner. Maybe I'd learn to fry pancakes for her shaped like snowmen. On special occasions, I'd fix her juice in a martini glass. I dump a soggy paper cone filled with spent coffee grinds. Starting a new pot, I can't shake the fear that the most interesting part of my life is only make-believe.

WHEN I WAS SIX AND MY SISTER, Josephine, was nine, my father left our family. He was a stockbroker, the kind who made cold calls to unsuspecting people in their homes or places of business to secure a sale. What I remember about my father during my early childhood, in suburban Cleveland, was how each morning he would shake open the newspaper and make small notations in the margins of the stock page. Seated at the breakfast table, he would punctuate each new discovery with a grunt. My sister and I were usually nearby spooning down sugary bowls of cereal. Our eyes would meet when my father announced, depending on the state of the market, "There goes your college fund" or "Don't be surprised to find a new Oldsmobile in the driveway tonight."

Mostly, my father was a man to whom we had a tenuous connection. He was not a bad person. Though he appeared to be someone who took little pleasure from being a parent. Or a husband. Special moments seemed not the by-product of industry but, rather, a thing upon which he had stumbled. He played poker on Thursday evenings. Once, I recall waking in the middle of the night to find my father standing at the foot of my bed. He was illuminated by a light from the hallway. Smiling, he reached into the pockets of his sportcoat and sprinkled fat decks of cash—his winnings—across my blanket. It was more money than I'd seen in my entire life. We began laughing together, and soon my mother and sister joined us. "We're rich," said Jo, again and again.

But we weren't rich. And for every shopping spree that accompanied a lucky night of cards or a splendid investment tip, there were a dozen days when he complained aloud about wanting to take a do-over with his life. I can honestly say that I still haven't the slightest notion what path my father might have chosen with his "do-over." I once heard him speak longingly about joining his cousin on a quarterhorse farm in Virginia. But given what I know about my father, it sounded absurd.

My mother took all of four days to erase our lives in Shaker Heights—a thirty-minute ride by rapid transit to Cleveland's downtown epicenter, the Terminal Tower—and move us near her family in Mill Valley, Michigan. She told me, years later, that as soon as she realized my father was gone for good she called a realtor, selected randomly from the Yellow Pages, to sell our house. The keys were left with our neighbors, the Gandys, until my mother returned nine weeks later to sign the closing papers. In the months that followed, the three of us lived in a series of apartments before settling into a small house the summer after Jo turned eleven. While we were in school, my mother worked as a receptionist for a family doctor.

It would have been easier for everyone if my father was gone *and* forgotten: a shadow swallowed by darkness. But there was a low-grade resentment in each of us, especially my mother, whenever his name was mentioned. "Do you know," my mother occasionally said at breakfast, "your father would eat cream cheese out of the tub with his *finger?*" She'd shake her head in disapproval and expect the same reaction from us.

Not long after I turned fifteen, my father resurfaced. I was shooting baskets in our driveway with Adam Sieglitz, who lived down the block, when my mother came to the door and announced, in the same voice she might use to call me for dinner, that my father was on the phone. As my father spoke, I remember staring out the window above the kitchen sink and watching Sieglitz fumble with the ball. My father asked me about school and girls and hobbies. Mostly, I listened while he glossed over his eight-year absence from our lives—something about a need to regain his sanity which, even at fifteen, I understood as rubbish—and then told me about how he was teaching English in Portland, Oregon. I don't know which part I found more unsettling, my father choosing to call us after all these years or the fact that he was responsible for educating a classroom of students the same age as me.

We saw him, finally, about four months after that first conversation. As much as my mother didn't want to grant him access again to our world, she recognized, she explained to Jo and me over pizza one night, it was necessary for the two of us to have a relationship with him on *our* terms. "I certainly don't want to be the one standing in your way," she said, peeling discs of pepperoni from her plate and stuffing them into her mouth. In fact, that's *exactly* what she wanted: to serve as a barrier when he reached out after this great chasm of time. But she couldn't rationalize the finality of her anger. She would tell me, years later, how she lost sleep agonizing over the proper way to handle his return. In the end, she put her faith in Jo and me, believing we would be able to discern for ourselves what kind of person my father had become in his new life.

I sat in my bedroom waiting to hear the sound of his rental car turning into our driveway. My mother never came outside, she never walked toward the front of the house to steal a glance. Simply, she straightened the collar on my shirt and brushed some lint from Jo's sweater. "Be good," she said. "Show him what magnificent people you've become." When we reached the door I looked back, and my mother, fighting herself, waved us away at the same time she announced, "You don't have to go."

Again, as during the phone calls in the months preceding his visit, my father chose not to discuss issues of significance. He took us to Ponderosa and told us, "Get whatever you want." He seemed disappointed when we both ordered the cheeseburger platter. He asked us questions about our classes and what kinds of things we enjoyed. During one stretch, he made comparisons between the curriculum at our school and the one where he worked until Jo, slightly perturbed, silenced him by saying, "Well, that's not how *our* teachers do it."

The worst part came near the end, once we got back to the house. None of us seemed sure what came next. Did we hug? Kiss? Would we see him again? I wanted a car for my birthday; I wondered whether buying me a Jeep might ease his guilt at missing most of my childhood.

Plans were made, tentatively, for some distant summer weekend. Then he shook our hands and, clumsily, leaned over to kiss us each on the cheek. As we walked toward the front door, Jo whispered, "Did you eat the last ice cream sandwich?" It occurred to me I should turn around, tell my father we weren't talking about him.

Sometimes I think the hardest thing about losing Flynn is that I never got the chance to be a parent and show her what I learned from *my* father's mistakes. Deep in my bones, I feel it's something I could do well. And now I'm terrified I won't have the opportunity again.

It's been a while since I've spoken to my father. Maybe last Christmas. He made a detour to come see me a couple years ago when he and his girlfriend, the mother of a former student, were headed for spring break to Hilton Head, South Carolina. They visited the station, watching in the wings as I muddled through the six o'clock forecast. Afterward, I peered at them through a Plexiglas partition as they wandered the set. I was pretending to take an important phone call. "Jo," I said. "What the hell am I going to do?"

"Oh, Christ," she said. "I'm just glad they didn't come to see *me*."

Later, they drank icy red daiquiris from enormous globes. Vacation drinks, my father called them. I listened to their plans for the coming week: sunning, swimming and as many rounds of golf as they could complete. Near the end of the evening, I turned suddenly irritable. My crankiness manifested itself in a comment about—of all things—golf. In fairness, I have been dispassionate about the game since my divorce; my ex-wife Annie worked as a teaching pro.

"It's such a marvelous way to spend a day," said my father's girlfriend. "When played properly, it's filled with such majesty"—she used that word, *majesty*—"and beauty. I get so angry when people say, 'Well, golf isn't a *sport*.' Do you know what I mean, Lucas?"

"To be honest"—and here's the jab—"I have difficulty calling anything where folks are dressed in trousers, walking at a shopper's pace, a *real* sport."

There was silence. My father's posture went straight. I had not intended for the words to sound as awful as they did, boring their way into our ears without something pleasant coming in close proximity to soothe the sting. Soon after, the evening folded predictably into the cordial exchange of promises to spend more time together in the coming year. Then I led them to the motel. I watched their arms curl from either side of the car, like crooked antlers, as they waved farewell. Because I wanted to do something nice, to leave them feeling good about their visit, I decided to call them in the morning with a few kind words. But I overslept. And the motel clerk confirmed what I already knew: They were gone.

SHORTLY AFTER ISABEL REACHES hurricane status, it appears as though she will burn herself to sleep along some distant meridian in the Atlantic Ocean. But hurricanes are illogical. And suddenly, in the time it takes to answer the phone, the National Weather Service reports the storm has gained another life. In addition, it seems Isabel has gathered enough strength, winds now in excess of 111 miles per hour, to increase its rating on the Saffir-Simpson scale to Category Three.

There was talk earlier today of making Isabel the lead story on the six o'clock broadcast. "We should wait," I said. "Let's see what happens in the next twelve hours."

While reviewing my notes before airtime, I take a call from Thom Guthrie, a guy I knew in graduate school. Until recently, he was a meteorologist in New Orleans. He's now working for the National Oceanic and Atmospheric Administration in Miami.

"You're on my call list," he says. "I was actually going to try disguising myself so I sounded like Earl Hanson."

We both laugh. Earl Hanson, who was in school with us, had the kind of grating, high-pitched voice that left you wondering whether his testicles had dropped. Every time he'd ask a question in class, our professor, Dr. Bergen, would wrinkle his face as though he'd ingested a bad clam.

"How's it going?" I ask.

"Pretty good, pretty good."

He tells me his wife's eight months pregnant with their second child and, for the life of her, can't get comfortable in bed. And if she's not sleeping, he's not sleeping. He also says yesterday afternoon he backed his new truck into a parking meter.

"That's always nice."

The conversation shifts to business.

"You know," he says, "we're tracking Isabel. The Weather Service has run some early SLOSH projections for a few spots along the coast."

SLOSH, an acronym for *sea, lake* and *overland surge* from a *hurricane*, is a computer program that maps the types of flooding that can be expected from major storms.

"They're already starting with that?"

"Sure," he says. "Because of the damage caused by Hurricane Gordon, there's lots of pressure to run the numbers as early as possible."

"And?"

"We've mapped a half dozen possible routes. It seems unlikely your region will get hit with anything more than high winds and heavy rain."

"That's what I keep telling people."

"My supervisor's pushing his better-safe-than-sorry spiel," he says. "I've still got another twenty of these calls to make."

"Nice way to spend a day, eh, Thom?"

"It beats listening to some guy's nine-hundred-dollar estimate to replace the bumper of my truck."

"Ouch." I take a drink of bottled water. "So, where do you think it's going to hit?"

"Flip a coin." I hear him speaking to someone else. Then, to me again, "I'm still betting she fizzles on her way south. Maybe Florida—Jacksonville, Daytona Beach, Melbourne."

INSTEAD OF LEAVING FOR DINNER BETWEEN the six and ten o'clock broadcasts, I remain at my desk. I eat a Milky Way and a bag of salt & vinegar potato chips. (My well-rounded meal also includes a vending machine turkey sandwich that's so awful it gets pitched after two bites.) I'm paying attention now. In the five hours since I spoke with Thom, the storm has begun to change its personality again. This evening I've already fielded calls from viewers concerned with Isabel's prospects for damage.

I reach into my wallet to tape a couple business cards beside my phone—contact numbers for Thom and a professor I know at Florida State who specializes in hurricanes—and a scrap of glossy paper falls loose. I haven't thought about the clipping in months, since propping it against a ketchup bottle on the bar at Stinky's one night while eating dinner. The photograph comes from a catalogue I received in the mail. It shows a little towhead, pigtails aimed like furry antennae, sitting on the end of a dock; she's clutching a fishing pole with both hands.

Her smile is crooked, unrehearsed. She has a pink blush to her cheeks.

I keep the picture, torn sloppily from the page, because the girl looks the way I imagine Flynn might if she had lived. Admittedly, the whole idea is kind of pathetic. I have nearly shredded the photo a bunch of times—bidding myself to rise from bed in the middle of the night and remove it from my wallet for good.

The only person who knows about the thing, frayed and folded behind my driver's license, behind Flynn's hospital band, is Kiki.

"Are you saving this for something?" she asked, lifting the picture as she sponged off the bar. "Maybe you planned on ordering yourself one of these little dresses?"

I was surprised by how easily it flowed; I hadn't realized I was ready to talk. And though I wasn't sure of the relevance, I explained how my ex-wife and I were never a good match. I described the way we argued throughout her pregnancy. Then two weeks before she was due, while I was drinking coffee, she sat at the kitchen table and admitted she hadn't felt the baby move in a whole day—maybe longer.

The next part was quick and merciless. We drove in silence to the hospital. As the doctor talked, I tried desperately to make sense of what he was saying. It felt as though he were speaking a foreign language and I was only capable of understanding every third or fourth word.

He couldn't hear a fetal heartbeat. Further tests revealed the baby—was she called a baby yet?—had become wrapped in the umbilical cord. She'd been asphyxiated. I remember thinking, *Just fix it*—you're *a doctor*. What followed seemed implausible, *impossible*. But he was describing the manner in which he intended to induce my wife. She was *still* going to endure labor; she was being asked to deliver a dead baby.

Even now, buffered by time and tears, it seems torturous, inhuman. (And, of course, it was.)

"I can't imagine . . ." said Kiki, unable to complete the sentence. She kept her eyes locked to mine, ignoring a guy at the end of the bar trying to order himself a drink.

Then she took the photograph in her hands, a catalogue snapshot designed to sell children's clothes, and gently smoothed out the creases. When her lips began to part, I expected to hear something else. But she only patted me lightly on the back of my wrist.

1 SPEND THE REST OF THE EVENING monitoring Isabel's progress. And though the story is not the lead at ten o'clock, we do move my update—based on viewer response—into the first five minutes of the broadcast. Maura Lease, who's substituting as anchorperson, looks alarmed when I announce the storm's most likely trajectory is along the Florida coast.

"How about Vero Beach?" she asks.

"A possibility," I say, grinning numbly into the camera.

"Oh." For a moment she looks genuinely lost, her eyes scanning the smooth news desk beneath her elbows. "My parents live in Vero Beach."

A few seconds of awkward silence tick past. It seems even longer because the large clock glowing above our director, Lynn Janda, actually turns a digit.

"I'm sure they'll be fine," I say, suddenly finding myself in the novel position of comforting Maura Lease *on the air.* When she fails to respond, her teleprompter locked at the ready with the beginning lines to a tease about the grand opening of a new bar-*slash*-laundromat called Suds & Duds, Lynn Janda motions for me to continue. "You know, it's more likely Isabel will slip south to the Miami area. I don't think Vero Beach will get much more than a thunderstorm."

When we break for commercial, Lynn marches across the set and begins massaging Maura's hand. She faces me and asks, "What're you thinking?"

"Pardon?"

"Come on, Prouty," she says, keeping skin-on-skin contact with Maura. She sidles closer to me as Kimmy Wilson leans across the desk to add another coat to Maura's rapidly fading makeup. "You don't tell somebody her parents are about to be swallowed by a hurricane. Especially on camera."

"That's not what I said." Walking toward the chroma-key screen, I begin preparing for the rest of my forecast. "I didn't know her parents lived in Vero Beach."

"I'm fine," says Maura. "I was just caught by surprise. My father's recovering from hip-replacement surgery. He has trouble getting around."

"Of course," says Lynn, whose voice, though comforting, has an edge that I'm certain is designed to make me feel guilty.

Seated on the counter of our weather set, Trip's doughy frame obscures most of the letters in a sign trumpeting DOPPLER RADAR. Instead, from my vantage point, it reads DO DAR.

"Nice going, ace."

I munch a few pellets of heartburn medication.

"You know how you're always hounding me about what I eat?" asks Trip. "Take a look at this."

He surrenders a stack of papers.

"My cousin—the one who lives in Sacramento—sent me a bunch of stuff."

At first glance, it appears Trip's cousin is encouraging him to join some dietary cult. For a not-insignificant sum (ranging from two hundred to nine hundred dollars), Trip will receive a membership packet in PowerEaters. His admission includes two one-pound canisters (chocolate and vanilla) of protein-shake powder, two videotapes, a calorie-counting guidebook, a pint of vitamin supplement and a dozen peanut butter snack bars. In addition, he will be mailed replacement products on the twenty-second day of every month, at which time his credit card will be duly billed, for a minimum of a single calendar year. Of course, if he chooses the two- or five-year program he will be "appropriately compensated in regard to the cost of said products."

"This looks dubious," I say.

"You're too cynical. Listen, my cousin lost *thirty-five* pounds on this plan. It's not a diet; it's a lifestyle change."

"Oh, Jesus."

"You should be more supportive," he says, snatching the papers from my hand. "You're the one who's always saying I eat like crap."

"Yeah," I answer, crossing my arms. "But I didn't mean for you to buy a sack of magic powder."

I listen to the flop-flop-flop of Trip's heavy-soled boots as he makes his way down the hallway. Remarkably, the rest of the evening is uneventful. I'm granted an extra fifty-five seconds of forecast time to discuss Isabel. Afterward, I hit the drive-thru window at Taco Bell and inaugurate Trip's new-found acceptance into the world of PowerEaters with three burritos and a Pepsi.

THIS IS THE LAST THING I EXPECTED. Standing beside a lamppost sprouting from Trip's lawn, I watch as his wife Ginny fastens their two children into the backseat of my car.

"You're *way* too sheltered," says Trip, slapping my shoulder with his open hand. "We're giving you a chance to see a whole different side of life."

Ginny backs away from the car.

"It wasn't my idea, Lucas."

"I'm sure—"

"Come on," says Trip, waving to his children through the windshield. "You're going to have a fabulous time."

"Seriously, Ginny," I say, turning away from Trip, "I don't think I've spent twenty minutes in my *life* alone with children."

"Exactly!" says Trip.

"We're not children," announces Nessa, who's maybe eight, from her place in the car.

For a moment, it appears as though Ginny is going to retrieve the kids: She's taken a decisive step forward, her right arm rising from her side. But before she can reach the safety straps—if indeed that is her intention—Trip closes the door and ushers me into the driver's seat.

"Have fun," he says, patting me on the head. "And bring them back if that hurricane gets close."

"Oh, Trip," says Ginny. She gives him a playful shove.

As we drive away, the three of us, I hear little Ryan sucking on the plastic spout to his spill-proof cup. When he's finished, it takes him a second to catch his breath. Though Trip and I have grown close over the past few years—killing time during location shoots, sharing meals beside one another in the van—I have been guarded with the details of my personal life. While he knows about my failed marriage, I have kept Flynn to myself. I make excuses: There hasn't been a good time; I'm afraid of his reaction. The last thing I want is for him to censor what he tells me—the way Jo sometimes does—for fear of ushering me into sadness. The death of a child, even a stillborn, has a way of changing how people relate to you. A slow ride past the schoolyard could easily inspire pity. *You okay? Wanna talk?*

"Where are we going?" asks Nessa, her feet kicking the back of my seat.

"I don't know." I notice a backpack filled presumably with kid supplies—snacks, toys, wipe-its, a change of clothes—that Ginny tossed on the floor. "Do you have some place in mind?"

"Huh?" says Ryan.

"He wants to know where we wanna go," Nessa says to her brother.

"The Globe . . ."

"What's that?" I ask.

"It's a video-game arcade," says Nessa. And then, to her brother, "Mom probably told him we're not allowed."

"Yeah," says Ryan, turning to face his window.

"Pretend he's Aunt Polly," she says, looking at Ryan. "We'll get something to eat and go home."

"I can hear you," I say.

We head in the direction of the beach, then loop around back toward town. A plume of Nessa's copper hair bobs in my rearview mirror. I swear to God I have *no* idea where I'm taking them. Suddenly, divinely, we trace a familiar route. We pull into the quiet parking lot at Stinky's.

"I'm going to run in for a minute . . ."

"You can't leave us here," says Nessa, unbuckling herself. "My parents would *kill* you."

"Kids aren't allowed in this place."

"Why?" she asks, taking her brother's hand.

"Why?" repeats Ryan.

Oh, Jesus.

I make them stand together on the front stairs while I peek inside. When I don't see any dancers—or much of anyone—I lead them against the side wall, telling them not to remove their eyes from the jukebox for even a second.

"Can we play a song?" asks Nessa.

"No." I look toward the bar. "We won't be here long enough."

As I start making my way across the room, Kiki emerges from the kitchen with a tuna sandwich. I give a quick nod and gesture toward the kids.

"Are you crazy?" she says, setting down her plate. "You can't bring them in here."

She slaps me gently above my right ear.

"I know, I know. They wouldn't wait in the car."

She escorts me to where the kids are standing. Their faces are illuminated by flickery red and blue light.

"I'm hungry," says Ryan, glancing across his shoulder at me.

I place my hand on his head and twist it like the lid to a mayonnaise jar, aiming him again at the jukebox.

"We'll get something to eat . . ."

"Take them outside," says Kiki. Though she's trying to sound stern, I can tell the presence of children has softened her. "I'll meet you out front."

Now Ryan is hanging upside down, his legs curled over the bar of the entranceway bannister. Nessa is sitting on the second step and leafing through a pamphlet about a nearby Indian tribe's casino. In a single fluid motion Kiki gathers the kids—objectionlessly distributing the pamphlet into a trash dumpster—and leads us to the car.

She says, "I've got a little over an hour."

She has a carefree, easy manner with Nessa and Ryan. There's a mutual respect they seem to have for each other—instant, absolute. As they settle into the car—Kiki crunched between the kids on the backseat—any tension that existed before her arrival has magically evaporated.

Some people simply know how to act around children; they have a way to connect. I'm not sure if the behavior is innate or learned—I'm trying to remember if Kiki ever said anything about spending time with kids. Either way, I'm clearly the outsider here. I thrum my fingers against the steering wheel.

Under Kiki's command, we order takeout from a Chinese restaurant called Jimmy Woo's. She nods knowingly when Ryan explains how he likes wonton soup without the soup part. When I call an audible, suggesting shrimp dumplings instead, Kiki casts her hand in a dismissive wave. "It's not the same," she whispers.

Because I'm now simply along for the ride, I follow Kiki's directions. We park beneath the enormous screen of an abandoned drive-in movie theater named the Waverly. Despite its neglected appearance—cracked concrete, beheaded speaker posts—the kids are thrilled.

"You mean people used to watch movies from their *cars*?" asks Nessa, breathless with excitement.

Kiki nods.

As we lay out the food on the hood of the Crown Vic, Nessa and Ryan race through the dozens of empty parking spaces. They are pitching stones against a boarded-up refreshment shack when we call them for dinner.

"That looks gross," says Ryan, pointing to a container of egg foo yong. (Naturally, it's my contribution to the meal.)

"You don't have to eat it." Kiki leads Ryan to a paper plate she has prepared for him. "I got you some wontons—the way you like."

Nibbling on a spare rib, it occurs to me that Trip's idea wasn't so misguided. In the short time I've been responsible for Nessa and Ryan, I have behaved—been *forced* to behave—in a more selfless fashion than usual. I filled their cups with root beer before my own. Twice already I've stopped stuffing my mouth to wipe sauce from Ryan's chin.

This thought passes through my head: It's a remarkable gift to watch Kiki demonstrate her maternal powers in all their glory. Several times I interrupt myself from being swallowed by what is only imagined. This is not my family. We have been bound together in a pretend game of house.

"You're good with them," I say to Kiki.

We watch Nessa and Ryan sitting across the lot, their backs pressed against the cinderblock base of the movie screen. Nessa is reading Ryan his fortune.

"What I try to remember," says Kiki, packing away the remaining food, "is not to treat them like children."

I'm grateful she has allowed the evening to spill forward under its own natural pace. Not once has she asked me if this is difficult, painful. She has a good sense about these things.

And, truthfully, it's been kind of nice—Kiki and the kids. A sober confirmation of something I already knew: I would've enjoyed being a parent.

Ryan takes a running start and then slides across the gravel in his sneakered feet. On the smooth white underside of Nessa's left forearm, Kiki is drawing a daisy "tattoo" with markers from the children's backpack. When Ryan sees what's happening, he comes over and extends *his* arm.

"I want a jet plane," he says. "No—a *snake.*"

"Can you handle that?" Kiki asks, looking at me.

"I don't think—"

"Just make two interlocking esses."

Cautiously, I start a green snake slithering upward from Ryan's wrist. I can't remember the last time I drew a picture. Junior high? Grade school?

"Give him big teeth," says Ryan. "With blood dripping off . . ."

Kiki smiles when she hears his request.

Then there's only silence, the four of us engaged in delicate activity against the hood of my car. Ryan's breathing has slowed; he holds it for a count, two, seemingly afraid any sudden movement will cause a mistake. As Ryan and I wait for Kiki to finish with the red, we blow air—*hwoo, hwoo*—on the lines squiggling across his skin.

SEVERAL DAYS BEFORE WE LEARNED ANNIE was pregnant, she and I spent the weekend in Missouri. We were visiting her grandfather, who was recovering from quadruple bypass surgery. He'd made arrangements for us to stay at the exclusive Cricket & Squash Club of Kansas City, where he was a longtime member. The walls of our room were coated in a sheen of red silk that matched the linens. Spaced equidistance from a tall armoire were four antique chairs displaying crushed-velvet cushions and elaborate carvings along their backs, arms and legs. Above the bed was a large canvas—wildflowers, green apples—in a gold-leaf frame. The hardwood floors were mostly hidden by a series of Indian rugs. Perhaps, in a nod to more cerebral times, the room had shelves of books and periodicals rather than a television.

The club offered a variety of complimentary services, including shoe shine, shirt pressing and high tea. Members (and visitors) were required to dress appropriately: jackets and ties for men; women were forbidden from wearing slacks. (Annie received a stern warning when she was caught retrieving ice in a pair of jeans.) In the basement, abutting an old-time barbershop that specialized in straight-razor shaves, was the men's grill. It was a room where local politicians and leaders of industry, concealed only by bath towels, would dine on cheddar and onion sandwiches. They sat behind giant circular tables, drinking scotch, their faces still flush from the sauna.

On our second night, we smuggled limes and a saltshaker from the bar. We lay in bed, propped upright by pillows, and took turns with a bottle of tequila. Later we filled a towel with ice, smashing it against the wall of our shower. We filled two glasses with ice chips, tequila and fresh lime juice for makeshift margaritas. By midnight we were dangerously drunk.

In the bathroom, I was wobbly and I didn't trust my aim to the opening of the toilet. I stood in the bathtub and urinated down the drain, gripping the towel rack for support. Though we both wanted to make love, we knew it wouldn't end well. (In reaching for the buttons on Annie's jeans, I nearly impaled myself on a lamp.)

We lay on a rug beside the bed. She told me about a time she'd gone fishing with her grandfather, the same one we were visiting, and while releasing an undersize bass he skewered his thumb with a hook. No matter how they jiggled it, the hook wouldn't come loose; it only became embedded deeper in the skin. They finally took him to the emergency room, where a doctor pushed the hook clean through to the other side and snipped off the barb.

"That's disgusting," I said.

"While I was waiting for him," said Annie, rolling onto her side, "a guy came walking down the hallway in boots and greasy jeans. He wasn't wearing any shirt. As he passed me, I saw that his back was bloody and raw. One of the nurses told us his motorcycle dragged him down a gravel road."

In kind, I described a remote shoot from a local farm where a guy drove a spike through the webbing of his fingers while tapping trees for maple syrup. He was a big mule of a man. And his reaction was so devoid of pain—as though he'd only popped a button on his shirt—that it had a rattling effect on me. I turned skittish and confused. In the distance I thought I saw something dancing through the woods. Birds, a deer. It took me a few seconds to gather myself for the camera.

I wasn't sure if Annie was still listening. She was breathing louder now. Finally, she broke the silence with a remark—

I can't remember the exact words—about my having to *expect* that kind of hokey accident working for a lesser station. (I'm certain she said the *lesser station* part.) I tried to push the alcohol from my system, if only for a moment, in order to gain my bearings. I wanted to make brief sense of this exchange; I needed to understand whether it was simply my drunkenness that made her comment distort to some outsize proportion. I waited. And when too much time had passed, we both fell asleep.

A few hours before dawn, I woke with a numbing pain in my back. I sat on the bed and watched Annie in the cidery streetlight. Everything seemed clearer now. She wanted more for me. And she needed *me* to want it too. It was important that I chase a piece of my life, some *thing*, with the same passion, the same burning-hot fuel, that she made use of as she ran after her dream of playing professional golf. But she had failed—and she wouldn't accept that again.

I'd like to work in a bigger market, I think. I always assumed I'd get there one day. But it doesn't drive me. I can't imagine the way it must feel to rise each morning with such a single-minded purpose—the knowledge that my every move is designated toward some larger plan. Surely the most significant turbine in this engine belongs to Annie: a transference of the part of her now teaching housewives to swing nine-irons instead of hitting them herself. She can't save herself from projecting that ambition onto me.

I wandered around in darkness. There was a sour smell coming from the corner—liquor, Annie's toppled sneakers. I can't remember the final moment when I chose meteorology as my profession instead of, say, becoming a dentist, astronaut or Indian chief. For me, it seems more like a childhood dream than a career. It's absurdly random, accidental. But maybe that's how most people make these types of decisions: A friend of your father's runs an insurance company and, yada-yada-yada, you're selling homeowner policies for the next thirty-five years.

Across the room, Annie muttered something in her sleep. I stumbled into my marriage in a similarly arbitrary manner. I simply allowed the momentum of our unspectacular relationship to carry me forward. We had little in common, Annie and I. There wasn't much I knew about her childhood, her past. Before our engagement, I'd only met one other member of her family. Several times in the weeks leading to our wedding I considered asking Annie, in a sober seriousness, whether this was something she truly wanted. It seemed like a dare, a game of chicken that one of us had taken too far.

From nearly the moment we moved into the same house I could feel us inching apart, like oppositely charged magnets. There was never a day when I saw signs, optimistically, that we might survive. The weight only got heavier—and we both understood our foundation would soon collapse. We grew increasingly distant. I began accepting more assignments from the station; I suggested location shoots that required a day's travel. We took turns lapsing into curious behavior: One night I heard a clacking sound coming from outside; I retreated to the backyard, where Annie was sailing wedge shots against the tarpaper roof. Likewise, during a particularly tense three-day period, I escaped to the garage—I slept on the cold floor wrapped in blankets—where I built nearly two hundred dollars' worth of plastic-model muscle cars. Once I had finished, I blew them apart with M-80 firecrackers.

On the street below our room at the Cricket & Squash Club I heard the voices of two men. Despite the late hour, they didn't sound inhibited. They were riding on the back of a garbage truck. Every few minutes came the slow squeal of brakes followed by the impact of glass, cardboard and empty soup cans. I felt guilty for the perfidious thoughts bounding through my head. I was ready to put this marriage behind me; I knew it was time to move on.

Sitting again on the edge of the bed, I was lost to this surge of sadness—a longing for the parts of my life that would soon be gone. It seemed strange to be missing what I still had, even the things I *wanted* to forget. I pictured myself in a lonely kitchen, not the kitchen I shared with Annie but one that didn't yet exist. I was buttering a bagel; I was waiting for Annie to poke her head over my shoulder and announce I was doing it wrong. ("It's not hot enough," she'd say. "That's why the butter won't melt.") Soon we would live apart. And, in time, the possibility existed that we'd never see each other again.

THE LAST THING I REMEMBER IS falling asleep in my bedroom. I have the window parted to breathe the ocean air. A breeze is tapping the blinds against the glass. In my entire life, I have had maybe a half dozen sexually explicit dreams. Now, in the wee morning hours—at least I *think* it's the wee morning; in truth, it's difficult to pinpoint the exact time a dream occurs—I have another hyperrealistic sex dream. I'm at the bar talking to Kiki and having a couple beers. For no discernible reason, Kiki orders me to take a seat on a couch in the back of the strip club. A woman, dressed in one of those short tartan cheerleader skirts and a cropped shirt, comes over and starts performing a lap dance. Though I can't get a good look at the woman's face, her body is fantastic. She grinds away. During her gyrations she gets really vocal. She moans; she says, "Feel my tits." Absurdly, I respond by saying, "I think the club rules are pretty specific about patrons not being allowed to touch the dancers with their hands." She shoots me a look. Again, she says, "Feel my tits." And, mercifully, this time I do. We start petting and pawing and kissing all sloppy and wet with our tongues. As I'm peeking over her shoulder, clumsily attempting to unfasten her brassiere, I see WYIP's own Maura Lease and Lynn Janda and, it appears, a young Dale Evans, sitting together drinking mint juleps. The thought of Maura and Lynn, especially, in such close proximity as I'm preparing to consummate my relationship with the exotic dancer is more than a little unsettling. But in my moment of pause, the dancer slugs her hand down my trousers and begins massaging my very erect penis. "Isn't this nice," she whispers into my ear. "Yes," I say, watching as Dale Evans rises and executes a series of tricks with a bullwhip for Maura and Lynn. The dancer, whose face I still can't see except for a collection of quick-hit glimpses (right eye, left cheekbone, glossy lips), has lowered her head into my lap and pulled my boxer shorts—I'm talking *real* boxer shorts: the bright, silky kind with a huge Everlast emblem across the navel—down to my knees. I watch the dancer open her mouth, in preparation, I believe, for fellatio . . .

And I hear Rick Fasco talking. It seems as if he's telling me the dancer's name is Bella, or perhaps he's speaking a bastardized version of Italian and English, saying, "She *is* bella." I'm holding something hard and curved—my dick? But I hear Fasco's voice, again.

And now I'm holding the phone.

"It's Isabel," he says. When I do not immediately answer, taking a few seconds to collect myself, he asks, "Are you *sure* you're awake?"

"What time is it?"

"You just asked me that." (I did?) "It's about five-thirty."

This next part is unsettling. I have not had a nocturnal emission since high school. But sitting on the edge of my bed, I look down to discover my underpants, a clingy hybrid of briefs and boxers, are sticky with semen. My penis is only now beginning to lose its stiffness.

"Did you hear—"

"Don't talk!" I say, not wanting to consider the prospect of a world where I'm listening to Rick Fasco's voice while staring at my own semi-erect penis. "Give me a minute."

The windows are dark. When the phone rang, I must have absently switched on the light on my nightstand. My bedsheet and blanket are twisted into the kind of rope you see movie prisoners use to escape from their cells.

When I'm ready, I say, "Go ahead."

"Twenty minutes ago they clocked Isabel's winds in excess of 131 miles per hour. She's been upgraded to a Category Four."

This is news. A Category Four hurricane is rare. Its potential for damage is classified as extreme. In August 1992, Hurricane Andrew reached Category Four status not long before slamming into Dade County, Florida. Within hours, the town of Homestead resembled a cavernous junkyard. I sat with a few colleagues and watched news footage of the aftermath shot from helicopters. We were speechless. "You know," I remember someone finally saying, "it looks like those film reels from Beirut."

I peel off my damp underpants.

"Have they revised their projections?"

"They're still not sure," says Fasco nervously. "But they think it's going to hit between Charleston and Jacksonville sometime tomorrow."

"Charleston? That's pretty high."

I can hear Fasco's uneven breathing.

"Take it easy," I say. "I'll be there soon."

Though I have no concrete evidence, I still believe Isabel will prove nothing more than an inconvenience to Bentleyville. I shower and shave, preparing for a long day. Should the predictions shift, like wind currents, and the nation's top forecasters begin suggesting Isabel may inch farther north, we have to be ready. There are both precautionary and mandatory evacuations. A Category Four hurricane is brutal, deadly; it has the power to change lives in a few short hours.

BY THE TIME I REACH THE STATION, the sun is fighting to burn a hole in the bleach-colored sky. There's still little definable darkness along the horizon. Standing beside the back door, one of the security guards has a cigarette cupped in his hand. He nods and removes a chair he's propped against the door to prevent it from locking shut. Almost immediately, I'm met by Kurt, who is hunched absentmindedly before a bank of vending machines.

"Do you like Lorna Doones?" he asks.

"Not really."

"For peanut-flavored M&M's, I pushed E19," he says, opening his fist to reveal a cellophane-wrapped package of cookies. "But it gave me Lorna Doones."

I nod.

"Too early. I may have hit the wrong buttons."

As I begin walking toward my desk, he asks, "Is this for real?"

It takes me a moment to realize he's no longer talking about snack food.

"Yes," I say.

He sighs. The last thing I hear before turning the corner into the newsroom is Kurt asking himself, or the vending machine, "Who *eats* Lorna Doones anymore?"

I am relieved to discuss something other than the hurricane. Bill Kayleigh, a cameraman, is sipping from a carton of grapefruit juice when I pass him. He tells me about a running back for the Carolina Panthers who, last night, was arrested for playing polo (!) with a bowling ball on the streets of downtown Charlotte. "*Allegedly*," says Bill, raising his forefinger to emphasize the absurdity of not presuming guilt—we have *video*—until Brady Carson, said running back, has been granted his day in court. "He was driving around in his truck while swinging a sledgehammer out the window at a bowling ball. When he got bored—cuz, for God's sake, the only damage the ball did was dent a few hubcaps—he started punching the hammer into the headlights and hoods of parked cars."

"Go figure," I say.

We both smile.

"Seems every time you hear about famous people these days," says Bill, "they're doing something stupid."

I can't take my eyes off his bulbous chin. It looks as though someone screwed a ball of putty to the bottom of his face.

I excuse myself. I watch Rick Fasco waving his arms on the monitor suspended above my desk. His cartoon dwarf, Goshen, again dressed in foul-weather gear, is driving a tiny car. Although I can't hear Fasco, I'm assuming he's telling our viewers they must prepare to leave. If I'd seen this broadcast yesterday, I would've been pissed at him for inspiring panic unnecessarily. This morning, though, I'm feeling different. The possibility now exists that Isabel, a major hurricane, will retain much of its strength as she moves in our direction.

Advanced technology be damned: The closer a storm creeps to land, the more difficult it becomes to track. Isabel will actually *gain* speed as she travels northeast along the coast. Naturally, meteorologists prefer to err on the side of caution. In the days before a hurricane strike, forecasters will tell residents of seaside communities to board their houses and move inland. But many people have started turning a deaf ear to these warnings. They've grown cynical, having returned home after past episodes to discover the storm missed their property by hundreds of miles.

When a storm's steering currents weaken, new levels of

unpredictability start to mount. It will travel in nonsensical parabolas, like beads of water on a hot skillet. I can already see what the day has in store: Despite the fact that it's not yet eight o'clock, the five phone lines with weather-department extensions are blinking furiously.

A few years after I finished college, I eliminated caffeine from my diet for nearly nine months. Though I'd like to claim some noble motive—embracing veganism, purging toxins—my reason for quitting coffee, cola and chocolate had everything to do with the woman I was dating. Her name was Clara Nye and she was convinced the single worst thing a person could put into his body was caffeine. For a while I'd been struggling to fall asleep without the assistance of medication. With Clara's encouragement I kicked caffeine cold turkey. Two days into my new life, I experienced horrible withdrawal: chills, nausea, an excruciating headache. But the worst part came *after* the physical stuff. I couldn't shake this dull, low-grade depression. Once I even snuck a Mountain Dew thinking it might make things better. But the rush of sugar and carbonation nearly caused me to vomit.

I'm reminded of that time because today I'm suffering from the same unquenchable malaise. Staring at my desk—papers, maps, Post-Its, stapler—I want to sit someplace else. I need my eyes to fall on a *different* set of objects. Anything unfamiliar. Though I would never admit it, never say the words aloud, part of me hopes the storm *does* land in Bentleyville. This tragedy as a cure for boredom.

By afternoon, expectations have risen at a dizzy pace. The town is filled with the same kinetic energy that ricochets through communities on the day of, say, a big game. My first year in Bentleyville, the Bandits played the Roanoke Mountaineers for the championship of their minor league. Storefronts were hidden beneath banners and placards wishing the team success. The mayor presented the Bandits' manager with a key to the city during a rally attended by nearly every Bentleyville resident. I couldn't walk a block without seeing some combination of team caps, pennants, T-shirts and bumper stickers. Many of the town's traffic signs had been defaced to read, "*Stop* the Mountaineers" and "*Yield* to the Bandits." For ten days, until the Bandits lost the series four games to three, the town was consumed by a common cause.

The supermarket is filled with shoppers loading their carts with canned goods, blue-tip matches (gone before noon) and jugs of distilled water. Two doors down, the hardware store has emptied its shelves of candles, flashlights and wood planks for sealing windows. Kimmy Wilson returns from a diner and announces the Kmart hasn't a single remaining umbrella, rain poncho or slicker. She says, "They don't even have those *huge* umbrellas you spear through patio tables."

Eager to clear my head—it's still throbbing—I decide to leave for lunch. There's a package store a few blocks from the station that serves home-cooked meals in a back room. They also offer tin cups of moonshine from a specially rigged water cooler behind the bar. Transparent as gin, it tastes the way kerosene smells. Because of moonshine's dangerously high alcohol content, it's consumed at a table designated for non-smokers.

I'm sitting at the bar eating ham steak, grits and biscuits.

Someone has threaded a bicycle chain through the handle of a small television, above the cash box, leaving it dangling from the ceiling like a comical chandelier. A snowy rerun of *The Andy Griffith Show* shares space with a constant crawl along the bottom of the screen warning viewers of the coming weather. I sprinkle salt and pepper onto my grits, already marbled with slippery streams of butter.

"Shouldn't you be somewheres?" asks Hollister Rozek.

He's using a small funnel to refill sugar dispensers. His left cheek is fat with chewing tobacco from a foil pouch in his breast pocket.

"I am."

He removes the funnel, snapping it against the air as though casting a fishing pole. Loose granules of sugar spray in my direction.

"Don' get smart."

I have seen this man commit atrocities against the human body, *his* body. It is not uncommon for him to together chew leaf tobacco *and* snuff, the kind that nests between lower lip and gum; he will smoke a cigarette at the same time. He seemed amused when I called it a goddam Mardi Gras of nicotine. On a bet, he once chugged a glass of moonshine in a single swallow. He claims his system is alcohol-proof.

"I'm taking my lunch break," I say, tapping fork to plate. "Do you have a problem with that?"

He smiles.

"You can kiss my cracker ass." He returns to his sugar dispensers. "Just thought a man like you might have someplace more important to be settin' on a day like today."

As I'm sopping my grits with part of a biscuit, I overhear two men seated behind me.

"Says these are *new* and *improved*," one of the men announces, waving a sack of potato chips at his lunch mate. "I think they're worse."

"How so?" asks the other.

"Used to be you could taste some potato," he says. "Now it's all drown out by barbecue flavoring."

They're briefly silent.

"You know what else?" he continues, not slowing for a response. "The bag was only half filled."

The premonition is unexpected, rising quickly like the swollen skin orbiting a sting. Isabel really *could* run aground in Bentleyville. Listening to the men behind me, I consider the way things work: It's guys like them who're yanked before the eye of a television camera to tell their stories. Explain to a national audience the way they existed only a dozen hours earlier. How the two of them were eating lunch on the very acre of land where Hollister's once stood. "I was tellin' Buddy," the one might say, "that Ran-Dee Potato Chips don't taste the same. And next thing we know the sky turns black as coffee."

My train of thought is interrupted by a loud ringing from my coat pocket. The cell phone I sometimes carry is hopelessly outdated. It's enormous, resembling the field phones used during World War II. Plugging my index finger into my uncovered ear, I talk briefly with Rick Fasco. I can see my reflection in the flaking mirror behind Hollister. The storm has again intensified, nearly reaching Category Five status.

"Everything okay?" Hollister asks.

"Work stuff."

He motions toward a foil-covered tray filled with plum cobbler. I shake my head. When he moves to the end of the bar to settle someone's tab, I wipe my mouth with a fresh napkin.

"I'm leaving," I announce to Hollister, tucking a few bills under my water glass. "Back to the office."

"Say you are."

I can't help noticing the song playing on a portable radio near the kitchen: "Speedoo" by The Cadillacs.

THE REST OF THE DAY CRUMBLES TO a savage inertia. Responsibilities accumulate at such a maddening rate, I'm left wondering how they'll be completed. Fasco and I wade through reams of information spread across our desk: print-outs, maps, computer diagrams and spreadsheets chronicling past weather patterns. We're in near-constant contact with both the National Weather Service and the National Oceanic and Atmospheric Administration. Because almost the entire ten o'clock broadcast is devoted to the storm, Fasco and I share on-air duties. Finally, four minutes before the news is scheduled to end, Isabel's barometric pressure drops below 27.17 inches, her winds surpass 155 miles per hour and she is classified as a Category Five hurricane.

"Since 1900," I explain to viewers during suddenly expanded coverage superceding a ten-thirty rerun of *M*A*S*H*, "only two Category Five hurricanes have hit the U.S. An unnamed storm crossed the Florida Keys in 1935, killing 408 people. Thirty-four years later, in 1969, Camille struck Mississippi, Louisiana and Alabama, causing 256 deaths."

In addition, we announce that the governor is preparing to issue a state of emergency for counties along the coastline. A decision on *mandatory* evacuation will also be made within the hour. After our broadcast is completed, we persist with screen-fillers during the regularly scheduled programming: A regional weather map is planted like a postage stamp in the upper right-hand corner, winking with reds and yellows; a small box beneath the map lists the counties affected by the governor's state of emergency; and a crawl across the bottom updates viewers on the hurricane's progress.

"You and Rick should split the workload," says Kurt. "We're going live whenever we get more definitive information. Even if that's three in the morning."

By the Weather Service's estimation, Isabel will make landfall somewhere between Virginia Beach and Savannah, Georgia, early tomorrow evening. The updated wind currents suggest most of Florida, even northern cities like Daytona Beach and Jacksonville, is out of harm's way.

Because I have seniority over Fasco, I decide it is probably better (for me, anyway) to take the second shift so I'll be fresher in the hours closest to Isabel's prospective arrival. I have enough time for a shower and a half night's sleep. At home, I can hear my neighbor, Hilary, pacing the courtyard while calling for her cat.

"Remy," she says, using her normal speaking voice even though most of the condo's residents have gone to bed.

I'm exhausted. Still, I have a restless sleep. I awaken on the couch at seven with no memory of moving into the living room during the night. When I call Fasco, I'm placed on hold for several minutes. He sounds awful, depleted. Each word is a chore for him to carry against his dry, gravelly throat. He tells me the storm is maintaining windspeed; he also says it's now being projected to strike Georgetown, South Carolina, north of Charleston, around eight this evening. It seems most of the heavy shit will miss us.

There's a sluggish, hangover quality to the day. We expected to be near ground zero of a major catastrophe and instead we'll encounter only strong winds and rain when Isabel makes news 350 miles down the coastline. Of course, this is a good thing—a *great* thing. But that doesn't change a lingering perception: We all feel cheated. The prospect of sitting in the storm's path was exhilarating. And now our chance for meteorological history has drifted south.

I walk Fasco to the parking lot, offering consolation before he lowers himself into his car. "You did a nice job," I tell him. He nods, rubbing his tired, puffy eyes. I watch him drive zombielike down the street. A warm breeze skirts through an orchard of pecan trees on the neighboring block. I can hear the frictiony swish of leaf against leaf. From farther still comes the smell of timothy hay, bound and baled for delivery. The sky is hidden by putty-colored clouds, turning and tumbling like smoke.

THE WHOLE THING TRANSPIRES WITH breathtaking speed and efficiency. I'm taking a piss when I hear one of the station's interns shouting for me to grab the phone. I have the switchboard forward the call to a wall unit beside our reference library. It's been six or seven hours since we last spoke to someone from the National Weather Service. I listen to a collection of mechanical clicks followed by the noise of human breathing, Hickman Barnes, who tells me Hurricane Isabel has abruptly changed its course.

"She's riding the coastline," he says. In truth, the storm is still nearly a hundred miles from shore. "The currents suggest she's going to veer left."

"Near *Bentleyville*?"

"That's our bet." He pauses to answer someone from his office. "She could bounce farther north. But you're in the hot zone. I spoke to the governor's office. They're going to reissue a state of emergency. They're also calling for the immediate evacuation of properties along the waterfront."

I'm silent.

"Lucas?" he says, making sure we haven't lost our connection. "You need to get on TV."

He promises to keep me posted.

We're forty-eight minutes from our six o'clock broadcast. I enter Kurt's office at the same time he's reading a fax from the governor.

"What's the deal with this state of emergency?" he asks. "On again, off again, on again—can't they make up their minds?"

I smile weakly.

"This is serious?"

I nod.

"We look like amateurs," he says, leaning back and lacing his fingers behind his head. "Our viewers will think we're idiots."

"Weather forecasting's not an exact science. Especially when it comes to hurricanes."

"Maybe we should wait for something definitive."

"Kurt," I say, moving to his desk, "did you watch any of our reports? This is a Category *Five* hurricane. I'm not exaggerating when I say it's one of the *three* most powerful storms to hit the U.S. in the past century."

He takes a few deep breaths.

"Now?" he asks.

"*Right* now."

He rises and together we head into the newsroom. He climbs onto a chair, cupping his hands around his mouth, and announces the new information.

"I'll find a cameraman," he tells me. "You've got five minutes."

I return to my desk, gather my materials. When I call the Weather Service for another update, Hickman Barnes tells me it's time to "batten down the hatches."

"Seven-thirty," he says. "You've got maybe two hours."

A message is left for Fasco. We're going to continue broadcasting until the storm reaches shore. We'll also rely on voice-overs coupled with on-screen graphics, weather maps, satellite shots and Doppler diagrams. For the first time in WYIP's history, it will run crawls *during* advertisements; it will suspend commercials entirely in the hour preceding Isabel's arrival.

Then comes something else: Once I have finished the first part of my broadcast, Kurt calls me to his office again. He's talking to someone on speakerphone, a network producer. When the Weather Service amended its prediction earlier today, network brass shifted around personnel. Now the majority of their reporters are stranded in Georgetown, South Carolina, or Myrtle Beach. Even if time wasn't a factor—to say nothing of rapidly deteriorating travel conditions—the National Guard has closed local airports and roadways to inbound traffic.

"What the network wants . . ." says Kurt, slowing to assemble his words. "They're asking us to help them cover the storm."

I nod.

"You and Trip will take the satellite truck."

The guy on the phone, the producer, suggests a few waiting-for-the-storm teasers from the beach. Then we'll move to higher ground for safety. Of course, the importance of doing good work isn't lost on Kurt. He's seized by the kind of caffeinated enthusiasm that comes from chugging a six-pack of Mountain Dew. He claws through a mound of paperwork and scribbles something onto a note card.

"This is for you," he says. "It's Garron Yulish's number in New York; he's the producer."

I'm beginning to gain focus; I'm running through a mental checklist of what needs to get done. In the time it takes to collect my things, maybe ten minutes, Fasco has returned to the station. He appears even *more* defeated. I'm certain he's considered how our roles may have been reversed—a throw of the dice—if he was working when the updated forecast arrived. Together we make our way to the back door, where Trip's standing in a slicker and rain pants. Poking from the corner of his mouth is a raw carrot stick.

"Ready?" he asks.

We leave Fasco beside a security guard in the cramped doorway, looking lonely and swindled.

THE SKY RESEMBLES A SHEET OF DAMP newsprint. A light rain begins to fall. We're driving east on Montesino Street. The horizon, mottled and streaked, appears as though it's been sprayed with motor oil.

"That looks scary," says Trip.

Gazing through the windshield, I watch a field of sugarcane deform with concentric ripples. The cool ocean air feels good on my face, smelling sweetly of orchard grass and surf. During the short time needed to complete our preparations, the tide takes an aggressive bead on the beachfront. Every few seconds a new plume of spray explodes against the concrete breakwall.

For our first shot, I stand in the middle of the boardwalk with the ocean at my back. The waves rise tall and white, making for dramatic television. I dial Garron Yulish with a soggy thumb and tell him we're sending something. He seems pleasant, relieved.

I think our early pieces work well. Admittedly, I'm feeling as nervous as I have since my first weeks in broadcasting. The prospect of my words and image being beamed far beyond the borders of Bentleyville is more than a little daunting. I consider the many people from high school, from *grade* school, who may have wondered what happened to me. Now a flip of their remote controls will provide them with an immediate answer. A couple times I stumble over a phrase, backing myself into an awkward corner. But Yulish comforts me. He insists everything we bounce to them will be taped and edited. "I promise," he says, "we'll make you look great."

During a break, Trip and I sit in the truck and stare at the ocean. For maybe five minutes a curtain of sky seems to part, offering the last vestiges of muted sunlight. Assuming you had just now awakened from a deep sleep, uninformed, you'd probably guess it was going to be a beautiful evening. "See there," says Trip, gesturing toward a section of singularly illuminated clouds. "Doesn't that look like a lantern?"

A recurrence of darkness is accompanied by slender spools of fog slinking across the waters. Near shore, the fog breaks into a fine vapor with corkscrewing tendrils that resemble fingers digging at the sand. If it were possible to squirt a giant drum of food coloring into the storm, marking its progress like some dye-induced medical test, I believe it would reveal that Isabel's frontal lobe is suddenly upon us. The truck begins to sway—it feels as though we're speeding down a banked racetrack, each turn threatening to spill us sideways. Trip braces himself against the dashboard.

"Let's get this," I say, opening the door.

He is slow to respond.

"Trip?"

He grabs his things reluctantly and steps outside.

I call Yulish, who suggests we go live. He tells me anchorman Mark Brown will break into network programming—*We interrupt this broadcast*—and toss it to me. Together, Trip and I make our way to an elevated patio near the beach, in the shadow of a boarded-shut restaurant, called Trixies, that's renowned for crabcakes and steamed shrimp.

The waves and wind are so fierce that many of the boats fastened to the pier are already threatening to unmoor themselves; their lines stretch vertically down to the submerged dock like ropes tethering lifeless balloons. We're both shielding ourselves against sharp pellets of rain. As we prepare to shoot, I tug a ballcap emblazoned with HOLLISTER'S PACKAGE STORE against my brow to keep the water from running into my eyes.

"Let's do this quickly," shouts Trip.

A cauldron of sounds—the hard flap of awning fabric, a flagpole's whipping cable—is lost to the blaring ignition of a hundred jet engines. We're momentarily distracted when a steel-weave garbage pail cartwheels into a brick wall. Trip looks repeatedly over his shoulder, fearing more debris. I hold my thumb against my earpiece to stop it from dislodging in the tiny flood washing through my ear canal. I can barely hear Mark Brown when he signals me.

"Thanks, Mark," I say into the camera. "As you can see, it's getting pretty rough here."

From the brink of my vision, I glimpse a wooden bench rattling fitfully; then it becomes a chubby javelin launched into the windshield of a parked car. The swoopy blur causes Trip to jump.

"Isabel came ashore a little while ago." I'm practically screaming. "This is only the third Category Five hurricane in history to hit the U.S. The winds—" A bullet-shaped life-preserver whistles past my head. "The winds in some sections of the storm are more than 155 miles per hour."

Even with the hood of my slicker cinched around the bill of my cap, my face is so wet that each time I speak, water sputters from my lips.

As I describe the way hurricanes are comprised of various bands of spiraling thunderstorms—we're presently in the throes of Isabel's earliest bands—I can see Trip lowering his head between his shoulders for protection. He looks ready to run.

For some strange reason, I'm not afraid. I feel a mighty surge of adrenaline tearing through me. This is a remarkable opportunity, kind of like having my demo tape played for every station manager in the country. If I can impress somebody—assuming I don't screw the pooch—I have a chance to land a gig in a better market.

"The hope," I say, holding the microphone against my

chin, "is that even with Isabel's sudden change in direction, most of Bentleyville's residents took the warnings seriously and departed."

On the word *departed*, Trip vigorously nods his head. Mark Brown is speaking into my earpiece, but I hear only fragmented static. The wind has a texture, bulldozing through us like wet cement. As I reach for a picnic table near my side to gain stability, it trembles, tap-dancing against the hard ground.

"This isn't good," shouts Trip.

"He's right," says Mark Brown faintly. And before he's lost to waves of crunching distortion, he suggests we sprint for safety.

I want one last panoramic shot of our surroundings, unhinged, while I narrate the scene. Let these viewers seated in their warm, windless living rooms have a little look-see. Hey, Garron. What's it worth to you? The glorious prospect of our final minutes on network television nearly makes me break into a smile. (That would be creepy.) I can almost picture myself being welcomed into a top ten—fuck it!—a top *five* market. After years of circling the drain, my ambition has wonderously resurrected itself. As I speak, wiping salt water from my burning eyes, I guide Trip with my elbow . . .

But he's moved . . .

Next comes a quiet in my head. Slow and fast. The earth violently ridding itself of debris: spitting loose trees and sailboats and huge plots of rootless land. I'm screaming Trip's name so loudly my lungs burn. He's farther away, watching the camera release from his hands like a paper airplane. There's nothing left to hold. Only blackness. And that ungodly sound of a thousand jet engines sucking everything back . . .

I reach for Trip, but the wind turns me around. And around. I'm instantly terrified in a way I didn't know existed. My right hand is contracting against the microphone with joint-popping force. The fear is thoroughly engulfing, maybe the only emotion I will ever have again. My body is shaking savagely, preparing to rupture from within. This time when I try to call for Trip I've forgotten how to breathe. There's no more oxygen. Nonsensically, my brain remembers "Come Go With Me" by the Dell Vikings. And every word of the song skates against my head at such terrific speed it's as though a ribbon of audiotape were yanked pull-cord-style through the player . . .

An amplified squeaking comes from a place beyond my left shoulder. I see a black monolith lifting and lifting. The roof from Trixies Restaurant is engaged in confetti somersaults. There's a moment when it freezes against the rushing wind. I call for Trip—*I scream, scream, scream* for him. But the loudness retreats to my ears and throat and mouth. In a single elegant motion, Trixies' roof climbs, briefly, before tucking into one of the currents and careening toward the ground. I can see events unraveling in deliberate order. I wave my arms in a fury, signaling Trip to jump out of the way. He's squeezing a bolted-down park bench when the roof tomahawks past. And I think it misses him. For there's no sound. Until I notice he's clinging to the roof, twirling above the pushed-flat trees. I reflexively gaze back to the place where he'd been standing. Rising from the sidewalk, partially obscured by a crosshatching of the seatback's wood and iron slats, is his lower torso—feet and legs and belted waist locked in position by more wind . . .

Oh, God . . .

To my left a pane of glass detonates from its frame, sending hundreds of glittery shards razoring through the air, stinging my cheek and forearm and calf. Each step's a series of trapdoors, the sledgehammer drafts permitting me to walk only in certain directions. I'm moving low to the ground, my eyes locked to a fissure in the back wall of Trixies. Surely there's a basement or storage locker in which to hide. Our truck's been turned upside down, flattened. An unholy maelstrom of objects wash past me, not unlike Dorothy's bedroom window in the *Wizard of Oz*: a steel garbage dumpster; a bicycle still padlocked to a lamppost; a charcoal grill; a pair of basketball sneakers. Rotating above the parking lot is a demasted sloop . . .

Something sharp bumps my left leg—an automobile antenna has skewered my thigh. After I tug it free, the antenna flies away without once skipping against the asphalt. A tsunami of trash sweeps along the street, clogged with spinning cans of tomato paste, shredded newspaper and empty boxes. Weirdly conjoined branches from differing trees are entwined in whirling, funnel-shaped motes . . .

A bottle of soda slugs the back of my head. I'm no more than forty feet from Trixies, but the distance seems impossible. There's nothing to anchor me on the journey. Suddenly the very earth appears to move, lowering itself by fractions; a correction. Another powerful lurch, and I realize *I'm* the one who is shifting, rising. Twin currents are now guiding my feet, pulling them in a reversal of gravity so they swing above my shoulders. Nature's shaking the change from my pockets. In a spastic rendition of the crawl stroke, my arms paddle the fast-blowing air. Though the fear is constant, I'm now experiencing a swell of pure debilitating panic. My heart is playing speed-bag against my sternum. There are stories about people who during monumental crises have moments of great clarity, an almost serene calmness spilling over them. But I'm devoid of such peaceful thoughts. Instead, I'm seized by a terror that's as absolute as anything I have ever known . . .

Blooming from the jagged crack along the wall of Trixies is the split trunk of a sugar maple. Somehow secured, it resembles a dragon's spiky tail. My survival seems suddenly linked to the tree: If I can reach its branches I can scale the wood, escape for the basement. In nearly the same instant the thought crosses my mind, another gust of wind drives me into a neighboring bait shack. Because I'm inverted, my skewed bearings lead me to protectively raise my arms against the wrong side of my body. The collision compresses my rib cage. And I'm certain bones have been broken. Even more remarkably, the grinding strength of the wind has pinned me sideways to the bait shack's outer wall. My mouth is filled with water and phlegm and the sourness of blood. I'm mounted like a hunting trophy; I touch my fingers to my lips, convinced the impact has lacerated one of my organs. Instead, I discover the injury is only a split tongue . . .

The pressure releases in conjunction with the door

beneath being ripped from its hinges, coming undone in time to strike me on the shoulder. I remember once hearing a retired football player talk about playing with pain—the constant soreness was as much a part of the game as slipping on his uniform. And those are my exact thoughts as I dump to the stony ground. I lean through the empty doorframe of the bait shack . . .

And the roar of an eighteen-wheeler barreling down the interstate bids me to retreat. A monstrous slipstream causes the bait shack to implode, *literally*, four walls collapsing against themselves in a tight stack of plywood and sharp corners. I avoid a sofa-shaped ice box tumbling weightlessly in the direction of Montesino Street, trailing potter's soil laced with nightcrawlers . . .

My forehead's seized with what I imagine is the start of a migraine. But my fingers, raw and red, remove a dagger of scrap metal from above my eyebrow. Again, I set my sights on the tree poking from Trixies. I watch a telephone pole bending, bending before it breaks with a sound no greater than a snapping twig. I squint against thick coils of muddy, sandy air . . .

A big Buick to my right has a fishing dinghy speared through its passenger side. The blowing wind breathes with a sort of waaahhh-*waaahhh* growl. The car is ready to roll sideways . . .

On the ground wet patties of sand are pushed, creepily, by some mysterious motion. Thunderheads clang with an intensity I can feel in my rectum. And I see the tree, so tantalizingly close, still holding its position. The storm's tide surge must be twenty feet high, reeling away our truck as though it were a rock crab. The tree's largest limb is slapping at the concrete. This *can* happen. When I'm nearly upon the branch, I notice a small fiberglass sailboat posited in the middle of the parking lot, paired strangely with a picnic bench—random items yoked in a confluence of matter and drastic wind. From my perspective, the picnic bench, now twitching, resembles the prisoner plank on a pirate ship . . .

As my hand grips the tree, I watch the sailboat scuff across the watery asphalt. It's headed toward me at a steady pace. I'm trying to shimmy safely along the trunk, but the tree's metronomic waggle is making it a difficult task. From the corner of my eye, I see the sailboat traveling faster, bouncing, bounding, before putting distance between itself and the ground. It's now airborne, a full three feet above land. There's a lunging wall of water and sand and pointy trash. When I realize the sailboat is bearing down on me, I decide against dropping low for fear of getting wedged beneath something heavy. Instead, laughably, I stand. I'm hoping to leap from its path at the last possible instant . . .

And the speed is greater than I anticipated. The sailboat clips my arm and chest. Even amid the fantastic vacuum noise of Isabel, I can hear the brittle splintering of wood as the bench dismantles against my body. Quills of oak are now sticking from my neck, breast and bicep; they're aimed awkwardly from my knee. A rubbery skin of bench-seat paint, peeled and perforated, is tacked to my nose and chin. I'm fighting to keep my footing. A freed poplar is caught against a section of fencing, its leafy foliage pawing loose gravel. The roots are transformed into whipping propellers. . .

Severed tentacles of power line scream in the awesome

wind, still attached to a hurtling traffic light. The air is congested with disintegrating oars, inner tubes, long ribbons of aluminum siding shucked from nearby houses. I fall to my knees and hug the tree, riding out its wobbly action. No matter how many times I spit, I can't rid my tongue of sand and saliva and pulpy wood chips. I feel throbbing pains, small and large, in every region of my body. Clinging to bark, I use each knot and branch to carry me closer to Trixies. The rain, the stinging, blinding rain, comes in weighted curtains . . .

I can see blackness where the tree disappears into the building. A leftover plane of roof has been slapped into narrow pleats. The floodwater is forming clouded rapids, the kind with whirlpools and steep, frothy humps of breaking surf. It won't be long before the tree too is washed away. I'm getting an awful stitch on my side, making me double over in pain. I'm now feeling a similar pang buckling against my spine . . .

There's not much farther to climb. The storm's pulse is maniacal. If I don't reach shelter soon I'll be pitched from current to current in a tantrum of centrifugal force. It'll dash me into the face of a cinderblock barrier. Only to repeat the process until Isabel burns out. I'm skirting upward, exhausted, allowing my cheek to drag against the coarse surface of the tree; I'm afraid to raise my head, lest some orbiting object decapitate me . .

And now I'm touching the sharpened petals of steel curling from the dark crease. If I can hoist myself to waist level, I should be able to squeeze through the gap not clogged by tree. As soon as I have committed, I sense movement. The tree groans; it rolls logger-style into the choppy flood. Without support, my torso drops into the tightening crevice until it finds resistance. The pain is immediate . . .

The toothy edge of sheet metal has sliced through my skin. And a V-shaped notch in the concrete has swallowed my hips. I know something cracked—my pelvis? more damage to my rib cage? Then comes the nausea—followed by more mind-numbing pain. A spume of vomit sprays from my mouth, mixing with rain and muddy salt water. Perhaps the retching is the only thing keeping me conscious . . .

I'm partially blinded. It's hard to know how much of my vision is distorted by dizziness and how much is the chaotic air. A bell. The *ting-ting-ting* of a bell. Driving through the inky room is a white truck, white and red and lime green. Pasted to its side are dozens of photographs promising a variety of frozen treats: Rocket Pops, Fudgesicles, Eskimo Pies, Krunch Bars. It's the Mr. Frosty wagon from when I was a kid. The same truck that would trundle through my neighborhood on hot summer days. *It's not real.* But I reach for it anyway. I arch my back and turn sideways, wriggling my thighs for leverage against the tines of crooked metal. Through, almost through. I swipe for the handle on Mr. Frosty's passing door— and plummet steeply down. Into four feet of murky water stirring against the inside walls of Trixies. . .

Somehow I'm able to lift myself above the surface. And the ringing continues. I can now see the sound is coming from a small bell the bartender uses to acknowledge tips, attached to one of the building's teetering beams. I slosh across the room, bracing myself against copper banisters and sliding tables. There are doors. I check them, jiggling the nobs—storage closets, bathrooms. My eyes grow fuzzy with the kind of black, spotty amoebas that arrive after staring into sunlight . . .

The basement staircase is hidden beneath a zigzag of rushing water. Standing in the hingeless doorway, my mouth fills queerly with the sweet taste of cinnamon . . .

It begins with a hollow report, the noise of pistols on a firing range. I turn in time to see a window on the far wall sucked in one pristine piece from its frame. A baritone howl of wind shear blasts through the skeletal roof, so loud it seems to knock the cilia in my ears completely flat. The whole thing unfolds in several long blinks. The wind ricochets off the floor, spreading water and exploding chairs before banking toward me. I'm elevated into the stairwell, my head slamming along the graded ceiling. But I don't release. Instead, the swirling currents batter me into the wall; my nails are scraping plaster as I'm carried into the basement . . .

Instinctively, I start running toward a distant corner. I'm moving drunkenly, my legs punching splashes that follow no discernible pattern—a crooked, confusing line. Hands splayed, I steady myself on a large furnace. I'm wheezing huge mouthfuls of damp, musty air. *This is a good place*, I think, taking a seat on several crates of stacked beverages . . .

And comes another mighty roar. Followed closely by shifting furniture and slamming doors in the room above. A beam punctures the basement ceiling. Then the bar itself falls through the floor, bringing columns of torrential water.

I hear something whistling.

And the side of my head explodes . . .

[9/18: Excerpts from story on front page of the *Bentleyville Barker* newspaper:]

HED: HURRICANE HORROR

Hurricane Isabel made landfall in the U.S. for the first time when it crossed Bentleyville beach yesterday at 7:56 p.m. EDT. The storm achieved the highest possible rating on the Saffir-Simpson scale, which measures strength, and became only the third Category Five hurricane to reach this country since 1900 . . .

Wind gusts of 164 miles per hour were reported at the height of the storm . . .

The governor has declared a state of emergency for all counties directly affected by Isabel. The National Guard has been mobilized to begin searching for possible survivors and assist with wreckage removal. Severe winds and flooding are said to be responsible for 17 deaths and 238 injuries, officials announced early today. With another 64 people still missing, the number of fatalities is expected to rise . . .

Among those still unaccounted for is WYIP Channel 7 weath-

erman Lucas Prouty, who was reporting from Bentleyville beach when the storm reached shore. His cameraman, Trip Elder, 33, was killed . . .

The Red Cross has set up a temporary shelter at the Bentleyville High School gymnasium, 2615 Farnsleigh Road . . .

Authorities estimate the storm has caused more than $1 billion in damages . . .

[9/20: Excerpts from story on front page of the *New York Times*:]

HED: SMALL TOWN STRUGGLES WITH BIG STORM

BENTLEYVILLE, N.C., September 19—In the wake of the most powerful hurricane to strike the U.S. in the past century, citizens of this pleasant seaside community are attempting to rebuild their lives. Only two days ago, Isabel washed ashore accompanied by violent rains, flooding and winds in excess of 160 miles per hour . . .

"It's a disaster," said Maggie Anselmo, 67, who has lived in Bentleyville for most of her life. "Entire neighborhoods were destroyed."

Mrs. Anselmo and her husband, Lester Anselmo, 71, lost their house to the storm.

"This is a catastrophe," said Bentleyville Mayor Tom Kopp at a press conference earlier today. "We will seek financial assistance from the government."

According to reports, 28 people are confirmed dead and another 261 injured. Among the 53 people still listed as missing is local weather forecaster Lucas Prouty of WYIP-TV, who was chronicling Isabel's arrival near the waterfront. Mr. Prouty's report was broadcast nationwide on N___ affiliates . . .

[9/21: Excerpts from story on front page of the *New York Times*:]

HED: ISABEL DEATH TOLL CONTINUES TO CLIMB

BENTLEYVILLE, N.C., September 20—Earlier this week, Hurricane Isabel killed 34 people and forced another 4,000 out of their homes . . .

The storm, which was among the most powerful to ever reach U.S. soil, caused three of Bentleyville's hospitals to confirm internal emergencies. It is responsible for more than $1 billion in damages . . .

This morning the President declared a dozen counties disaster areas, including Pender, Brunswick and Onslow. Employees of the Federal Emergency Management Administration were en route to the city by nightfall . . .

Officials have used boats and helicopters to save thousands of residents trapped by fast-rising floodwaters . . .

Bentleyville's sewage system is ventilated to allow for the discharge of potentially hazardous methane gas. But excessively high waters are now passing through these grates and releasing sewage into the streets.

"People need to understand they're at risk of acquiring dangerous infections if they wade in knee-deep water," said J. P. Brown, the director of the city's Department of Public Works.

In addition to 34 deaths, there are still 41 people listed as missing. A focus of national attention has been the recovery of local meteorologist Lucas Prouty, of WYIP-TV, who disappeared while broadcasting during the storm. He remains unaccounted for . . .

[9/21: Excerpts from story on front page of *USA Today*:]

HED: ISABEL SURVIVORS LOOK TO REBUILD LIVES

BENTLEYVILLE, N.C.—Under a cloudless blue sky, Adrian Parker surveys the damage Hurricane Isabel inflicted on his Moonlight Inn Restaurant. The floor is hidden beneath nearly two feet of water. Part of the roof is missing. And his elaborate barbecue pit has been rendered a pile of useless scrap metal.

"This place was built by my grandfather," said Parker, 41, a former lineman for the Washington Redskins. "It's going to take some work, but we'll put it back together."

Gil and Ruth Stevens are less fortunate. Their house was demolished by the storm. "We have kinfolk in Georgia," said Mrs. Stevens. "We might move down there."

Authorities are estimating that Isabel has caused more than $1.5 billion in damages . . .

[9/21: Sidebar accompanying preceding story; page 7A of *USA Today*:]

HED: "HE GOT TOO CLOSE"

On that terrifying night last week when Isabel made landfall, one man was there to greet her. Meteorologist Lucas Prouty, of

WYIP-TV in Bentleyville, N.C., chose to report on the Category Five hurricane at close range.

But Prouty may have underestimated the storm's strength. During his broadcast, a national audience watched the awesome power of Isabel firsthand until their TVs filled with choppy static and went momentarily black. It was the last time anyone saw Prouty.

"He got too close," said Garron Yulish, a producer at N____ in New York. "He was doing a great job for us. But we expected him to find shelter."

"I was watching from the studio," said weather forecaster Rick Fasco, a colleague of Prouty's at WYIP. "Even inside our building I could feel the wind gusts. I kept talking to the monitor, telling him to take cover."

Although rescue efforts will continue throughout the week, the prospect of recovering survivors is growing remote. A few days ago, Prouty's cameraman, Trip Elder, 33, was found dead.

"We'll keep looking," said Lt. Gregg Park of the National Guard. "But we know it's unlikely that we'll find someone alive after five or six days."

[9/22: Partial teleprompter transcript from ten o'clock broadcast on WYIP Channel 7:]

WENDY: We'd now like to take a moment to talk about something very personal.

ZANE: The WYIP family would like to thank the many concerned *viewers who have sent cards and e-mails over the past few days. We know Lucas Prouty is a very popular part of each newscast. He ventured into the heart of the storm to provide you—and the rest of the country—with the best possible coverage, risking his life in the process. He's a true professional with exceptionally high standards; he's also a special person. We are all holding out hope for a miracle.*

WENDY: Yesterday, we reported a body found near the marina was believed to have been Lucas. That turned out not to be the case. We hope you will join us in keeping Lucas in our thoughts and prayers . . .

[9/23: Excerpts from story on page 26 in the October 1 issue of *Time* magazine:]

HED: EYE OF THE STORM

BENTLEYVILLE, N.C.—Nearly a week after the Storm of the Century leveled parts of the North Carolina coastline, many are still struggling for answers. Why did weather experts have such a difficult time predicting where Isabel would strike? How can authorities convince people to take hurricane threats more seriously? Have we learned anything from the way information on Isabel was disseminated? . . .

Still scratching our collective heads, we are now left to pose yet another question: Is our nation's preoccupation with storms and other natural disasters requiring those who cover these events to place themselves at risk for the sake of increased ratings? The query seems especially relevant in the wake of several recent incidents.

• Last February, Derrick Burden of CBS was covering a series of avalanches near Silvercrest, Colo., when he was nearly killed

by a cascade of snow. It took a team of rescuers five hours to dig out Burden and cameraman Floyd Hahn.

• In July, Anne Mason, a reporter with KSDA-TV in Wichita, Kan., suffered a punctured lung, broken ribs and a sprained wrist while trying to track several tornadoes. The van in which she was traveling was blown onto its side.

• A month ago, Clarence Gooden of CNN nearly drowned after high waters knocked him from a dock in Ft. Lauderdale, Fla., as he was attempting to broadcast on Tropical Storm Glenda.

Many were riveted to their televisions last week when Lucas Prouty, of WYIP-TV in Bentleyville, N.C., reported on the arrival of Isabel. But viewers did not expect the image of Prouty, in blue slicker and ballcap, to disappear into darkness. They waited for the words technical difficulties to appear on their TV screens. Surely the storm had only interrupted his signal . . .

Prouty remains missing. His cameraman, Trip Elder, 33, was found the next day, his body sliced in half . . .

"Certainly there are inherent dangers in covering violent weather," says Donald Wagner of the Weather Channel. "But we do our best to minimize the risk . . ."

[9/24: Excerpts from story on front page of *Bentleyville Barker*:]

HED: THE SEARCH FOR SURVIVORS

The National Guard and teams of volunteers continued digging through wreckage from Hurricane Isabel in the hopes of locating survivors. It is unlikely someone found among the rubble will be *alive a week after the storm, conceded National Guard spokesman Bud Hartnett . . .*

Of course, much of the attention still centers around missing WYIP weatherman Lucas Prouty, who was reporting on Isabel when he was presumably washed away. Because Prouty's broadcast was carried on national television, the recovery of his body has drawn significant interest from the rest of the country. Six days ago, the badly mutilated remains of Prouty's cameraman, Trip Elder, 33, were discovered.

"This is a very difficult time for our family," said Prouty's sister, Josephine Tepper, of Lincoln Park, Il. "We are trying to stay optimistic."

A memorial service for the 43 people who were killed by the storm will be held at 7:00 p.m. tomorrow at the Bentleyville Civic Center, 11642 Hampton Pass . . .

[9/24: Unscripted dialogue between sportscasters "Easy" Ed Miller and Dave Cranepool during ABC's *Monday Night Football* game: Carolina Panthers vs. Tennessee Titans:]

DAVE: This was a tough week for the Panthers, Ed. Their practice facility was nearly destroyed by Hurricane Isabel. (Pause.) —Pudge Henkel takes the snap and rolls right, throwing for Reggie Donley along the sideline and . . . incomplete. Just out of his reach— Anyway, Coach Willie Harrod told me they spent more time than usual reviewing film as they waited for the turf inside their practice dome to be replaced. They even traveled to Georgia so they could get enough reps.

ED: Sweet molasses! That sure makes a mess of a team's game plan. Reminds me of the time I was playing for the Packers and we got hit with a blizzard. Dumped more than four feet of snow onto Green Bay. The worst part was that most of us couldn't even get out of our driveways. The general manager hired a fleet of buses to come get us all. (Chuckle.)

DAVE: —Third and four. Henkel's lined up in the shotgun. Takes a long snap count. He drops back to pass. He's got Chris Ahman sneaking across a seam in the middle. Oh, Henkel's blindsided. A hard sack by Rooster Lee. Ouch! That looks like it hurt— So, how'd you guys practice?

ED: One thing you can say about the Packers: They're ready for snow. They had these enormous tractors waiting to plow the fields.

DAVE: —The punt team comes out— Yesterday I was talking to Panther running back Shawntae Green. He said the new game room in his basement was flooded by the storm. —Ooooh, that's not a good punt—

ED: He shanked it.

DAVE: —The Titans will let it bounce out of bounds. Twenty-eight, maybe thirty yards if he's lucky— We should take a moment here to say that all of us at Monday Night Football *would like to extend our prayers to the many people whose lives were affected by Hurricane Isabel.*

ED: Just terrible. (Pause.) *And we're burning a candle for that weather fella, Luke Prouty. Here's hoping for some good news* . . .

[9/25: Excerpts from weekly ratings release, Nielsen Media Research:]

For more than 45 years, Nielsen Media Research has measured television audiences on both the national and local levels . . .

The rating is the percentage of the nation's estimated TV homes (102.2 million) watching a particular program. Each rating point represents one percent (1.022 million) of those TV homes. The share is the percentage of TVs operating at a given time that are tuned to a particular program . . .

Top Five Network Shows for the week of September 17–23:

1. Expanded Coverage of Hurricane Isabel, N___
    32.4 rating/39 share, 33,112,800 viewers

2. Monday Night Football, ABC
    24.8 rating/28 share, 25,345,600 viewers

3. Dentist's Chair, The, CBS
    20.6 rating/24 share, 21,053,200 viewers

4. Fred Hersch Jazz Hour, The, N___
    19.1 rating/21 share, 19,520,200 viewers

5. NewsLine, ABC
    18.7 rating/21 share, 19,111,400 viewers

[9/25: Boxed announcement on bottom of front page, *Bentleyville Barker*:]

HED: VIGIL OF HOPE

Tomorrow evening at 9 p.m. a candlelight vigil will be held for Lucas Prouty near lifeguard tower No. 4 on Bentleyville beach. "This is not a memorial," said event organizer Kimmy Wilson, who is a coworker of Prouty's at WYIP Channel 7. "We are simply coming together to pray."

[9/26: Partial transcript from Breaking News coverage on N__ at 1:17 p.m. EDT, interrupting *Days of Our Lives*:]

ANCHOR MARK BROWN: We're preparing to send you to Bentleyville, N.C., where Paul Kirkhart, who has been covering the aftermath of Hurricane Isabel, has a significant development. Paul?

REPORTER PAUL KIRKHART: Yes, Mark . . .

MB: What can you tell us?

PK: Only moments ago, a team of rescue workers from the National Guard and the Bentleyville Fire Department were clearing debris from the site where a restaurant called Trixies once stood. And they heard a voice coming from the basement. It now appears the person buried beneath the wreckage [PK motions with his left arm; a brief picture on TV screens shows men stepping gingerly between the skeletal frame of a mangled building] *is local weathercaster Lucas Prouty.*

MB: Any word on how he's doing? Do we know the extent of his injuries?

PK: No, Mark. They discovered him only about forty minutes ago. As you can see [the camera again pans across PK's shoulder to show men in the background] *these crews are working feverishly to try and get closer. But there is* [he's startled by the sound of something being dropped] *lots of garbage to be moved.*

[9/26: Partial transcript from a Special Edition of ABC's *NewsLine*, a magazine-style news program hosted by Will Wolcott and Sarah Keeler; 8:37 p.m. EDT:]

REPORTER LIZ MOFFITT: The spotlights you see behind me were installed by rescue workers as they continue their efforts to free Lucas Prouty, who has been trapped in the basement of Trixies Restaurant for nine days. As I mentioned earlier, Major Ryan Castle of the National Guard is optimistic that work crews will be able to reach Mr. Prouty within the hour.

[Split-screen broadcast with New York studio on left and LM on right]

WILL WOLCOTT: Liz, does Major Castle have any idea how Lucas Prouty is doing?

LM: Late this afternoon, rescuers managed to lower a walkie-talkie down to Mr. Prouty. They've remained in constant contact with him since about five-thirty. I'm told he's in pretty decent spirits, all things considered.

SARAH KEELER: Oh, that's wonderful.

WW: Liz, any idea how badly he's hurt?

LM: His injuries are significant. Initially, they were hoping he might climb out on a rope ladder. But it now appears they'll be forced to cut a hole large enough to accommodate raising him on a stretcher.

SK: Do you think—

LM: Hang on a minute, Sarah. There's something . . .

[Amid the darkness and klieg lights, the camera focuses on a small crane in the bed of a pickup truck. It's surrounded by dozens of rescue team workers. A body strapped to a red stretcher is greeted by sustained cheers]

LM: Can you get a good shot? [LM is speaking to her cameraman.] My goodness. I've got gooseflesh.

[9/27: Excerpts from story on front page of USA Today:]

HED: HE'S ALIVE!

BENTLEYVILLE, N.C.—Nine days after weathercaster Lucas Prouty disappeared during Hurricane Isabel, he was found buried in the basement of a seaside restaurant by a team of rescue workers and lifted to safety . . . Many who had been following the story believed Prouty was dead . . .

"We heard a ringing noise," said Mitch Hewson of the National

Guard. *"He was hitting a bell with the broken leg of a chair. When we called to him he answered."*

Prouty is listed in serious condition at Bentleyville's Bayside Hospital. No additional information was made available . . .

"Considering what he's been through, he's in remarkable shape," said hospital spokesperson Allison Eckhart.

The nation has been captivated by Prouty's story in part because so many people watched his disappearance unfold on TV . . .

"It's a miracle," said Prouty's mother, Violet Prouty, who traveled to Bentleyville last night along with his sister Josephine Tepper . . .

[9/28: Press release from Bayside Hospital in Bentleyville, N.C.:]

Over the past several days, our switchboard has been inundated with calls from people requesting information on the health of patient Lucas Prouty. The statement that follows includes as much material as we are legally permitted to provide at the present time. We trust you will respect our immediate need to return to business as usual. Please understand how important it is for Bayside Hospital to keep its telephone lines available for those requiring genuine medical attention. In addition, we would ask for your assistance in reserving the hospital's parking spaces for Bayside employees, patients and visitors . . .

On September 26 at 9:18 p.m., Mr. Prouty arrived at Bayside by ambulance and was admitted. His condition was recently upgraded from serious to stable. Dr. Jeremy Metzel, who has been a member of Bayside's staff for the past eight years, is overseeing Mr. Prouty's care.

Mr. Prouty's injuries include a nondisplaced fracture of his right leg, three broken ribs, a punctured lung, fractures to his right cheekbone and orbital bones, a hairline fracture to his collarbone, lacerations to the face, hands, arms and legs, shock and dehydration.

"We expect Mr. Prouty to make a full and complete recovery," said Dr. Metzel.

We will provide further details as they are warranted.

[9/29: Excerpts from story on the front page of the *Bentleyville Barker*:]

HED: MEDIA MADNESS

The small plot of real estate near Bayside Hospital known as Pryor Park has become the temporary home to a collection of media personnel from across the country. Some were dispatched to cover the aftermath of Hurricane Isabel. But many more of the visiting journalists are eager for information about WYIP Channel 7 weathercaster Lucas Prouty, who is recovering in the hospital after being discovered three days ago in the basement of Trixies Restaurant. Prouty disappeared while reporting on the storm's arrival . . .

During daytime hours, traffic along Ford Drive has slowed to a standstill as drivers attempt to navigate their way through a clutter of double-parked satellite trucks stretching as far south as Jesper Street.

"It's a real hassle," said attorney Rudy Coleman, who is now planning to ride his bicycle to work . . .

But some locals have taken a more neighborly view of Bent-

leyville's guests. "Keep them coming," *said Lyle Lambert, who owns and operates Big City Deli on Ford Drive.* "This has been unbelievable for business."

Among the visiting newscasters is Mark Brown, one of N__'s primary anchors. "This is a very compelling story," *said Brown.* "You have a man struck down in the line of duty. On television. For over a week the entire nation was captivated by his disappearance. And now, thankfully, we've got a happy ending."

[9/30: Excerpts from front-page story in the *New York Post*, jump on page 10:]

HED: GINGER ALE FOR WEATHER MALE

BENTLEYVILLE, N.C.—Nearly two weeks after local weatherman Lucas Prouty was swallowed by Hurricane Isabel on national television, he showed further signs of improvement by asking staffers at Bayside Hospital for solid food. Said one nurse who requested anonymity, "He was very hungry. He wanted a Swiss cheese sandwich and a glass of ginger ale."

Prouty, who is in a private room on the hospital's fourth floor, is listed in stable condition. He has a variety of injuries, including a punctured lung, a fractured leg and several broken bones on the right side of his face. He was also treated for shock and dehydration.

"I think he's a real hero," said Ellen Daum, 43, who was among the nearly two hundred well-wishers gathered across from the hospital. "He risked his life for us."

A nearby park is crowded with print and television journalists from around the country. Twice each day, a spokesperson from Bayside Hospital holds a press conference to update Prouty's condition . . .

[10/1: Partial transcript from Marlon Kellogg's monologue three minutes and nine seconds into the late-night talk and variety show *NightTime with Marlon Kellogg*:]

MARLON KELLOGG: Are there a lot of visitors here tonight? [Loud applause.] *Be careful. This is a very strange town. I was walking down Sunset Boulevard yesterday when a guy comes running past me and tackles a nun from behind. He stands up and says, "You don't feel so tough now, do you, Batman?"* [A smattering of laughter.] *Oooooh. Did I just see tumbleweeds blow through here? This is a dangerous audience. I feel like Lucas Prouty preparing to shake hands with Hurricane Isabel.* [Loud cheers and applause.]

[10/2: Excerpts from story on front page of the *Washington Post*:]

HED: MEDIA MAELSTROM

BENTLEYVILLE, N.C.—For nine days local weather personality Lucas Prouty was entombed in the basement of a beachside restaurant. He was driven underground by high winds and flying debris that accompanied Hurricane Isabel, arguably the most powerful storm in U.S. history. Now, a week after Mr. Prouty was discovered by rescue workers, he finds himself a captive of a different sort. This time he is trapped inside one of the rooms at Bayside Hospital, surrounded by hordes of journalists . . .

"There's a tremendous appetite among our readers for anything about him," said Kent Caldwell, a reporter for the Chicago Sun-Times. *"I've been down here since last Thursday."*

The city of Bentleyville was obliged to close one of the streets near the hospital, Ford Drive, to accommodate the increasing number of TV trucks . . .

"Despite the damage caused by Isabel, we haven't had an available room since last Friday," said Lily Moore, who manages the Seaside Courts Motel. "And I know it's the same for the other places."

Two reporters from the tabloid newspaper The Dirt *were arrested on Sunday when they attempted to sneak into Mr. Prouty's room disguised as hospital orderlies . . .*

[10/2: Blurb in the Vanities section of the October issue of *Vanity Fair* magazine:]

"It" Weather Whiz:
Out: *Ned Shields;* In: *Lucas Prouty*

[10/4: Excerpts from story entitled "Letter From Bentleyville" on page 37 of the November issue of *Harper's* magazine, written by Russell Fulton Everett:]

The occasion for this article is a visit I recently paid to Bentleyville, N.C., a small seafaring community that's been at the white-hot epicenter of our nation's regard since it was bitchslapped[1] by

---

[1] Some readers will undoubtedly disapprove of the word-choice "bitchslapped" to categorize Hurricane Isabel's actions. In context, however, I believe the term is wholly appropriate. Consider: "bitchslapped" is a derivative of rap music, which is at present an extremely popular brand of contemporary entertainment. Likewise, all things Bentleyville/Isabel are currently at the core of our country's collective consciousness (see: *Time* magazine, *Newsweek* magazine, et al.).

the mother of all hurricanes, Isabel, in mid-September. My editors bid me not to write about the survivors in that patronizing, hey-I'm-a-bigtime-magazine-writer-from-up-north-sent-down-to-feel-your-pain sort of way.[2] Instead, I was asked to focus on local weather personality cum burgeoning national icon Lucas Prouty, who, as nearly everyone of reading age living in the continental United States is aware, was reporting from a nearby beach when Isabel struck and, thusly, was pursued by fleet winds until he found refuge for nine days[3] in the basement of a popular eatery. So intent were my editors on including some byte of information about Mr. Prouty that they held open the November issue—virtually unheard of[4] in the high-dollar world of glossy magazine publishing—for my story . . .

From the moment[5] a team of burly[6] rescue workers hoisted Mr. Prouty to safety, he has been ensconced in a fourth-floor room at Bayside Hospital. It is not possible to speak with him. Paid sentinels stand guard at each of the hospital's entrances and at various intervals along his floor. He is given a new pseudonym each day,

[2] This in no way is meant as a knock against the fine people of Bentleyville, N.C., or other communities struggling to put back the pieces of their lives after hemorrhaging under the awesome might of natural disaster. Quite the opposite: I'm deriding myself and, of course, the countless other hey-I'm-a-bigtime-magazine-writer-from-up-north-sent-down-to-feel-your-pain types.

[3] Obviously, Mr. Prouty was not seeking "refuge" for the entire nine days he was consigned to the basement of Trixies Restaurant. In fact, once the storm passed he spent much of his time attempting to escape.

[4] On occasion, *Sports Illustrated* will hold its Monday night close until Tuesday to include the NCAA basketball championship game, which is traditionally played on a Monday evening. Also, when breaking news dictates, other weeklies—*Time, Newsweek, People*—will accommodate by altering their closing schedules.

[5] I'm leaning here on hyperbole. Actually, I spoke with Lt. Gregg Park of the National Guard, who said it took about four minutes to load Mr. Prouty into an ambulance and another seven minutes to navigate the debris-ridden streets of Bentleyville, N.C.—a time I confirmed by making the drive myself—to reach Bayside Hospital.

[6] Naturally, this is a generalization. I'm sure some of the rescue team workers are of slight-to-moderate build.

not unlike a motion-picture star checking into a tony hotel,[7] for use by hospital staffers and law enforcement agents. It also terminates an obscene number of phone calls from being unnecessarily routed to his room.[8] Moreover, pedestrian traffic near Bayside has become so heavy that in order to gain admission to the facility you must be wearing a plastic, laminated wristband not unlike those traditionally exhibited by patients.[9]

Three times I have tried to speak with the person who speaks with the person who serves as one of Mr. Prouty's primary nurses. Moments into our final attempt at holding a conversation,[10] scheduled over "coffee"[11] in the hospital cafeteria, she departed after receiving a page on her beeper . . .

[10/5: Partial transcript from the syndicated, celebrity-themed TV program *Today's Entertainment*, hosted by Brandon Little and Mimi Maxwell:]

---

[7] I once wrote a feature on a very famous movie personality who told me he was fond of choosing cartoon characters (Barney Rubble, Elmer Fudd, Wile E. Coyote) as his alter ego when he was residing in a hotel on the East Coast and literary figures (Binx Bolling, Tyrone Slothrop, Bill Gray) when staying out West.

[8] Bayside spokesperson Allison Eckhart insisted the obscene spike in phone calls has forced the hospital's administration to hire two new operators to assist with switchboard duties.

[9] The bracelets also resemble the ones given to prospective concert-goers so they may reserve passage among long queues of ticket-buyers.

[10] I'm fearful this entire story is beginning to read like one of those loathesome magazine features where the author makes himself/herself an integral part of the tale (i.e. "[Rock star] and I repaired to a Mexican restaurant. Together, we got wicked-drunk on tequila.").

[11] I actually had my heart set on a slab of lime Jell-O, replete with bloom of whipped cream, that I'd spied the previous day.

BRANDON LITTLE: More on pop diva Courtney Evans's breakup with Dentist's Chair star Toby Rodgers in a moment. But right now we've got a special report from Mimi Maxwell, who's on assignment in Bentleyville, N.C. And Bentleyville can only mean one thing, right Mimi?

MIMI MAXWELL: Absolutely, Brandon. Today we've landed an exclusive interview with one of Lucas Prouty's neighbors. Joining me is Hilary Gibbs, who lives beside Lucas Prouty at La Vista condominiums. Thanks for talking to us on T.E., Hilary.

HILARY GIBBS: Thanks for having me. I just want to say that Today's Entertainment is one of my favorite shows. I watch it every night during dinner.

MM: That's very kind of you. Now, let me ask: How long have you known Mr. Prouty?

HG: About a year or so.

MM: And what can you tell us about him?

HG: He's a really nice man. One time, I was hanging out with a few friends and we were making screwdrivers. We ended up running out of orange juice. When I went over to ask him if I could borrow some, he gave me a whole never-before-opened carton. That's the kind of guy he is.

MM: Does the rest of the community feel the same way about him?

HG: Sure, sure. I think everybody likes him.

MM: [Smiling and raising her microphone-free arm] *What's not to like?*

HG: [Smiling] *Nothing. But sometimes he gets a little upset with my cigarette smoke. And my cat, Remy. He might be allergic.*

[10/6: Top Internet search terms according to Crynos 50; 50.crynos.com:]

1) Courtney Evans
2) Lucas Prouty
3) Halloween
4) Hurricane Isabel
5) Costumes

NONE OF THE SOUNDS ARE FAMILIAR. Odd bleatings. The muffled squawk of words filtered through a tinny intercom speaker. The measured breath of something artificial, a *machine*, sucking and huffing. There is movement: easy, unhurried. And it seems the violence is gone . . .

A nebulous pain kicks at the side of my head. When I reach for my face, it takes an eternity for my hand to leave my waist and make contact with the strange, spongy surface around my eye. I feel wa-*thump*, wa-*thump* in a new place, several inches below my armpit. A clear tube is sprouting from my side. The touch of human fingers on my left wrist. In a fury, vomit rises along my throat, its warmness creeping across my jaw and neck. There's talking and talking. Voices I don't recognize . . .

Somebody has put an ice box on my chest. More movement near the sharpness on the back of my left hand. Then comes a lover's sleepy-sweet embrace that I want to last forever, forever . . .

My sister is slinging herself headfirst down the slide in

our backyard. The swing set's legs are candy-striped like the pole outside a barbershop. Twice already my mother has turned the sprinkler against the slide's hot metal facing to cool it down. I'm eating a peanut butter sandwich on bread that is whiter than aspirin. Our neighbor, Mr. Girner, is leaning across a pine fence with a Pall Mall poking from the corner of his mouth. My mother is stirring her Bloody Mary with a celery stalk. The two of them are discussing the son of a mutual friend, a boy who was recently expelled from college for stealing stereo equipment from his classmates.

"He's going to spend the summer lifeguarding at Oakmont," says my mother. "Cynthia hopes a year off will do him good."

Mr. Girner nods.

Again, Jo mounts the slide. She waves to a small yellow bird perched atop one of the swings.

I'm wearing a pair of navy-blue swim trunks. I lie back in the soft grass and stare at the sky. The clouds crawl past like raw cotton dragged through the tines of a comb. In the distance, I hear the sound of exploding firecrackers. Our other neighbor, Mr. Overstreet, is listening to a ball game on the radio as he washes his Oldsmobile.

The gate to our yard squeals open. Petey Kirkwood is pushing his bicycle, an orange ten-speed with a banana seat. His mother has threaded red, white and blue crepe paper through the spokes of his tires. She has also tied colorful streamers to the handlebars. Petey removes two comic books from his basket, *Captain America* and *Iron Fist*, and tosses them onto the lawn beside me. He unrolls a crumpled paper sack, revealing assorted penny candy—fireballs, peppermints, wax lips, Bazooka gum, Pixy Stix.

I take one of the paper-straw Pixy Stix, pouring purple sugar into my mouth. I massage the granules with my tongue. I sprinkle a pinch on the final bite of my peanut butter sandwich. Jo makes her way to us, choosing the fat wax lips. Flashing her new red mouthpiece, she marches around the yard with an exaggeratedly hippie walk. Every few steps she fluffs her hair, starlet-style.

Petey and I are lying on our stomachs, chins in hands, reading comic books and snapping gum.

"Lucas," says my mother, "if you boys can't chew more quietly I'm going to ask you both to get rid of the gum."

We chew softer. Mr. Overstreet howls at something from the ball game.

"Did you hear that, Bob?" he calls across to Mr. Girner. "LeFlore just got doubled up at first on a short fly ball to center."

Mr. Girner shrugs.

The sun warms the tops of our heads, our shoulders, our bare arms and legs. My mother takes a long swallow from her drink. I know from listening that she likes lots of horseradish in her Bloody Mary . . .

And Petey is saying something to me about one of the villains in his comic book. But his words are jumbled. I can't understand him. Suddenly Mr. Overstreet has hopped the fence. He's carrying an axe, chasing my sister. I start screaming for help, but Petey's wrapped boa-like around my legs, my torso. I'm having trouble breathing. My mother's sitting calmly in her lounge chair, her teeth foaming red. When she turns to face me, her mouth has morphed into Jo's wax lips . . .

Again come the unfamiliar noises. The slurpy machine. A lisp of metal against wet metal. A vague collection of notes that sound like something I should know. Calling me. Maybe Petey, in a strangely formal tongue. *Mr. Prouty* and *Lucas* and *Mr. Prouty* again. A penlight flickering against my right eye. More fussing along the back of my hand, followed by that wonderful warmth. The kicking in my skull has melted away.

"Mr. Prouty," says the voice. "Can you hear me? I'm Dr. Metzel. I want you to tell me if you see this light."

"I do," I say, my cheeks stuffed with clouds of steel wool.

Is there water? Can I have a glass? I'm not sure whether I speak these words aloud . . .

MY SISTER'S NO LONGER DRESSED IN A swimsuit. She's standing beside me. And so is my mother. A man wearing a pale blue shirt, striped necktie and long white lab coat is leafing through a clipboard at the base of my bed.

"How do you feel?" he asks.

"Lousy," I say.

My head aches. So do my leg and wrist and rib cage. It hurts when I breathe.

"You've been through a lot." He makes some notations on the chart and returns it to a hook below my feet. "You're lucky to be alive."

"I don't feel lucky."

My sister smiles. My mother strokes my hand, which has an intravenous tube screwed into its backside.

"Do you remember anything?" asks my sister.

I do; I think I do.

Dr. Metzel describes my injuries. He says my ability to follow his flashlight is a good sign.

"You took quite a blow to the head. There was damage to the orbital bones surrounding your right eye."

He runs briskly through the rest of it. I was treated first for shock and dehydration. (Though there were several containers of clean drinking water in the basement of Trixies, I didn't ration them properly and they were gone in a couple days.) He explains stable pneumothorax—the ice box on my chest. I have a small puncture in my lung. The dull pain I feel every few breaths is a result of a decompression tube snaked through my ribs, rubbing against the tender lining of my lung.

He believes my right eye did not suffer any loss of vision. Nor was damage done to the ocular muscle. They also placed a cast on my leg, cleaned my lacerations.

"Since you've been here," he says, gesturing toward my left hand, "we've had you hooked to an I.V. of saline and morphine. The latter for discomfort."

We talk some more and then they leave, all three, so I can rest. There's a mechanism that floods my system with a measured portion of morphine every hour. I sleep soundest during the moments shortly after the medication merges with my bloodstream, entertained by sugary dreams in bright, cartoonish colors. When the narcotic begins to fade, my thoughts grow edgy and desperate.

A nurse comes regularly to check my vital signs. On those occasions when I'm awake, or nearly awake, I notice a policeman standing outside my door. At least I think that's what I'm seeing. Because of the morphine, it's hard to know what's real and what's only imagined.

Eventually, my memories tumble back to the night of the storm. A muddy cocktail of time, trouble and medication has left the details a garbled mess. I need someone beside me to parse fact from fiction.

THE WORDS LEAVE MY MOUTH BEFORE I'M fully awake. (Did I dream them?) The nurse nods. She tells me she will run it past my doctor. I've asked for a Swiss cheese sandwich and a glass of ginger ale. With ice.

I hear voices in the hallway. There's no clock in my room. Time has caved meaninglessly on itself. Not unlike the days I spent in the basement of Trixies. My watch stopped during the storm, either the result of a ridiculously low barometric pressure or a collision with some flying object. Until I was informed, I had no idea I'd been down there for nine days. I ate when I was hungry. I used shards of glass to carve eating utensils from splintered wood. There was a storage closet stocked with canned goods—baked beans, corn, peaches in heavy syrup. I dismantled pieces of shattered furniture for nails, hammering them into the lids of aluminum cans to create openings.

For diversion, I pitched wood chips into the empty cans. I invented basketball teams; I scratched the players' names and statistics into a pine door. I had a series of make-believe conversations with Flynn, imagining how she might sound at four, nine, seventeen. I also sang as many doo-wop songs as

I could remember. Tunes like, "One Summer Night" by the Danleers, "16 Candles" by The Crests, "Walking Along" by The Solitaires.

I rarely considered my mortality. Deep down, I knew someone would find me. The things that scared me—shortness of breath (from the punctured lung), pains in my head and leg, rats scurrying across the floor—bolted through my subconscious like scenery from a moving car. The worst thoughts featured Trip; I couldn't shake the image of his upper torso stuck spookily to that twirling hunk of roof. The only time I cried was when I imagined his two children without him. On the day I was discovered, I awoke to the sound of huge, earthmoving vehicles overhead. I began ringing a bell attached to a fallen pillar for attention. I hit the bell so hard, so often, I worked my way through three chairs.

Near the end, I could feel my grip to reality starting to unbind. Dr. Metzel called it delirium induced by shock and dehydration. I remembered attending an overnight camp in Wisconsin. Our cabin, Joppa, had a heavy chain fastened to its rafters. As punishment for disobeying a rule (or simply to amuse the counselors), a camper would have the waistband of his underpants strung through a towing hook on the end of the chain. The device was nicknamed the Joppa Jim. And counselors would take turns spinning the kid until his underpants ripped, depositing him on the floor. It was called an atomic wedgie.

I remember a time before my father departed. The two of us had traveled to rural Ontario with some of his friends to go fishing. We sat together in a small boat during a rainstorm and then, afterward, the group of us packed into one of the trailers for card games. There was Canadian beer, roasted nuts and cloves of peeled garlic. Every half hour one of the men would depart for a different trailer. Years later, I learned the others were having sex with Indian girls from a nearby reservation. As hard as I racked my brain, I couldn't recall whether my father had gone.

In the final days before they lifted me out, I allowed my pretend life with Flynn to weave together with more pragmatic thoughts I'd been having about Kiki. I kept picturing a little girl running through Kiki's yard. I was chasing her around the porch, hiding behind a pyramid of stacked firewood. We crawled on our knees like commandos to scare a squirrel from a birdbath.

I imagined tucking Flynn into bed. As I moved down the staircase, I would see the hazy glow of her hummingbird night-light. I would listen to her tender breathing—soft, peaceful, the way Trip described his sleeping children a few weeks ago: the most wonderful sound in the world. Then Kiki and I would sit in the cool grass, drinking highballs of gin and cranberry juice. She would let me rub the soreness from her bare feet. We'd grow hungry from the smell of a neighbor's grill. But we'd wait, drinking in the evening stillness. I'd lay with my ear pressed to her lap, feel her fingertips in the creases of my forehead. She would whisper a song I don't recognize, soft as a prayer, before we moved to the house. On the back steps we'd reach for the screen door at the same time. And our fingers would overlap. I'd pull her toward me, kissing her sweetly on the nose and chin. She'd turn around, my arms still wrapped across her, and we'd shuffle into the kitchen bound together like some strange beast . . .

I dreamed this again and again. Or some variation. By myself for nine days, in a cold basement. Memories from childhood, from college. Some only invented. I forgot to eat. Maybe I didn't. The water was gone. Then the great noise from above. And somehow I managed to fight the madness, ring the bell.

THIS MORNING THERE'S A BRAN MUFFIN, orange juice, cornflakes and a withered half grapefruit. Despite repeated requests, they won't bring me coffee. Bridged across my chest is a narrow table on wheels. A small, droopy transistor speaker is held to the bed frame by a lariat of insulated wire. The speaker has knobs for controlling the television's channels and volume. The first station plays a continuous loop of information for new and expectant mothers. Next comes children's programming. Then I recognize a local newscaster standing outside a hospital—*this* hospital. More coincidental still, when I stop on a national all-news network I see *another* reporter posted beside a sign reading, BAYSIDE HOSPITAL. Could both stations *really* be covering Hurricane Isabel so many days after its departure?

Suddenly the reporter speaks my name. And I fumble with the controls—I want to make it louder. Though I only catch the broadcast's final moments, I'm able to determine his reason for visiting Bayside: *me.* He's updating a national audience on *my health.* Improving the bed's angle, I sit in a silent stupor. Ideas enter my head with the speed and clarity of ply-wood targets springing to life in a shooting gallery . . .

I was dead. At least that's what people must have believed. The last time anyone saw me, I was clutching a microphone as Isabel blew me horizontal. There was rain and wind and pinwheeling debris. Then darkness. And everything that followed was left to conjecture and drama. Viewers held their breath, inhaled by the immediacy of the moment. *He's okay*, they whispered to one another. This is a medium of happy endings. Aloft in their dirigibles of optimism, newscasters sweet-talked audiences into pleasant dreams. (Tune in tomorrow when we're *sure* to have better news.) But in the passage of days—three, six, *nine*—doubt crept into their collective consciousness. I was dead. All that remained was the formality of recovering my body. Found maybe in the surf. Or the tangled-branch webbing of the trees. Or perhaps even dismembered, like Trip's. If the wind had bent differently, I'd have been the one riding that wooden kite. And Trip lands here in this bed. They *must* know about him by now. (My stomach contracts in a bundle of sharp knots.) I've got to see Ginny, the kids. Fabricate a story about how he died quickly, peacefully. Do I have the strength to tell them it was *my* fault? (My thoughts drift to honey-pie Nessa. She refuses to look me in the eye, instead scratching the faded daisy on her arm.) Trip never wanted to cover the storm. He knew better. We should have filed a single report, two, then rushed to safety. He wasn't interested in advancing his career; he only wanted to see his family again. Did I get greedy? There's no explanation for my survival. I watched Isabel thread a Chevrolet through a second-story window. The damage must be catastrophic. I haven't been home in weeks. Do I still *have* a home? A small elm from the courtyard may have been spiked through my patio door. (Time for another shot of morphine.) That's incredible—where'd they find a photograph of me? It was taken five years ago. In Ohio. I'm back from the dead. I wonder what people said about me. (I change channels again.) Game show. Commercial. Commercial. And . . . *me.* File footage from—oh, I lost that necktie in Iowa. I begged Kimmy to hide the zit on my chin with more and more concealer.

BODIES FORM A PICKET FENCE AROUND my bed. The group includes Jo, my mother, Dr. Metzel, Kurt Cadarette and Garron Yulish. (Still no Kiki.) I'm propped upright by pillows. Expectantly, I await news of my health. Yulish has flown down from New York. Because my mouth has lost its ability to produce saliva, I'm chronically sipping iced water from a straw. I fidget with the bedsheets. A small tray of Prahti's cookies rests on the table near my right elbow. Yulish's nibbling at one with purple sprinkles.

"My part's easy," says Dr. Metzel ominously. "You're recovering nicely. And I see no reason to keep you here. I'd like to take a final look during my rounds tomorrow morning. Assuming we don't encounter anything unexpected, you'll be discharged."

There's a blue spider of ink on the breast pocket of Dr. Metzel's lab coat. He crosses his arms and dissolves into a shared quiet.

"You did a wonderful job for us," says Garron Yulish. Two sprinkles are mashed between his incisors like caraway seeds. "I *am* sorry about Trip." More awkward silence. "I have spoken to Kurt and Gil Vickers about this next thing . . ."

My mother squeezes my hand.

". . . We would like to offer you a job. In New York. For the network." He smiles and I can't take my eyes off those stupid sprinkles. "In fact, we're damn near *pleading* with you to accept it."

Sensing my confusion, Jo intercedes.

"A lot has happened in the time you were . . . away."

"Here," says Kurt, flipping a copy of the *New York Post* onto my lap. "But there are plenty of other examples."

The headline reads, *Ginger Ale for Weather Male.*

"This is about *me?*"

Several nodding heads.

"It's very strange," says Yulish. "Maybe because so many people watched your disappearance. There's also the length of time you were missing, the severity of the storm. But you've generated a great deal of curiosity."

"We're getting hundreds of calls each day inquiring about your health," says Kurt. "I'm told it's the same here at Bayside."

The whole thing seems invented, illogical. I'm having difficulty wrapping my brain around the news of these last few days. Stumbling upon station-to-station coverage of my hospital stay filled me with anxiety. And now there's more. It's like some episode of a science fiction program. What possible interest would a family in, say, Boise have in *me*, a meteorologist a half continent away? I scan a few lines from the *Post* story. *Said one nurse who requested anonymity, "He was very hungry. He wanted a Swiss cheese sandwich and a glass of ginger ale."* My lunch made the *news*?

"Consider the offer," says Yulish. "We can talk about it more this afternoon. Or tomorrow."

"In the meantime," says Kurt, "it might be a good idea if we thought about a press conference."

"A press conference?" I wave the newspaper as though fanning charcoal. "For what?"

"Lucas," says Yulish, "I'm not certain you appreciate the enormity of the public's appetite for Prouty-related stories." *Prouty*-related? "We've had Mark Brown on location here since last week. As the network that carried your report on Isabel, we've seen residual bumps in ratings every night since. For the first time in three years we're the *leading* news network."

"You're suggesting I had something to do with that?"

Leaning across the bed, Yulish grabs the tethered remote and turns on the TV. Of the fourteen channels carried by the hospital's cable provider, eight are showing stories somehow related to me. Even the all-sports network cuts to a tight shot of a football crowd in which three fans are wearing cardboard masks of my face.

"Now, *that's* scary," I say.

"Are you beginning to understand?"

Deep sigh.

A nurse enters and announces it's time for me to rest. Before they leave, my mother and Jo huddle around the bed.

"We thought you were dead," says Jo.

"—Don't say that," snaps my mother.

"*Ma* . . ." Jo rolls her eyes. "He's *not* dead. I'm just telling Lucas how it seemed."

"I'm sorry, sweetheart."

"You don't need to apologize, Mom," I say.

As though by design, they both touch one of my arms.

"What's it like out there?" I ask, turning toward the window.

"Very weird." Jo covers the plate of cookies with crinkled cellophane. "It's impossible to watch TV or read the newspaper without seeing something about you."

"That won't last."

"Maybe," says Jo, breaking into a smile. "But I called Patrick this morning. He said the guy from *Newsweek* only left *four* messages yesterday."

"Get some sleep," says my mother, patting me softly on the foot.

"I'm going to do you a favor," says Jo. She unties the remote and threads it over an I.V. stand across the room.

THEY WON'T LET ME WALK. EVEN with crutches. Hospital policy mandates that until I'm officially discharged later this afternoon, I must travel the corridors seated in a wheelchair. Jo's rolling me down to the first floor. I was told the cafeteria is the only room in the building large enough to accommodate the number of reporters who requested credentials for the press conference. Custodians dismantled many of the tables in order to make space for the extra chairs, some of which were rented from a nearby party center.

This morning I showered with my leg cast stuffed into a plastic bag. I shaved with a deliberate hand, avoiding several freshly sutured cuts—chin, cheek, lower lip—that continue to heal. Blood draining from the broken orbital bones has turned the skin beneath my right eye into a purple and black dumpling. I'm wearing a white dress shirt and untapered khakis with room for the bulky cast. My hair's slicked down with tap water.

We are led secretively to the cafeteria by Bayside spokesperson Allison Eckhart and three security guards. We use a key-operated service elevator, navigating hallways clogged with laundry baskets and drums of waste. As we prepare to enter the dining room by way of the kitchen, several members of the cooking staff stop what they're doing to watch our procession. There's an awkwardness to the way they stare at me—it's almost as though they're afraid to make eye contact. One woman drops her head quickly when I smile at her.

We wait for a signal to mount the dais. My mother squeezes beside Garron Yulish, who's dressed in a dark pinstripe suit. With the hospital's chief executive officer preparing to introduce me—he's not going to miss his chance to address *this* group—my mother whispers in my ear.

"Lucas," she says, offering me her outstretched hand. "Give me your gum."

I had found a linty piece of Juicy Fruit in the overnight bag Jo brought from my apartment. The moment I surrender the gum, serendipitously, I hear them call my name. Jo rolls me through the doors. There is applause. And dozens of exploding flashbulbs. I'm seated and it's difficult for people to see me. When a few journalists rise from their chairs, the others follow. The scene bears an odd resemblance to a standing ovation.

I had been told to expect a large crowd. But this is overwhelming. Every goddam seat is taken. Bodies are stacked two-deep against the side walls. Television cameras mounted on tripods are pressed so tightly together they seem a contiguous piece of machinery. Reporters sit with small notepads nestled in their palms, pens at the ready. Because there's such a vast collection of microphones and tape recorders fastened before me, the table has been tied to the dais for fear it will tip unbalanced into my lap.

I have attended my share of press conferences. Before I was a full-time meteorologist, my job included taping sound bites for rebroadcast during the evening news. Still, I have never seen anything like the mass of people congregated in this room. Every pair of eyes is locked on me. A simple scratch of my nose will send them all scribbling intently. They wait— eager, anxious for words. Whatever I say next—*my ass hurts; this hospital has shitty rice pudding*—is going to make news.

"Well," I begin, my voice swallowed by feedback until a frantic technician corrects the problem. "Here I am."

Scattered laughter.

"Thanks for coming." I take a sip of water. "I guess."

A few smiles.

"I'm not sure what I can tell you that you don't already know. But I'll give it a shot . . ."

When enough silence passes for them to realize I have

completed my brief introductory remarks, dozens of hands spike into the air. Questions are shouted out.

"Let me remind you," says Allison Eckhart, interrupting, "Mr. Prouty will only call on you if your hand is raised."

I point to a smallish woman in the front row whom I recognize as a resident of Bentleyville.

"Catherine Selway, *Bentleyville Barker*," she says. "Which was worse, being caught in the middle of a hurricane or trapped for nine days in a basement?"

Is she serious?

"They were both pretty lousy."

The questions are endless. A reporter from a newspaper in Wichita, Kansas, wants to know what a hurricane looks like at ground zero. The guy from the *Los Angeles Times* asks what was the most frightening moment. A woman from a TV station in Chicago is curious about how I passed the time in Trixies.

There are false finishes, extended periods of silence that deceive me into thinking we're nearly done. Until, inevitably, amid the hundreds of hairdos comes a raised hand with something else. As they burrow deeper into their lists of queries, the subject matter becomes more personal, more aggressive. Have I ever been married? Did I feel pressured by the network to remain outside when the storm hit? Was I trying to make a name for myself?

Finally: A variant of a question I was hoping wouldn't get asked. One of the reporters (there are two!) from the *Washington Post* wants to know about Trip. I lie; I tell them he was killed by a hurtling park bench and only later his body was cleaved apart.

"Do you feel any guilt," the reporter continues, causing

a lump to rise against my throat, "about surviving the storm when your partner was killed?"

Mostly, I'm relieved. I feared he would speculate that some of the blame for Trip's death lies with me. Surely he knows—they're professional journalists, they *all* know—that it's not the cameraman who suggests working through the ugly stuff.

"Yes, I feel guilty," I say. "He was my friend; I miss him." My voice cracks on *him*. "He has two incredible kids." I can feel my eyes go moist. And then I'm just talking for the sake of talking. The words leave my mouth in a therapeutic rush. "I had dinner with them before the storm. His boy, Ryan, likes wontons without the soup; that's not the same as dumplings . . ."

As a flurry of hands stab skyward, Allison Eckhart leans into the microphones.

"We're going to end it here," she says. "Please keep in mind that Mr. Prouty has been through a trying ordeal. He needs his rest."

Everyone rises at once. Jo steers the wheelchair down a ramp snaking from the dais. Several yards before the exit, we're intercepted by a scrum of reporters elbowing for a *true* final question. Security guards lock arms to create a wall near my left shoulder. I watch my mother's eyes grow wide as hubcaps. They scream out like hungry children. "Don't answer them," whispers Allison Eckhart.

"What's next for your career?" someone asks.

Yulish can't resist. The prospect of all this free publicity sets his face aglow.

"I have asked Mr. Prouty to come work with us," he says, grinning.

This triggers a chain reaction of other inquiries: *Have you accepted? What will you do for them? When are you scheduled to start?* Eckhart leads Jo back into the kitchen. I listen to Yulish through the door—his remarks are practiced, polished. "Mr. Prouty has not yet committed to anything," he says. "And neither has the network." But he insists everyone is hopeful.

We wait until a team of guards confirms that the route back to my room has been cleared. I'm short of breath. I wipe the perspiration from my hands. One of the cooks offers me a can of cold soda.

Surely that's the worst of it.

MY BATHROOM STINKS FROM AN APPLE core I tossed in the wastebasket the day before the storm. Floral arrangements crowd the counters and tabletops. Dozens and dozens of bouquets, sent by "fans" and well-wishers, had blocked the front landing upon my return. This afternoon a truck will come to haul most of the greenery to local charities. There were also notes, paintings, cards and hand-lettered poems. A homemade cake was decorated with a confectionery likeness of me standing beside a weather map. My mother filled five pages of a spiral-bound notebook with phone messages. For my protection, Yulish hired several off-duty police officers to wander the grounds. I reluctantly agreed to certain precautionary measures—in ballcap and oversize sunglasses to shield my injured eye, I was led from the hospital using routes normally traveled by delivery personnel. Still, news of my departure was leaked and the streets surrounding my condominium were lined with TV trucks and reporters.

I'm now seated on my couch with the blinds drawn closed. My mother has returned from a visit to the supermarket, where she was shadowed by a bodyguard. On the coffee table rests my casted leg. To one side is a cellular phone the size and weight of a Zippo lighter. It was a gift from Yulish; I think he wants to know he can always reach me.

"Relax," I told him last night. "I'm not going anywhere." But he's a hot coal of nervous energy. Does he think I'll get a better offer? The financial portion of the network's offer is breathtaking. During my ride home from the hospital, Yulish scribbled some incentives on the back of his business card. Besides my salary—seven majestic figures—they're including a driver, apartment and the use of a corporate beach house in St. Croix.

Tomorrow we leave for Los Angeles. I'm making a ridiculously hyped appearance on *NightTime with Marlon Kellogg*. But I'm having mixed emotions. Part of me sees it as a public affirmation of my new career—a voucher against the network's brass welshing on their job offer. The other part of me thinks it's too soon. I want to spend time with Kiki; I need to visit Trip's family.

My mother rises, poking her head behind the blinds. She half expects it all to have disappeared. I think I've come to terms with the inevitability of what's next. Surely that explains the sharp stone of fear in my chest: What will I *say* to Kellogg? Most nights his couch is filled with movie stars, models and pop singers. I'm a *weatherman*. Was I booked for levity? For comic relief? I may as well be the guy from Delaware who carves U.S. Presidents from cakes of bath soap.

SWOOZY WITH PAIN PILLS, I LISTEN to my mother and sister in the bathroom preparing themselves for bed. The spank of sink water against their skin. A glassy twisting sound like the lid on a jar of facial cream. The rise and rake of a toothbrush. Spit, sneeze. Jo asks my mother if I'm asleep yet. And in my darkened bedroom, I see a lemon light seeping from beneath the door. It's blurred by footsteps, then extinguished.

From the great stack of words in my mother's handwriting appears the only one that matters. I have lasted this long— *made* myself wait until day's end. Excitedly, I misdial the digits; I try again. I feel like a teenager. *Should I hang up if her father answers? Will her mother like me?* I'm breathy, tense.

Then comes the familiar sound of her voice—gentle, reassuring.

"I was worried about you," says Kiki.

I don't know what I expected. But this is nearly enough. Suddenly the storm doesn't seem like such a bad thing.

"They wouldn't let me in the hospital."

I have pursued her without mercy. Thrown myself at her night after night. And for the most part she's kept me at a safe distance. But something has changed. I'm trying to decode the truth from this jumble of thoughts in my head. During my time in Trixies' basement, I used my imagination as a crutch; I created a make-believe world with Kiki that was based on fantasy. But the spark for those daydreams came from her. I *know* I could feel Kiki leaning toward me in the weeks before the storm. *Am I remembering this correctly? Did I invent that too?*

I'm ashamed of what comes next. I start questioning

Kiki's motives. Though nothing I know about her would lead to this conclusion, I can't shake the lingering doubt that maybe she *wants* something from me.

"So . . ." she says, clearing her throat. "How do you feel?"

"A little banged up."

"The amazing part . . ." she says, letting the rest of her words collapse into quiet.

I'm having trouble reading her—is she emotional or just tired?

"I wanted to see you," she says, turning over the sentiment that carried me to her several times a week. "You were gone. They said you were dead. And all I wanted was to *see* you."

Until Isabel, I'd led an exceedingly boring life. I'm a creature of habit. I don't have many friends and, deplorably, I'm not interested in expanding my circle. During visits to Stinky's, I paid special attention to the things Kiki said in hopes of gaining a better insight into her personality. I relied on my skills as a reporter to gather information; I was anxious to cast light on the shadows.

Shortly before we met, Kiki had a boyfriend who ran his own construction firm. Several times he promised to build an addition to Kiki's house so she could sell the Airstream in her yard that she uses for an office. One Christmas, he even had a friend draw some architectural plans. (Kiki still has them tacked to the side of her refrigerator.)

His name was Derek. And, to his credit, he convinced Kiki to return to school. She said Derek would prepare "fantabulous" brunches on Sunday mornings: country French toast, butcher-shop bacon, eggs with basil. "Honestly," she once told me, "I thought we were headed to a good place."

But she started noticing a gradual change in his attitude soon after they moved in together. It's not that he drank or gambled; he wasn't abusive. But the more time they spent with one another, the more he resented her. He acted as though he'd been snookered into the whole arrangement. (In truth, it had been *his* idea to cohabitate.) On evenings when he planned to watch football with his buddies, he'd announce his intention in the form of a challenge. The implication being that if Kiki had a problem with it, she should *try* and stop him.

One night while she was working, he moved out. "Why are men *like* that?" she asked me several months later. "Why do they make everything so goddam hard?"

I threw my hands into the air. I told her I wasn't sure I could give an objective answer. ("In case you hadn't noticed," I remember saying, "I'm a man—a very *manly* man.") Then came the part that has me thinking about this now. She insisted her next meaningful relationship would be with a man who had more to offer than a plate of eggs and a nice ass. She wanted someone who could take her places, literally *and* figuratively.

She was still hurt, angry. (That morning she'd discovered that Derek had taken her bicycle pump; she didn't want to call him to get it back.)

Now, years later, my brain is firing on all cylinders to interpret her comment. I've always assumed she meant she was looking for a guy who'd rise above his inclination to behave like a jackass. But what if we're breaking new ground here? (Is that what's happening?) I'm wondering when her feelings for me began to carry more than the weight of friendship. I'm spooked—and a little insecure. Am I nuts to think she's interested in me because *now* I've got something to offer?

"Kiki," I say, bracing myself against the headboard of my bed, "what's going on?"

"I don't know, Lucas," she says. "I swear to God, I don't know."

She tells me that while I was gone, she couldn't forget this one image of me from the drive-in: I was hunched over Ryan's forearm, drawing a snake. She said my tongue was curled between my lips in a posture suggesting deep concentration. She said I looked more like a boy than Ryan.

"When I heard about Trip," she says, "I cried for days."

The next part makes her laugh. Admittedly, she's horrible with analogies. But she explains it's like your whole life you hate tomatoes. Until one summer day you try a juicy, fresh-picked tomato from somebody's garden. Maybe there's a splash of olive oil. And suddenly you're thinking about tomatoes in a totally different way.

"So now I'm a *tomato*?"

"You could be . . ."

I hear a clicky noise, like the phone bumping against her teeth.

"Let's talk in the daytime," she says. "I'm tired. And I'm probably not making any sense . . ."

SECURITY SPECIALISTS HAVE WRAPPED my condominium with streamers of Day-Glo crime-scene tape. They've created a narrow channel, approximately sixty yards in length, leading from my front door to the parking lot. Signs posted to trees and telephone poles warn trespassers they'll be prosecuted to the full extent of the law. "This shouldn't take more than thirty seconds," says the main guard. The instant my door is opened we're greeted by a wall of noise: reporters shouting questions and jockeying for position with video cameras, still cameras and boom microphones. (Many use the endearing sobriquet, "Hey, Weather Guy.") I'm wheeled briskly down the sidewalk by uniformed officers. The stuttery *thwop-thwop-thwop* of helicopter blades causes one guard to unfurl an umbrella, creating a barrier against bird's-eye lenses.

The journey is keenly efficient. In a few rapid blinks, I'm resting comfortably on the backseat of an elongated sport utility vehicle. The windows are tinted. Four police-issue motorcycles sit imposingly beside each tire. As we drive away, I let my eyes devour the scenery. There are *hundreds* of journalists. Screaming and lunging and poking their cameras at awkward angles. Some, in danger of being ingested by the rest of the pack, raise their lenses straight-armed into the sky, snapping blindly in our general direction. Behind the windshield, one tangle of reporters resembles figurines in a life-size diorama. As we turn onto Dansby Road, nearly a quarter mile from my apartment, photographers continue sprinting beside us with their index fingers curled around trigger buttons.

Arrangements have been made. We're permitted to drive on the tarmac at Bentleyville Airport. A small white network-owned Learjet awaits us. I'm met by the captain, an attendant and Yulish. This is my first time on a private plane. The interior is blindingly beige. There are rotating leather seats with padded headrests, carpeted walls, mahogany tables and personal video monitors. Below my window is a linen tablecloth draped over an adjustable service tray. It holds a stylish silver bowl, filled with cashews, almonds and honey-roasted peanuts; there's also a crystal decanter of iced water. Several feet away is a bolted-down coffee table displaying a collection of current newspapers, magazines and the network's annual business report. Our attendant, Lisa, asks if I'd like a beverage.

"I'm fine," I say.

Without provocation, she removes two pillows from a closet and stacks them beneath my casted leg. As she prepares to stand, she leans with her lips near my ear and whispers, "It's an honor to meet you."

The remark catches me by surprise. I can think of no reasonable way to respond. I thank her, quietly, and pretend to examine the magazines.

Once aloft, I study cloud formations with my head propped against the window: Stratus, Altocumulus, Cirrocumulus and, finally, Cirrus. Music plays softly from a series of discreet speakers. The song sounds vaguely familiar. When the engines ease to their cruising speed, lessening the noise, I can make out the words: "So Fine" by The Fiestas. I turn to Yulish and smile.

"We did our homework," he says, raising a glass of grapefruit juice in mock toast.

By proxy (Yulish), the network is pitching woo. It's strange to be the object of someone's desire. I can hardly remember how it feels. All this newness. They know what's possible in these first fragile days. And they rue being misin-

terpreted, making a clumsy advance. It should all be perfect—
the lighting, food and drink, even the music. With these stakes
everything takes on outsize proportions. A media conglomerate has come courting, bouquet of fresh-cut flowers in its
sweaty fist. I can smell wintergreen breath mints . . . to hide
the stink of what's beneath.

"This must be rather exciting for you," says Yulish.

I nod absently. I'm hoping to conceal my emotions. But
it's all too intoxicating. Sometimes it seems I'm able to watch
this crazy show from a measured distance. *Gosh, Mr. Yulish.*
This sure is a nice aero-plane. They've gone to great lengths
to impress me. And I fear it's working. For sport, I'd almost
like to test the elasticity of their boundaries, see what I could
get away with. Would it queer the deal if, say, I confessed that
I've always wanted to make love at thirty thousand feet?
Maybe Yulish wouldn't bat an eye. What if he excused himself for a few delicate words with Miss Lisa in the galley?

Even when I *force* myself to think about something else—
Kiki, bills that accrued during my absence, half-orphaned
Nessa and Ryan—I'm slapped back to my new reality. Lisa surrenders a frosted goblet filled with shaved ice and, hooked
evenly around its rim, peeled shrimp the size of chicken
wings.

"These are the best shrimp you've ever tasted," says Yulish. "I think they're flown in from Boston."

"Maine," says Lisa politely.

"Maine."

I remember my family taking a trip to Key West when I
was very young. The airline had overbooked our flight and,

lotterylike, the four of us were upgraded to first class. Ridiculous as it now sounds, until my teenage years the food we had on that plane was the best I'd ever tasted. Likewise, today's offerings—strip steak, lobster tail, long-grain rice, crème brûlée and, of course, shrimp cocktail—seem to belong in a four-star restaurant. Yulish tells me Lisa took special courses in learning the proper ways to prepare the preprepared dishes. He also informs me a famously cantankerous food critic from a glossy men's magazine once gushed in his column about the chef's foie gras. (I haven't the heart to reveal I couldn't name a single foie gras ingredient with a gun to my temple.)

The flight is smooth and unhurried, lacking the headaches associated with commercial travel. I watch network-sanctioned video—the morning show, Marlon Kellogg, episodes from various sitcoms—and Yulish talks on the telephone. A couple times, he announces to whomever he's speaking with that, indeed, the "weather guy" is beside him at this very moment. The statement's followed by a quick wink, as though we're sharing some intimate secret. Two men on the cusp of a remarkable journey.

Before landing, Lisa brings me a hot towel and a basket of assorted toiletries: single-serving pouches of hydrating lotion, aftershave, hand cream, mouthwash and lip balm. At Yulish's request, she removes the lid on a black leather box filled with pharmaceuticals—analgesics, anti-inflammatories, painkillers, stimulants, relaxants—because, as she says, "Air travel doesn't agree with everyone." To be courteous, I take a couple aspirin "for my injuries." I'm afraid dipping into the more potent medications might send the wrong message.

In Los Angeles, we're greeted by a spunky publicist standing between the parted door to a limousine.

"You're ruining me," I say.

"That's the idea," says Yulish.

The "short" trip from the airport to the soundstage where *NightTime with Marlon Kellogg* is filmed seems to take longer than the plane ride. For the majority of the drive, we're parked in a prairie of motionless automobiles. Every car we creep past is empty except for the driver, who, invariably, is talking into the type of headset favored by telephone operators. I'm offered more spirits, more food. I drink as much bottled water as my bladder permits. The publicist, Brandy Howe, expends inordinate amounts of energy telling Yulish how wonderful he looks. She's convinced he's lost weight. As he's shaking her off, she leans across the seat and asks dangerously, "Have you had a tummy tuck?" When they're interrupted by Yulish's cell phone, she turns to me and, without breaking stride, says, "You're a marvelous man—a *true* inspiration."

We're waved through the studio gate by a pair of sun-soaked security guards. In fact, they're so perfect-looking I nearly ask Brandy Howe if they're actors researching a role.

"Oh, Jesus," I say aloud, as movie-star Julie Rust swaggers past my window.

"Do you know her?" asks Brandy.

I shake my head vigorously.

"She's a sweetheart. They're shooting a period piece in No. 22—that's why she's dressed that way." Brandy lowers her window. "Julie, honey!"

I'm seized by an overwhelming desire to poleaxe Brandy

Howe with one of my crutches. This has the potential to be excruciatingly embarrassing. I can already hear Howe's introduction—meteorologist, movie star; movie star, meteorologist.

Julie squints into the shaded limousine, crinkling her perky nose.

"It's Brandy Howe." Long, painful silence. "From *publicity*."

Slowly, uncertainly, Rust offers the lifeless wave of a beauty contestant. (The gesture appears to bring her great discomfort.) For a moment, it seems she's finished with us. She pivots in the opposite direction. But something has caught her eye. She starts walking toward the car. A few feet away she lowers her head and smiles.

"That's *you?*" she says, stabbing the air with her index finger.

I wait for one of the others to respond—Howe or Yulish. But when Rust's heavily painted face breaks the open plain of our window, I realize she's talking to *me*.

She extends a begloved hand for me to shake.

"I was *very* moved by your work," she says.

Brandy and Yulish nod in agreement.

"Oh, God. I was just speaking to Tilly about you—about your *commitment*. She's going to *die* when I tell her you're here."

In this case, a last name would be superfluous, redundant. We just saw Tilly Dayton's likeness on a massive billboard during our ride from the airport; she's starring in a western.

"Are you on holiday?"

"He's taping for Kellogg," says Brandy.

"Be careful," says Julie. "He can get pretty rough."

She sighs, shaking her head in apparent disbelief. Then she asks where I'm staying.

"At the Royale," says Yulish. "But we're leaving for New York tomorrow."

"What a shame."

She finally excuses herself. ("Jesus," she says. "They're probably calling for me on the set.") She makes me promise to give her a "jingle" the next time I'm in town.

WE EVENTUALLY REACH OUR DESTINATION. My crutches are constructed of space-age polymer; they resemble inverted question marks. Their rubber-tipped ends squeak against the linoleum floor. As we advance down the hallway, it feels as though people are leaning out of their office doors for a peek.

I have my own dressing room. There's a rack of clothing along the back wall. A narrow table is crowded with refreshments—sliced fruits, cheeses, breads and crackers, nuts, finger sandwiches, pastries and a variety of beverages. Yulish talks to someone outside the door. I'm told to make myself comfortable. A television flickers with the direct feed of a program being shot in a nearby soundstage.

A young woman named Cory enters my dressing room to discuss Marlon Kellogg's questions and my intended responses. It's called a preinterview, and Cory's goal is to keep guests from looking unprepared or, worse, from looking foolish.

"We'd like to get something really *fresh* on today's show," she says.

"That shouldn't be difficult," I say. "I haven't been any-where else."

She smiles.

"Right. But we're also competing with the immense media coverage."

Cory rifles through a stack of index cards. A legal pad rests against her lap. We spend the next ninety minutes talking about Hurricane Isabel, Trixies' basement and pretty much every goddam thing that's ever happened to me. She dismisses most of my stories rather abruptly. ("I'll try to be more *interesting* over my next thirty-five years," I say, only half joking.) The tales she categorizes as "keepers" are refined again and again. She makes me repeat them six or seven times.

"You should be able to recite these in your sleep," she insists.

If we keep this up, I *will* be reciting them in my sleep.

When it appears we're nearly finished, she informs me the anecdotes will be surrendered to the show's writing staff for further embellishment.

"They're going to improve upon my *life*?"

"Only to make you look better."

Cory is replaced by a woman from wardrobe. Despite the pain in my leg, she moves me to a small chair so she can arrange several outfits against the couch. She stands on a table to redirect the lighting. "This will give us a sense of how the clothes will look on TV," she says.

We—*she*—settles on a black three-button suit and pow-der-blue shirt. Before the show, she wants to make a couple slight alterations—lengthening the sleeves, lifting the crotch.

"This is a magnificent suit," she says. "It's a Hans Berber."

I nod, pretending to know what that means. A *Hans Berber*. She views my legcast as an imposition, an *insult*. "I guess you'll only need one shoe," she says testily, holding the spare in her hand. We nearly come to blows (do we?) when she suggests painting the cast to match my outfit.

At last I'm alone. I fill a glass with ice cubes and beer. Mounted along the walls are framed photographs of Marlon Kellogg and guests. Some shots were taken during the show, others were unposed candids in the hallway or dressing rooms or backstage. My cell phone rattles and rings. Annoyingly, it's Yulish calling from an office down the hall. He wishes me luck.

I accidentally strike a button on the phone that displays the previous few numbers I dialed. Earlier today, I called Ginny; I'd been trying to reach her since I left the hospital. She was taking a nap so I spoke with Nessa. Her voice—strong, confident—caught me by surprise. I couldn't string together the right words. I didn't know where to begin. How much does she understand? Should I apologize?

"Hey, sweetie," I said.

She told me the house has been crowded with visitors—lots of relatives she doesn't remember. In a child's honest appraisal, she admitted it bothered her that everyone was asking how she's doing.

"I miss my father," she said. "How do they *think* I'm doing?"

She had overheard some of the adults. They doubted whether Ryan knew what was happening; he's too young. "He expects his father will walk through the door any minute," said Nessa's aunt.

That's not true, said Nessa. She described the way she and Ryan shared a bedroom those first couple nights. They had talked about never being with their father again. One morning, before Ginny or any of the others had awakened, Nessa played a videotape of Trip. She and Ryan wanted to see their father— they studied his movements, they listened to his voice.

She recited the story without sadness. She simply obliged me with the details of their new world. The two of them, Nessa and Ryan, seemed to understand the way life worked. They embraced this sudden truth in the same stoic manner as they accepted the mass of other things over which they had no control: attending school, eating cauliflower, completing daily chores.

I wanted to leave something for Nessa, lift her spirits. I recounted a story from her past—a story that *showed* how dearly her father loved them. Before Christmas one year, Trip was disturbed that Nessa had grown so cynical. He was upset she no longer even *pretended* believing in holiday magic. He decided to rent a Santa Claus costume for Christmas Eve. But Nessa's a perceptive girl; he knew she'd recognize him if he got too close. So he devised a plan: The two of us borrowed a half dozen klieg lights from Channel 7; we pointed them at the Murphys' house across the street.

In the middle of the night, Ginny would wake the kids. Trip, who'd been granted permission by the Murphys, would waddle in tiny circles around their chimney. He carried a bed-sheet stuffed with crumpled newspaper across his shoulder.

"I don't remember my dad playing Santa Claus," said Nessa.

"That's because you never saw it."

The Murphys' roof had been severely damaged by rain. Several steps away from the ladder, on the backside of their house, Trip hit a swatch of soft tarpaper; he was swallowed into the Murphys' master bedroom.

"I was scared he injured himself," I said. "When we ran upstairs—me, the Murphys—we found your father lying on the bed, his fake beard shielding his eyes like a blindfold."

Nessa had the kinds of questions that interest a young girl. Did her father pay for the hole? Were the Murphys angry? Did the noise wake her friend, Libby Murphy?

Before ending the call, she told me the drive-in theater where Kiki and I had taken them for dinner was destroyed by the storm. I didn't know what to say; I asked her to find a new place for our next picnic.

THE RENOWNED "GREEN ROOM" IS NOT green. It's pale blue. And I'm seated in a padded chair watching Marlon Kellogg deliver his monologue on a closed-circuit TV. Near yet another food buffet—couldn't they have simply wheeled it down from my dressing room?—members of the rock band Soft Bunz are "getting loose" by passing around a joint. Singer Ed Dorley is tactfully asked to extinguish his "cigarette." Dorley's blond hair, styled in ragged dreadlocks, fans out from beneath a backward ballcap. He's wearing a cropped St. Louis Rams football jersey and dungarees that appear four sizes too large, exposing the waistband of his black and gold underpants. Diamonds the size of molars are twinkling from each earlobe. One of his bandmates, in black-leather trench-coat, is mesmerized by his own reflection in a full-length mirror. Seven-year-old golf prodigy Casper Oris sits across from me, nibbling on a peanut butter and red jam (strawberry? raspberry?) sandwich; his mother leafs nervously through a magazine.

Though the room's as cold as a meat locker, I can't stop perspiring. I follow Yulish, Brandy Howe and a production assistant to a spot where I await my televised introduction.

"I'll point to the curtain after he announces your name," says a guy wearing a headset. "You'll walk—" He catches himself and smiles. "You'll *crutch* out there like during rehearsal."

I'm half paying attention, trying to soak it all in. Then comes a sound like my name—the right notes spoken by a voice that's vaguely familiar. It's Marlon Kellogg's baritone stretching four syllables as impossibly long as they'll last: "*Luuuuuuuuu*-cas Pr-*ooowwwwwww-tee*." Headset-guy pokes the curtain. But I momentarily freeze. He nudges me through a fissure hidden in the fabric. I'm immediately engulfed by the types of spotlights used for landing airplanes. The crowd, partially illuminated, is standing; they applaud, they hoot and whistle. A couple yokels in the front row have raised their index fingers. (I'm number *one*? At what?) I take a second to gain my bearings. A few paces to my left is Marlon Kellogg, also clapping frantically. The whole thing is overwhelming. I maneuver the crutches toward Kellogg, hoping the sound will erase once I reach his couch.

But the applause continues even after I've taken my seat. In fact, the noise endures for such an embarrassingly long time I'm actually bade to stand again and acknowledge the sustained affection with a brief wave. As Kellogg motions for quiet, I remove a small mug from his desk, near my armrest, and drink a sip of water.

"*Goodness!*" says Marlon Kellogg emphatically. "That was *incredible.*"

I nod. A woman seated near the back of the auditorium screams, "We love you, Lucas!"

Kellogg assures her the feeling is mutual, thereby inciting another short swell of applause.

And then we talk. There are no surprises. Except for a couple new jokes, everything is exactly how Cory said it would be in my dressing room. Kellogg is hotly curious about the way a hurricane looks from the inside. There's a smattering of laughter when I compare the experience to climbing into a washing machine. (The analogy was suggested by one of the show's writers.)

As we return from commercial, I'm distracted. I have broken a cardinal rule of the TV biz: I'm actually *paying attention* to the audience and cameras (about five times as many as for my weathercasts) and bustling staffers behind the scenes. What a terrible time to discover I'm out of my element, overmatched. Kellogg asks me a question I don't quite hear. A cascade of blurred figures rushes across my pupils, followed by a shortness of breath. Comes now an excruciatingly long silence that I don't have enough perspective to measure. Have three seconds elapsed? Nine? I can feel myself blush beneath the crust of makeup. Even Kellogg senses trouble; his face erupts with a compassionate smile. Again, his lips move but I'm not certain whether he said anything. Fourteen seconds? Twenty?

The words trickle from my mouth at a glacial pace. I manage to tumble back to our scripted conversation. And I can feel the room heave a collective sigh of relief.

Most guests remain beside Kellogg for two complete segments, sandwiched around a break for advertisements. However, he insists I stay on the couch for the entire program—Cory mentioned this was a possibility—thereby bumping diminutive golfer Casper Oris to another night. I was also told by the show's director that "in order to preserve spontaneity, he won't speak to you during commercials. And he *always* watches the musical number by himself."

But we continue chatting, albeit awkwardly, when filming is suspended. ("This must be crazy for you, huh?" he asks.) Likewise, he doesn't allow me to leave during Soft Bunz. ("Stay right here," he says, slapping his armrest. "You'll like this band.") Once they finish performing, Kellogg thanks them and cuts to break. He leans toward me, shielding his mouth, and says, "The singer's a complete *asshole*. Last time we had them on the show, he got drunk and fondled one of the interns."

Afterward, Kellogg declares I was wonderful (his word) and promises to bring me back. Yulish and several others are drinking champagne in my dressing room. Now there's a tray of deli sandwiches and wobbly tin troughs of side salads. I'm thoroughly exhausted; it's been a long day. I'm singularly focused on the bed in my hotel room. If I can muster the energy, I'll take a hot shower—I remind myself to find a plastic bag for my cast. I'd order room service, but I doubt whether I'll stay awake long enough to eat it.

In the industry, this is called a grip-and-grin. Lots of handshaking, back-slapping and small talk. I'm trying desperately to cut the session short. But each time I try to get Yulish's attention—I need some *sleep*—I'm greeted by another "admirer." I have already posed for a dozen pictures, meaning a dozen strange arms draped across my shoulder. I'm acutely aware of the way people are staring at me—I feel like there's a giant stain on the crotch of my trousers. I'm a novelty— a spiny fish that's washed ashore; they're poking me with a sharp stick, turning me over in the sand to examine every angle. Three snooty entertainment types are standing beside the booze, sucking highballs and whispering. Every few minutes they cast a collective glance in my direction and erupt in machine-gun giggles. *Listen*, I want to scream, grabbing the tallest by his pointy lapels. *This wasn't my idea. I know I don't have anything to say.*

When Yulish and I finally make it outside, we're surrounded by paparazzi. My patience has grown thin. I'm tired, irritable. I wanted to leave before I got here. But rather than whisk us into the idling limousine with its phalanx of security guards, Yulish displays me like a trophy date. "A photo op," he says. "Your picture in a thousand newspapers tomorrow morning. Do you know what that's *worth*?"

Newly motivated, we battle our way from the curb—for a second time today photographers chase us, inexplicably snapping pictures of a retreating limousine. Thirty minutes later we arrive at the Royale. In my previous life, I recall reading an article about this place. Small, elegant and obscenely popular with celebrities. The instant our car reaches the courtyard, bellmen descend upon us with the precision of a drill team. Hidden amid the shrubs, a "secret" door yawns magically open and we're escorted through a series of illuminated passage-ways. My induction requires nothing more than a signature during our journey on a private elevator.

Though it's probably my imagination, I feel like I'm being judged again. This time it's the hotel's staff. (These aren't even my own *clothes!*) And, much like at the after-show reception, I can't shake the notion that I'm woefully inade-quate; I'm somehow not meeting their expectations.

You're a freaking weatherman!

My room is ridiculously large. In fact, I'm certain it's got more square footage than my apartment. I listen as the hotel manager (not merely some bellhop) explains their amenities: six telephones (including one in each of the three bathrooms), fully appointed wet bar, fax machine, computer, televisions (four), terrace with courtyard view, high tea at two p.m. (should I so desire, they will bring a *harp* to my room for musical accompaniment), valet, cellular phones, personal tailor, full-service spa . . . And more and more and inhumanly more. He wins back my attention when he introduces me to a middle-aged man dressed in navy suit, white shirt and navy necktie. His name is Dixon Boyd. I'm informed that during my stay, Mr. Boyd will be at my disposal. Day or night. When I tell them I think we're leaving tomorrow, the two of them nod synchronistically and surrender a small card embossed with Mr. Boyd's numbers (work, home, mobile).

That's everything. They depart—apparently, Yulish has an apartment not far from here.

"I'll call you later," he says.

"I'm sure you will."

I'm finally alone. And the first thing I do—before taking a piss, before undressing—is call her. Kiki's voice sounds as though she's speaking through a cloud of cotton. I'd forgotten about the time difference. On those evenings when she's not working, she'll read until she passes out. I'm trying to interpret the intricacies of her pitch, the fragile underpinnings behind each word. Is she happy I called? Would she rather go back to sleep?

"How'd it go?" she asks groggily.

"Hard to say," I answer. "You can tell me when you see it tomorrow night."

"Did you fall on your way to the couch?"

"No."

"Did you drool?"

"Don't think so."

"Well," she says, making soft, breathy noises as she adjusts herself in bed, "then it sounds like everything went fine."

"I guess." Lighting a match, I drop it into an ashtray; I watch it burn down to a crinkly black tapeworm. "I lost my head for a minute. There was some dead air when I couldn't remember what I was saying."

"Oh, they'll edit that out."

"Probably."

"It's never as bad as you think."

We don't talk for a moment. It would be nice to have her here with me. I'd impress her with the room and food and Mr. Boyd. Or, better yet, I'd like to be home on her couch, spooning with our bare ankles rubbing together. I picture my arm draped across her belly, my cheek pressed against the cool skin of her neck. After a while, we'd start breathing to the same rhythm; I'd let my fingers lace through hers.

I want a sign that, yes, it's important she sees me again. *Soon.*

But she's tired.

"It's been amazing," I say. "But all day I've had this image of Trip in my head."

"That's natural." I hear the creak of her bedsprings. "He was a good friend."

For the most part, I was able to block out his memory. But, strangely, I thought I saw him a couple times: in a passing car during my conversation with Julie Rust; and later, on the Kellogg show, I was positive he was seated in the audience. That's why I lost my train of thought, turned agonizingly silent.

"He wanted to go inside," I say finally. "I think . . . I think I *made* him stay in the storm with me."

"You didn't *make* him do anything. He was a grown man."

I feel better having spoken the words. I return the phone to its cradle. My eyes are sleepy. They stare into space before coming to rest on the closet's shiny gold doorknob. Actually, it looks more like a comma—a long, horizontal one.

DO I DREAM THE CONVERSATION? (A brief exchange on the telephone.) Can I *really* have visitors? Then comes the sound of another storm. A pounding from across the room, metal against wood. In darkness, I'm able to locate my crutches. Someone's knocking on the door with the force of a jack-hammer. I almost expect to hear a maid's heavy Latino voice, "*Ow*-skee-peen." I turn the knob and a light in the vestibule automatically illuminates. I'm greeted by three perfect faces.

"Howdy," says Julie Rust. She adjusts an enormous ring on her right hand. Apparently, it shifted while she was punching her arm through the newly dented wood. "I hope you don't mind a little company."

Though introductions are made, they're hardly necessary: I immediately recognize movie actors Tilly Dayton and Achilles Loeb. This would be disorientating even if I weren't half asleep. It's nearly midnight.

"Did we wake you?" she says.

"—"

"Oh, sugar. I'm sorry. But you're leaving tomorrow." (Pause.) "And we just *had* to see you."

Again comes the now-familiar notion that I'm being cast as entertainment. A *diversion.*

Through no fault of my own, I have seen dozens of news stories about Achilles Loeb. He was once arrested for urinating on pedestrians from the balcony of his New York hotel suite. Presently, he's seated on the end of my bed with two airplane-size bottles of scotch removed from the minibar. His shoulder-length hair is greasy and unkempt. He's wearing a weathered black-leather sportcoat and a white V-neck undershirt that looks as though it's never been washed. His jeans are so porous I can see the colorful tattoos along his legs. On his feet are a pair of chunky motorcycle boots. Despite signage posted every few feet warning THIS IS A NO SMOKING FLOOR, he's puffing a ceaseless chain of Marlboros.

I'm fatigued. And cranky. A few weeks ago these three wouldn't have tolerated my existence within a half dozen bodyguards of them.

Still dressed in my Hans Berber suit—"We spoke to Mr. Berber's *people,*" said the woman from wardrobe. "They want you to keep the clothing"—I reluctantly agree to join them for a quick drink. I ride shotgun in Loeb's Mercedes. As we pull to the curb, a crooked river of onlookers shoots an anticipatory glance in our direction. Most are waiting behind a velvet moat for admission to a nightclub called the Saturn Room. A man with biceps as thick as holiday hams sees Loeb and clears us a path. The crowd's now crackling with the enthusiasm of having spied some real celebrities. But as we reach the door, I hear a voice say, "*Omigod* . . . It's that guy from the hurricane." I can't tell if it's a compliment or insult.

Loeb's a regular here. Julie and Tilly are chatting purposefully as we plunge through a haze of cigarette smoke to
reach a circular booth in back, with a RESERVED sign mounted
on the table. A bottle of expensive-looking red wine is
brought without provocation. It's followed in close order by
several platters of appetizers—calamari, oysters, braised ravi-
oli and tiny pea (!) pancakes topped with sour cream and
caviar.

"How'd you like Kellogg?" asks Loeb.

"He seemed okay."

Loeb grimaces.

"Achilles hates him," says Julie. "But he hates *all* talk
show hosts."

I'm having trouble enjoying myself. I'm jittery, uptight. I
keep thinking I'm going to say the wrong thing, knock a drink
on someone's lap. I feel the way I used to when I'd get called
into the station manager's office: I'm waiting to be appraised.

"Were you scared?" asks Tilly suddenly.

"I was a little nervous," I say. "But one of Kellogg's assistants went over the questions with me ahead of time."

The three of them laugh.

"No," says Tilly, using her pinkie to remove a crumb
from the corner of her mouth. "I meant *during the storm . . .*"

I feel myself turn red.

"Sure, yeah," I stammer. "I was afraid."

I tell them what they want to hear—maybe the only thing
I truly have to offer. A story that grows more refined each time
I deliver it. I'm trimming the fat, polishing away rough edges.
They're ravenous for details in the same way as Marlon Kel-

logg, his studio audience and the viewers at home. What was it *really* like inside that fucking storm? And I give them everything—the noise and wind and wet-your-pants terror. I watch their eyes expand as I describe the conjoined sailboat and picnic bench hurtling toward me at cartoonish speeds. The tumbling cars and biting rain. I let them picture the way the wind currents lifted me into the sky like Peter Pan—it's an analogy åI rehearsed so listeners can relate—and then slammed me into the wall. Lastly, I surrender something new. I don't know if it's because they're famous, *very* famous, and I want to absolve myself of the notion I'm only here on a lark, a take-the-homely-girl-to-prom dare, that I provide them with what's personal, a currency toward being *accepted*. It's cheap and dirty; I feel sick as soon as the words leave my mouth. I tell them about Trip, every gruesome detail. I speak about the park bench and rooftop and his mangled, lifeless body. I explain how I yelled into the rancid wind before he was sliced apart.

This is my shot at learning their secret handshake.

When I have finished, I'm breathing heavily. Julie takes my hand in hers and strokes it across the knuckles. Tilly has gooseflesh on her forearms. Shaking his head, Loeb twists out a cigarette.

"Man," he says.

We can't leave soon enough. I have violated a compact of decency—with Trip, with his family. I'm disgusted by the ease over which I offered them my secrets. Blinking my eyes—once, twice—I envision Nessa munching an egg roll; I see Ryan leaping from the bumper of my car.

There's not much else. The room is crowded and for the

first time I notice two large men standing near our table. Presumably, it's their job to keep people like *me* away from people like *them*. Velvet ropes within velvet ropes. To bridge the silence, Julie asks me what I thought of Soft Bunz.

"They were fine. It's not really my type of music." Inappropriately (*again!*), I continue talking. "During one of the breaks, Kellogg called the lead singer a complete asshole."

I have lost the mechanism in my brain that would normally filter such comments.

"Nice," says Achilles.

This ignites another sick, burning sensation in my belly. I can't erase the image of me collecting a bulb of cash from the nightstand. I wish Kiki were here. Not because, again, it would be nice to have someone share the experience, someone to reel me back to reality when we returned to the hotel room—do you think Tilly saw a fucking *thing* with those sunglasses on?—but because Kiki would have remained grounded. She'd deliver a swift kick beneath the table to keep me from saying too much. Surely she's a voice of reason during this unreasonable time.

They drop me at the hotel. From the backseat, Tilly says, "Don't be a stranger." I thank them three times, once for each of them, and crutch self-consciously up the stairs. Inside, I'm greeted by the night manager, who asks me, by name, if there's anything I need.

"How about a couple Weather Service maps?"

He looks confused and I tell him I was only kidding (though part of me yearns for a link to my previous life). Sitting on the suitcase stand beside my bed, I'm pinched between emotions. I feel like I've returned home from a strange first date, a ribbon of promise stretched out before me. Will we do this again? Did they have a nice time? Did I? I consider calling Kiki, sharing the good parts of the evening. And the bad.

I caught a glimpse of what my (celebrity) future may hold in store when our Saturn Room waitress brought us a meringue dessert and I announced, roused by drink, that the fluffy topping looked exactly like a photograph I have tacked above my desk of a Lenticular cloud formation. The observation was met with equal parts amusement and animus. In fact, Julie Rust, seemingly stupefied, nearly hocked a mushroom cap across the table. Then I was stranded in the same smog of dead air as during the Kellogg show. Again, I had no perspective on how long the silence lasted. But my fingers turned enamel-white as they gripped my knees.

THIS MUST BE HOW PEOPLE OF spectacular means awaken on a common weekday. Mr. Boyd is standing near the foot of my bed with a breakfast tray. The room smells of freshly percolated coffee and warm croissants. A few hours ago, I abandoned my suit on the bathroom's tile floor. Sometime in the brittle hours of early morning, Mr. Boyd steamed and hanged the outfit. I believe it's no small victory over my personal neuroses, given my compulsion against unlaundered clothes, that I'm going to wear the Hans Berber for a second consecutive day.

"We need to have you ready for departure in forty-five minutes," he says, adjusting the tray across my thighs.

Lying on the bedspread is the day's newspaper and, incredibly, several National Weather Service maps. Mr. Boyd can read the astonishment on my face.

"A courier brought those pages from a local television station," he says. "I hope you'll find them suitable. The request came from our night manager."

"Jesus Christ," I say, folding a pillow against the small of my sore back. "Talk about *full service.*"

This is a dangerous game. I could get used to this type of treatment. I imagine my life with a round-the-clock valet. Every list of errands pasted around my apartment—on the fridge, beside my bed, on the mirror in my bathroom—would actually become a call to action. For somebody else.

I let the concept twirl in my head like a rotisserie chicken. Each morning I could have Mr. Boyd retrieve my research material from the station. That would allow me to wake at a leisurely rate: I'd leaf through my paperwork over eggs benedict, home-baked muffins and pulpless grapefruit juice (Pop-Tart toxins begone).

As I half seriously consider a way to crowbar the idea into my network contract, I stumble over my newly buffed shoes. (Fantastic!) On the toilet, I flip through the morning newspaper. My stomach drops when I notice a photograph of me and Achilles Loeb entering the Saturn Room, beside a headline that reads, simply, *Overheard.* The hair along the back of my forearms stands rigid. I scan the piece, quickly, before going back twice more. *Huddled in a rear booth at L.A.'s hot* Saturn Room *with* Achilles Loeb, Tilly Dayton *and* Julie Rust, *weather wonder* Lucas Prouty, *fresh from his appearance on* NightTime with **Marlon Kellogg,** *shared this spicy nugget with his dinner-mates. Prouty told the threesome that during taping, Kellogg referred to* **Soft Bunz** *lead singer* **Ed Dorley** *as "a complete a——."*

I spoke the comment less than a dozen hours ago. It seems implausible that one of my "dinner-mates" would leak the story. Which means someone, indeed, *overheard* our conversation. I'm trying to remember if I said anything else inflammatory. A wave of nausea passes through me. I talked about the storm. Of greater significance, I described Trip's *death* in the storm. Now I'm frantic. How will I protect Ginny and the kids against the possibility that at this very moment some weasel is tapping the keys on a story—*nay:* an item, a *blurb*—about the dismemberment of Trip's torso?

The worry stays with me on the sidewalk outside the hotel. I speak distractedly to four autograph hounds from Atlanta. Wagging shiny black pens, they ask me to sign the backs of their business cards and, when I oblige, one of them suggests I draw a curlicue with the tail of my Y. "It'll look like a tornado," he says. "Which is almost a hurricane."

During the limo ride to the movie studio—they've scheduled a nonsensical meeting—I call Kiki three times. (She must be in school.) I open my wallet and stare at the photograph of an imaginary Flynn. When I screwed up back in Bentleyville—insulting one of the anchors, using indelicate language—I had only myself to blame. I was able to apologize, move on. But what happens here? Do I have to look over my shoulder every time I speak?

I fiddle with the air vents in the limousine.

"I'd like to tell you it gets easier," says Yulish, who interrupts a teleconference to take my call.

I lie down on the backseat, my feet pressed against the door.

"You got reporters out there who make a living digging through people's underwear drawers."

Yulish excuses himself. I don't know what comes next. I suppose I proceed with caution, pin back my ears and try to enjoy the ride. I'm knee-deep in designer clothes and high-end hotels; I enjoy a fancy meal as much as the next weather guy. Sitting upright again, I watch the sprawling landscape from my window and decide I need to visit Bentleyville. Even if it's only for a couple days. I'm so distracted by thoughts of home—what can I buy for Kiki?—I hardly notice we've arrived at the movie lot.

The lobby walls are filled with framed posters of the studio's more successful films. I'm surrounded by a herd of low-level employees; it's a surprisingly pleasant sensation. They attend to my every need. In fact, they attend to needs I didn't *know* I had. (Who would've guessed that guava juice tasted so good?) I've already been asked three times by three *different* people whether I'd prefer additional refreshments or alternate reading materials.

Granted, the financial remuneration of my network job and other sundry deals—endorsements, sponsorships, impending film—is overwhelming. And I'm thrilled my forecasts will now play to a national audience instead of a few hillbilly towns in coastal Carolina. Still, I can't rid myself of the laughable notion that the most inebriating part of my new life is the seemingly endless parade of free *stuff*. When I was a kid, I remember thinking it was really cool that professional athletes received complimentary sneakers and tennis rackets and baseball gloves and track suits. Years later, I read a story about the "goody bags" certain awards shows provided to their celebrated presenters. It seemed illogical that the people with the largest bank accounts were magically hitched to some graft-churning pipeline.

During my entire weathercasting career, I can't recall more than a couple odd gifts that bear repeating. The clock-radio from Shockley's. And each holiday season the company who services our Doppler radar sends me a desk calendar highlighting the most important events in weather history (March 12: New York City is buried beneath nearly two feet of snow in the Blizzard of 1888). There have also been embossed pen-and-pencil sets, refrigerator magnets, ballcaps and tins of flavored popcorn.

But you can't compare those trinkets with the merchandise that's come my way since the storm. My transition into the world of executive travel has been swift and seamless: private planes, hotel suites, idling Town Cars for carefree passage. And the network's simply a small piece of a giant conglomerate. There's a music division (free compact discs), a manufacturer of audio and visual equipment (portable CD player, TV), a publishing arm (books) and an online service provider. I feel like a game show contestant. *Congratulations, Mr. Prouty. You've won what's behind curtains one, two and three.*

Consider: I have yet to engage in a single discussion with the movie people and *already* they've placed beside me satchels of videotapes, T-shirts and ballcaps. (Does this sound horribly shallow?) As I flip through my new collection of DVDs, a young woman interrupts and leads me into a gleaming conference room.

The other day Yulish warned me what to expect during my visit. "Swallow hard," he said, patting me on the chest. "And keep thinking about the fat paycheck."

The producer's name is Ben Willocks. He's an amalgam of every parodied movie executive I've ever seen. He's wearing a black T-shirt, beige trousers and narrow rectangular eyeglasses. His perfectly tended toenails peak out from beneath a pair of brown mules. For the first part of our conversation, I have trouble paying attention because I'm watching him eat a variety of grotesque-looking foodstuffs from Tupperware containers. His assistant explains that Mr. Willocks is bravely attempting to shed a "smidgen of unwanted weight" by submitting to a carefully orchestrated dietary regimen.

I'm reminded of Trip's weight-loss program. And how, depending on my mood, I'd tease him about his size—clucking my tongue when he ate fast food, slapping desserts from his pudgy fingers. I feel crummy, until Ben Willocks distractingly hits his stride.

His vision for a "picture" based on the recent events of my life, a biopic, is remarkable in its seemingly comprehensive disregard for accuracy. According to Willocks, the studio *loves* the idea of setting the film in the Midwest. When I inform him of the mathematical—not to mention geographical—implausibility of a hurricane occurring in the heartland, Willocks dismisses my apprehension with a wave of his hand.

"We've focus-grouped this thing to death," he says, plying the noun *focus group* into a verb. "The Midwest tests very high. It's wholesome."

Other liberties include changing my name—"Just for the movie," he says reassuringly—to Ned Kansas and contriving a love interest (either a stewardess or schoolteacher). They've tentatively titled the project *A Star Named Kansas* because, in his words, "it works on so many levels. Like the whole *Wizard of Oz* thing. You remember the song, right?" He sings a few wretchedly off-key bars: "Kansas she says is the name of the star/ Kansas she says is the name of the star."

I'm amazed. *Thunderstruck.* Is he *serious*? A spark of anger rinses through me at such a rapid speed I notice my arms have started trembling. To compound matters, he appears to be glowing with confidence; I think he's actually *pleased* with himself.

The only good comes when he reaches to shake hands. My mouth has filled with fluid. He says something—honestly, I wouldn't have heard him if he offered to blow me under the table—and when I thank him (!) a small pearl of saliva is slingshot from the nave of my tongue onto his surgically enhanced cheekbone. Right below his eye.

The rewarding image of my spittle leeched to his face is all that keeps me from weeping during the ride to the airport.

REFRACTED SUNLIGHT CASTS A colorful bracelet against my kitchen floor. I watch as particles of dust tumble and swirl. My apartment is crowded with mementos: more

flowers, greeting cards, gifts. (Evidently, the building's superintendent grew tired of the mess and dragged the stuff inside.)
I leaf through my mail while sitting on the toilet. For the first
time in what seems like many, many weeks, I am truly alone.
Only a few people know I have returned to North Carolina.
Even my new cell phone is recharging. I collapse on the couch
and fall into the innocent sleep of a child.

I'm awakened by a familiar noise: Outside a group of
raccoons is examining the contents of trash cans, tipping
them into the hard concrete. It happens every couple days
when someone doesn't fasten the lids with a tight seal. I rise,
stretch and move to the window above my kitchen sink. Now
it's dark. Because I have no interest in seeing the rodents, I
prepare to shout down the alley—sending them scurrying
away—before heading outside to clean the spill. But when I
reach the screen, I hear voices. Two men talking back and
forth in hushed tones. I peer through the blinds. Their figures
are illuminated by a small security light. They are foraging
through the garbage, *my* garbage. One of them is collecting
discarded mail, empty food wrappers.

"Hey!" I say, for lack of something intelligent. "Can I
help you?"

As though characters in an old Bowery Boys film, they
exchange panic-stricken looks (eyebrows raised, mouths
agape) and move several steps back. In the time it takes me to
work my way from shadowy kitchen to patio to alley, they've
reached the parking lot on the opposite end of the courtyard.
I watch their twin-disc headlights retreat into blackness like
synchronized fireflies, drunk and harried. Then comes the

sound of their car spraying a rooster tail of gravel in advance of hitting the hard-paved road. Pathetically, I throw my crutch after them.

Later, I recount the incident when I'm speaking to Yulish.

"I've heard worse," he says. "They probably work for one of those supermarket tabloids, like *The Dirt.*"

"What the hell were they looking for?"

"Who knows?"

"Listen," I say, enunciating to the best of my TV-trained ability. "I'm a meteorologist. From a place *I* can barely find on a road map. Does anyone really care what kind of toothpaste I buy?"

I hear him inhale a loud mouthful of air.

"Look, this is a zero-sum business. Every time somebody does a negative story about you, like the nonsense between Kellogg and that stupid band, it potentially replaces a good one. They can only devote so much space to *weathermen.*" He rustles some papers near the mouthpiece of his phone. "Infatuations are short-lived. We need to capitalize on this buzz, keep it going. Because it'll be over sooner than you think."

"Sure," I say. "I just didn't expect *this.*"

His secretary squawks something over the intercom.

"Have you seen the promos we've been running?"

I have not.

"They're really inspired. We shot a handful of N__ personalities—news reporters, anchors, sitcom stars—on the sets of their respective shows. Each says a few words about your arrival."

The question has been bumping around my head for a

few days. In truth, I haven't asked it because I'm afraid of his reply. *Why did you hire me?* Surely it hasn't a goddam thing to do with my talent as a forecaster.

After I ask it, I can practically hear him organizing his thoughts, spinning his reply. His voice disappears into a bramble of sputtery sound. Of course, I already have my answer. It doesn't matter to them whether I can tell the difference between an Icelandic low and a Bermuda high. They care about one thing: my popularity. The network will ride me like a booster rocket. My success owes everything to timing. I could easily be Rick Fasco. Or, had the storm taken a different route, I could be Toby Lansing from WVBO in Virginia Beach.

Before ending the conversation, Yulish encourages me to relax. He claims in a few weeks I'll be knee-deep in the swing of things. "Enjoy yourself," he says. "It beats shooting a remote from the National Okra Festival."

I walk to the bathroom and gaze at my reflection in the mirror. My skin's in dire need of elixirs—the red flakiness between my eyebrows has become worse; my scalp is ripe with nubs and sores. I know there's one last spritz of solution remaining in my medicine cabinet to soothe the itching along the seam of my skull. And I remind myself to peel away the bottle's pharmaceutical label, shred it into a hundred indistinguishable pieces before tossing the confetti into the trash for fear of reading about my maladies in one of the next day's tabloids.

I GREET THE NEW MORNING WITH A series of lower back exercises in my living room. The movements are made infinitely more difficult by the heavy cast; my proportions, familiar from half a lifetime with nearly the same dimensions, have suddenly shifted. When I oafishly knock the telephone onto the floor as I'm crossing my right leg against my left hip, I fail to hear a dial tone. I follow the wires. Before my mother and sister departed, it seems they unplugged the receivers.

More than anything, I'd like to meet Kiki for breakfast. We could sit on her porch, my fingers massaging the sleep from her body. But she's not home. She told me she was spending the night in Raleigh to complete a seminar for school.

I bravely decide to abandon my cocoon for the outside world of Bentleyville. The ignition in the Crown Vic turns over on the second try. Driving with a leg cast takes some practice and, after a few blocks of herky-jerky motion, I discover I'm most successful when I use my toes to grip the pedals. Still, I nearly rear-end a delivery truck in the parking lot at Hollister's Package Store.

I prop my sunglasses on my head. It takes a moment for my eyes to adjust in the room's perpetual darkness. I don't recognize anybody and, for the time being, no one recognizes me. I intend to order a plate of ham steak and grits as I have done, in my spot at the bar, a hundred times. There's something strangely reassuring about sitting behind one of Hollister's translucent jars of homemade pickles. I tap the greasy glass with a fingernail.

The woman who takes my order is a new employee. She's slow to leave my side for the kitchen. I drink a sip of water, then coffee. As I'm blotting a coin of spilled cream with my napkin, I hear Hollister's booming voice and the skin along the back of my neck turns prickly.

"Christ almighty," he says, snapping a dish towel against the air. "Oh, *Christ* almighty."

"Hey . . ."

"You sumbitch. I can*not* believe you're settin' right here."

"Came for breakfast."

He skips around the bar and, surprising both of us, plants a stubbly kiss on my right cheek.

"I didn't think I'd ever see you again." He crosses his arms and gives me a long look. "First I thought you were gone to that storm; then I thought you were gone to them fellas from New York."

He's speaking loud enough so the others in the room are now driven into paying attention. Even the waitress cuts loose with a slow nod. (He's jogged her memory.) She slides me her order pad across the bar and I inscribe my name, twice if you count the carbon paper.

"We can't stock them fast enough," says Hollister.

Sensing I have no idea what he's talking about, Hollister disappears briefly into his office. He returns with a women's fashion magazine folded against itself, revealing a glossy page bookmarked by a paper clip. Lifted from television is a small photograph of me broadcasting during the early hours of Isabel. The magazine's editors have highlighted my ballcap, bearing the HOLLISTER'S PACKAGE STORE emblem across its crown. The accompanying caption reads, "Hot Accessory."

"You've *got* to be kidding."

"Nope." He hooks his thumb toward a small stack of caps behind the cash register. "There's six of 'em. And that's our *third* batch. We're mailing hats to folks all across the country."

It seems inconceivable that anyone living outside Bent-leyville would have the least bit of interest in wearing one of Hollister's silly ballcaps. Even more perplexing is the con-struct that most of these people, from fashion meccas like Manhattan and Los Angeles, are pairing the headgear with designer outfits costing more than Hollister's flatbed truck simply because I happened to choose one, randomly, to keep the rain from running into my eyes. And because a magazine is telling them it's "hot."

"The apocalypse is surely upon us," I say.

"Maybe so. But that ain't stoppin' me from cashing in."

Betwixt a gentle stupor and something requiring actual medical attention, I finish my meal. As I drink the remains of my coffee, tepid and grainy, I spy Hollister on the phone; he acknowledges me by pointing to his cap. Presumably, he's made another long-distance sale. I smile. I tip my head and pretend to knock it clean of cobwebs in a motion not dissim-ilar from what a swimmer does to flush water from his ear.

Lacking any pressing duties, I decide to take a slow drive through town. I'm hoping to inspire the same pleasant feelings I had upon returning home to Mill Valley during my first Thanksgiving vacation from college. I remember wanting to make sure nothing had changed in my absence. There was a light glaze of snow; I guided my mother's car through the silent streets. An odd monologue ran through my head, as though I were narrating my own adolescence: *That's Danny Wheeler's house. Over on those monkey bars, when I was twelve, I watched Tom Orkin break his arm so badly he was placed in traction. Oh, see the small shop on that corner? It's*

Hooper's. We used to buy comic books and candy from them. When I was a senior in high school, I ripped off a box of rubbers from the pharmacy next door.

Now, in Bentleyville, I'm longing for a similar steady comfort. The whisper in my ear of a friendly voice telling me everything's going to be okay. A history with some place, *this* place, to provide ballast in a choppy time. *See?* the voice would offer. *No matter how crazy things become, you're grounded by* that *tree—recognize it?—and* that *stoplight*, that *donut shop*.

But the gentle touch never arrives. Nothing's the same. This is my first extended look at the damage caused by Isabel. I have visited other cities in the aftermath of powerful storms. And the raw emotion from survivors, who often stand for hours amid the scabby wreckage of their houses, is difficult to witness. This is worse. Now *I* am the survivor; this is *my* home.

Wandering from street to street, I feel violated. Not unlike the victim of a crime or, more specifically, an assault. Every block is active with people rebuilding their lots, their lives. The backstop from the high school's baseball diamond is a mangled mess; it resembles the chicken-wire frame beneath a papier-mâché iceberg. A statue of the town's founder, Emmitt Bentley, is battered so severely—by a trash dumpster? a car door?—its head looks like a collapsed soufflé. The picket fence demarking the house at the northwest corner of Percy and Dunkirk is now a sloppy white pyramid of cordwood. Farther still, a child's swing set has been uprooted in a massive somersault. At first glance it appears to be a gigantic dog's corpse with four paws aimed skyward.

Near the center of town is an ubiquitous coffee-chain shop, opened less than a year ago. There was a long, arduous battle among city council members about whether or not to allow the franchise in Bentleyville. Many residents were against its arrival, fearing it would be the first step toward the homogenization of the town's commercial landscape. They wanted to preserve originality, uniqueness. Alas, sizable donations to the local library and elementary school by the chain's founder, who summered in Bentleyville as a youth, served their purpose. At the time, I was very much against the shop; I even encouraged a full-scale boycott by WYIP employees (which was suitably ignored).

Driving quietly past, I stare at the dim storefront, hidden behind heavy scrims of plywood. From some place I don't fully understand, I begin to cry. The tears arrive one by one, in the precise, protective manner of the human eye turning damp after coming into contact with a powdery substance. In fact, I'm so startled I think maybe I *did* catch a fleck of dirt. But soon the sadness seizes hold of the rest of my body: My hands are jiggly along the wheel; my breath grows short; and deep in my throat rises a whelpy moan. I'm compelled to pull off the road. It's the kind of hysterical *yaw-yaw-yaw* attack normally reserved for children, leaving them incapable of forming plain sentences, words. I remember something I was told by Dr. Metzel in the hospital. He said it's not uncommon for those who have lived through a severe crisis like a hurricane to experience depression in the weeks and months that follow. Often, he continued, the survivors feel *guilty* about surviving.

I wipe my eyes with my shirtsleeve, my shoulder. I can't seem to find the root of my emotions. Mostly, I think I *do* feel guilty; I feel guilty that I don't feel worse about living—about *succeeding*—when others (like Trip) died. It's the same sense of helplessness that enveloped me while standing over Flynn's body. How could it *happen*? We listened to the experts, did everything right. And now we only wanted what was promised us—a way to reverse this horrible, horrible momentum.

I roll down my window. The air is wet with humidity. It will probably rain this afternoon, this evening. Some days it's enough to have a symmetry imposed by simple routine: Awaken at the same time; shave with a familiar brand of soap; purchase a muffin (corn) and coffee from the corner bakery; and take the same left, left, right, left path to work. And that is exactly what's been missing from my life since the storm: *order*. The steadiness that comes from everything ordinary.

Suddenly it's as though I'm playing an arcade-style driving game, the kind where you climb into a replica seat, and my thoughts have erased my peripheral vision; I'm now focused only on a black ribbon of roadway that's leading me to the lot behind WYIP. I sit in my car and stare out the windshield at the studio's rear entrance. I crutch my way to the door and greet the guard, a man I have seen many, many times. He shakes my hand, twice, and pats me on the shoulder. Even when I'm halfway down the hall, his eyes remain locked to my back; he calls to me before I turn the corner and jogs to make up the distance. From his breast pocket he presents a black-tipped marker, asking if I will autograph the visor of his cap.

The first couple people I pass don't pay attention to me. They're deep in conversation. My stomach is filled with the same queasy flutter as before my early days working in this building. I'm not sure why I feel so nervous.

I smile when I make eye contact with Maura Lease, who's pouring milk into a mug of tea. She jumps. *Literally.* And the cloudy liquid from her cup splashes across her hands and onto her black leather shoes. Resembling the onset of trauma, her mouth locks into a perfect 0. She fails to respond when I say hello.

"Sweet Jesus!" says Bob Gates, fresh from today's episode of *Breakfast in Bentleyville.*

We shake hands. And Maura, snapping awake, uses a paper towel to dry her fingers without once looking away. Soon I'm surrounded by other station employees. They're reaching, touching, petting and hugging. With each new person comes another tale. They all feel compelled to offer their unique versions of my disappearance and, with greater enthusiasm, my rescue. The gathering brings vaguely to mind a group therapy session in the aftermath of a major catastrophe: *Where were you when . . . ?* Unexpectedly, the person who appears most delighted by my revised career path is Rick Fasco. I suspect he considers our good fortunes inextricably linked. By default, my departure makes him the station's main meteorologist.

As we all begin making our way in an amoebalike clot toward the center of the newsroom, I glimpse the bulletin board outside the kitchenette. It's littered with all things . . . *me.* Press clippings, photographs from newspapers and magazines. This is the spot where a year ago the station posted a letter of congratulations from the network to anchor Zane Grobbit on his regional Emmy nomination. (He lost to a guy from Asheville.) Though the news articles may not seem like much, I recognize that until recently many of these same people considered me an underachiever (for lack of a better description).

I'm told of the great procession of reporters who continue digging for information about me. They call, they visit. Many of the stories are hijacked for further retribution on my unofficial website. (I have a website?) It's a creepy revelation.

They pepper me with questions about my visit to L.A., the movie deal and my new job. It feels as though there's a transparent membrane between us, one that permits diffusion in only a single direction. They seem reluctant to reciprocate when I ask about the daily events of *their* lives. (How are the ratings? Is camera No. 3 still on the fritz?) Somehow, I sense they believe this news is now beneath me.

They slowly begin excusing themselves. More slaps on the back, handshakes. One by one they break from the pack. A finality settles over the closing strands of conversation, as if I'm bidding them—this *place*—a last farewell.

Though Kurt's not around, I peer through his open door on my way out. Not long ago, I spent an afternoon every other month in his office listening to mostly negative appraisals of my work. Today, the only thing my eyes catch upon is a framed photograph of Kurt holding a string of lifeless fish.

I'm not proud of what happens next. As I maneuver through the parking lot, I see sportscaster Wes Nichols climbing out of his car. He's holding a briefcase in one hand, a fast-food hamburger in the other. He doesn't notice me. The moment he lifts the burger to his mouth, I lay on the horn. He jumps, smashing the sandwich into his nose. When he bends down to get a good look at who's driving past him, I raise my fist into the window and extend my middle finger.

THE CROWN VIC MOVES AS THOUGH on rails. It snakes through a flattened cable of roadway, low-slung foliage slapping off the sideview mirrors, the windshield. Acres of wobbly land, wooded and green, rise to meet the horizon. The air is dense with moisture. It could be from last night's rainstorm or the cool perspiration of nearby water. I hear the trickley chime of a creek hidden in the underbrush. As the car slows to a crawl, stones and dry branches pop beneath its tires. To my right is a flightless dirigible, a sausage of weathered steel. The Airstream trailer sits on a hump of yard between a small Georgian-style house and the road.

The trailer is half covered by a lattice of unkempt vines. The windows are glazed with soot and red, sandy dirt. Above the door is a string of holiday lights braided through a pair of frowning antlers. A gravel path leads to the house, marked by wildflowers and brightly painted rocks. Skewered into a rectangle of black soil are bamboo shoots with tiny cellophane-wrapped tags detailing a variety of crops: snap peas, tomatoes, basil and rosemary.

I remember the owl. On a night nearly a year ago, when the bar was practically empty, I helped her convert an old denim shirt, feathers, wire coat hangers and a set of false teeth into a stuffed-owl scarecrow. She's got it bolted to the hood of a disembodied Plymouth. The contraption looks like a picnic table with an elaborate centerpiece.

Her birdbath is the severed heel to a metal beer keg. It's screwed atop a fence post of cross-cut oak or pine. She has returned from Raleigh. The engine of her truck is freshly ticking.

"Is that you?" she says, from a place I can't see.

I turn my head and scout for movement.

She uses the trailer as an office. The storm door squeals open; her face is flush against the puckered screen. Then comes the most genuine emotion I've felt in a long time: I'm seized by a desire to throw my arms around Kiki and draw her close to me.

She lowers herself onto the stacked cinderblock steps.

I want to push my face against the soft skin of her neck.

She tucks a strand of hair behind her ear and I notice that the buttons of her shirt, a man's blousy oxford, are misaligned. This would have bothered me with Annie. But now, peering into Kiki's pale gray eyes, I find it endearing.

She's not exactly rushing to shorten the distance between us. I'm probably getting ahead of myself. I have trouble separating the pretend part of our relationship—all the fantastical thoughts I had in the basement of Trixies—from reality. I almost died. And she's offered neither passion nor deliverance nor a yearning even to embrace me back. Instead, only the practical response of a friend: the necessity to see for herself that I'm truly fine.

"You're alive and well," she announces, punching a fist into her hip.

"Alive . . ."

"Oh, *please*," she says, turning to chase a rabbit from her garden.

It's hard to believe this is the first time we've been together since the storm. I catch myself staring at the smooth tendon striping the back of her foot. I've had this thought on a hundred nights: What would it feel like to lean forward and kiss her deep on the mouth?

But I settle for a squeeze on the wrist, a quick peck above my chin.

I guess I expected something else. I'm trying to recall her comments from the other day; I'm now considering what *she* wants. (Does she even know?)

"Before you start talking," she says intuitively, "I'm not good with boys. I always screw things up. I'm agog–that's a word, right? agog?–whenever I see a couple that's been together for more than, say, a few years."

I nod unsurely.

"I watched you on Kellogg," she says, changing tacks. "The whole bar did. We turned off the music and everything."

We're sitting together on a distressed bench behind the trailer. She cocks her head, swats at a yellowjacket.

"I can't offer you anything more than this: I missed you," she says. "During the couple days when I'd given up hope, when everybody thought you were dead, I began to realize– " She breaks off, crossing her arms over her lap. "Every day I'd catch myself looking toward the door, expecting you to walk in. Like it was all okay."

Neither of us knows what this means. But it confirms what I took from our last few conversations: She's modifying the terms of our relationship (however slightly). The possibility now exists that we can become more than friends. Maybe it's nothing; maybe it's everything.

I wonder what I can say to move things along. This is fragile stuff. If I talk too much I may scare her away.

Last spring, Trip and I drove to Fayetteville for work. We were shooting a remote with some guy who was riding his bicycle across the country. On our way back, we stopped for lunch at a hot dog stand across from Jernigan's Kiddie Park—about twenty minutes outside Bentleyville.

Because the season was still a few weeks away, the area was mostly quiet. Trip and I were sitting on a picnic table, watching a couple guys doing groundskeeping around the park. I had just dripped mustard onto my shirt; I was blotting the stain with a wet napkin when Trip said, "Geez, what do you make of that?"

A lean figure was twirling a lasso, flinging it over the head of a wooden horse on a stationary carousel. Something about the way the person moved looked familiar—a recognizable gait and posture. I jogged across the street. I followed the chain-link fence until I found an opening. Behind me, Trip scuffled along with his hot dogs in one hand and his Pepsi in the other.

"It's Kiki," I said.

"Kiki," responded Trip, as though it were the most logical thing in the world.

We made our way past the miniature steam engine, the cup-and-saucer ride and the go-cart track. I could hear the rope whistling against the air. Kiki did a nifty little trick where she slapped the lasso off the asphalt and leaped through its whirling mouth.

"*Yee*-haw," I said, coming up from behind.

She smiled; she removed a pair of deerskin gloves and wiped the sweat from her forehead with her shirtsleeve. She took a long swallow from Trip's drink, munching on some ice chips.

"My brother used to compete in rodeos," she said.

She told us she loves to "swing rope" when she's feeling stressed—it helps to clear her head, get the blood pumping. She didn't seem bothered by our company. In fact, I think she enjoyed the attention. She executed a couple slick maneuvers—was she showing off?—before asking if we wanted to give her some live targets.

"Tempting as that sounds," said Trip, "I think I'll pass."

"That's probably for the best," said Kiki, twice missing an elf statue—YOU MUST BE AS TALL AS ME TO ENTER THIS RIDE—with her throws. "I'm not very good."

"Oh, come on," I said.

I leaned down and tightened my shoelaces. I started a drunken gallop, making horse noises—*clippity-clop, clippity-clop*—as I moved through a series of crooked figure eights.

She was hesitant at first, casting the rope in ridiculously soft parabolas, like a child lofting a softball. But the faster I skipped, the more competitive she became. (I taunted her with exaggerated whinnies and brays.) Finally, she got me around the shoulders; she waited for the lasso to settle across my chest before snapping her wrist, like an angler setting his hook.

I was between gallops and my feet got tangled; I lunged forward. Of course, this wouldn't have been a problem if my arms weren't bound to my sides. But I couldn't raise my hands to break the fall.

Fortunately (for my teeth), I turned my head at the last second and struck the ground with my ear. I screamed and, symbiotically, so did Trip. It seemed as though my ear was on fire; I was certain blood was oozing down the side of my jaw.

"Oh, shit," said Kiki, rushing to loosen the rope.

By the time Trip reached me, he was laughing so hard that snot was leaking from his nose. I was fine. There was no blood, no injury. Only a throbbing redness in my right ear that made me feel strangely asymmetrical. Kiki apologized twice as she helped me to my feet.

"It's my fault," I said. "It's my own damn fault for being clumsy."

Trip was still giggling. But now he was examining his hot dog—it had also fallen to the pavement—and deciding whether it was clean enough to eat. As the three of us squeezed onto a bench, Kiki fished more ice from Trip's drink and dabbed it against my ear.

What happened next is the part I remember best: Because the coldness started to hurt my ear, I reached to stop Kiki. But somehow as I was moving her arm away, our fingers laced together. They stayed that way while we lowered our hands to my knee. And we sat there, silently, skin against skin, for enough time to make it mean something more than a splendid accident.

I dig my heel into the soft dirt of her yard. During moments when I surrender to my imagination, I rarely dream about the impossible—a network job, a motion picture about two weeks in my life. Rather, I wish for the kinds of things that are seemingly within my grasp—practicing meteorology in a respectable market, having a family of my own.

Now it feels like everything has been spun on its head.

I lean my body into a funnel of light. The sun on my face feels warm and pleasant. This new information has made me anxious—I want to get on with it already. I've waited long enough for this relationship with Kiki; I'm ready for us to see what's on the other side.

I suppose the worst thing would be to speed forward with reckless abandon, mislead myself. This might be all there is.

"Okay, then," I say, newly content to move at her responsible pace.

I sock her playfully in the arm.

SOLACE COMES WITH A RETURN TO RIGOR, the actions that once provided structure to my day. Resting in bed, I guide the emery board through a palindromic pattern: pinkie, ring finger, middle finger, index finger, thumb, thumb, index finger, middle finger, ring finger, pinkie. As I peer across my stocking feet, I see Rick Fasco's dwarf, Goshen, armed with sunglasses and a tumbler of iced tea, smiling from my television. His presence, thusly, is synonymous with an uninterrupted string of fine weather.

Waiting for the varnish on the nails of my left hand to dry, I surf from channel to channel. After rapidly passing something I recognize, near-subliminally, I return to discover

Tilly Dayton engaged in a red-carpet interview. She's been absconded by Mimi Maxwell of *Today's Entertainment* who, near a tsunami of photographers, asks several inane questions ("Where are you going for dinner?") before permitting Tilly to escape for the premiere of a high-budget action movie. I've missed most of their little chat. But more remarkable than anything I hear Tilly say is what she's wearing. On her head. It's a gold satin ballcap by a designer whose name I can't pronounce. The cap's crown is aglitter with a combination of gemstones that replicate the emblem from Hollister's Package Store.

Tomorrow I'm headed to New York. The network's been running promos for a magazine-style show in which I'll be interviewed—*exclusively!*—by Emmy-winning anchor Mark Brown. Likewise, an obscenely long list of other media outlets—magazines, newspapers, online services, *competing* networks—have requested time with me. In preparation for my arrival, I've been granted a personal assistant; her name is Gitchy Outzen. Despite the thrill that came from watching Mr. Boyd tend to my every need, I'm not particularly comfortable knowing somebody's going to scuttle about in my shadow. (Can I get you a caffe latte, Mr. Prouty? What time should I make those reservations for? I had your dry-cleaning delivered to your apartment.)

In fairness to Ms. Outzen—she *is* counting on the job—I'm keeping an open mind. I figure it will be nice to have some of the clutter excised from my life. (Can I get you a caffe latte, Mr. Prouty? What time should I make those reservations for? I had your dry-cleaning delivered to your apartment.) I've even caught myself fantasizing about her; I'm pretending she's French. Or maybe Australian. Something with a sexy accent. She's got impossibly black hair cropped cutely short. And enormous green eyes. Because I've never had a personal assistant, I'm at a loss for ways to occupy her time. (I can only eat so many danish.)

I dial her number while watering the ficus above the sink. Though hardly exotic, her voice sounds vaguely mid-western. ("Oops," she says. "You caught me drinking a glass of *orn*-juice.")

Gitchy is copious in her praise for me. She says she's a "totally huge" fan. She has a videotape of the broadcast in which I disappeared and claims to have watched it "a hundred times." She graduated from the University of Missouri's jour-nalism school last spring. "It's such a privilege to be working with you," she says. "I was so excited I didn't sleep at all last night."

In response, I express a not-insubstantial fear of disap-pointing her. "I'm serious," I say when she breaks into a con-vulsive laugh.

"Tomorrow you'll be landing at five-twenty-five," she says. "Look for a man holding a sign reading Mr. Pibb *before* you take the escalator down to the baggage terminal. Mr. Pibb is your code name—it was my favorite pop when I was in high school."

"Nicely done."

I pack my suitcase with the oldies station playing on my radio, the Boss-Tones singing "Mope-itty Mope." Near the door are three sacks of mail filled with what I'd reluctantly describe as mash notes. When I was a kid, I wrote one of these to a member of a popular band. I waited weeks for an answer, each afternoon asking my mother—*assaulting* her upon my return from school—if anything had come for me in the day's post. On the evening I finally abandoned hope, I announced at dinner that if I ever became a rock star, I'd write back to every single kid. Now, I can't imagine anything more repulsive than reading those silly letters—*Oh, Mr. Prouty, I'm not the kind of person who normally writes to a complete stranger* or *I wanted you to have this picture of my dog Winky* or *Please, please, please call me the next time you're in Duluth*—other than actually having to reply.

A cardboard tube the size of a sprinter's baton is poking from the mouth of the second sack. I remove the plastic seal and unroll a sketch of me standing behind a microphone. (In truth, the drawing more closely resembles a circus clown with its arched eyebrows and bulbous nose.) I'm suddenly testy; I don't know if it's my impending travel or leaving Kiki behind. The first line of the accompanying card reads, "You're a real inspiration." *Inspiration?* What exactly did I inspire you to do? Drag your friend onto the beach during a hurricane? Get him sliced in half? I try to blink away the final image I have of Trip. Reaching into the top drawer of my desk, I withdraw a small booklet of photographs. It was a gift commemorating my second anniversary at WYIP.

I leaf through the pages. There's a picture of me standing beside Miss Corn Queen at the state fair; in the background Trip has plugged a corncob between his unzipped fly. Another shows me lying face-up on a snow-covered parking lot. I'd slipped on a patch of ice and thrown out my back, forcing me to deliver the forecast from a prone position. The next one I *love*: I'm dressed like a hobo for Halloween; and Trip's wearing a child's Spider Man costume, the kind that fastens from behind. Because he's much too wide, the costume runs down the center of his body like an oversize necktie.

I miss him.

Not enough time has passed to make his loss seem permanent. It feels as though he's gone on vacation. Maybe to visit his mother in Knoxville. And I've got all this stuff to tell him when he returns. We'll take our lunches, park down by the water. I'll scream at him when he feeds our leftovers to the gulls. He's going to enjoy the stories from L.A. *Kellogg really called the guy an asshole?*

I spent every day with him. Every stupid, stupid day.

It takes me a moment to realize I'm crying.

I wipe my eyes with a pair of folded boxer shorts. And then I move without granting thought to my actions. Three stops in my car. I'm parked against the curb, steeling myself. I'm afraid I won't be strong enough. Mostly, I fear the smaller things: Her little voice will crack, his lip will tremble. And I'm scared of seeing their faces. I know if I start weeping again I won't be able to stop. I knock my forehead into the steering wheel. Two, three times.

In the doorway they fight over the bag. This turns out to be my saving grace: A sternness reverberates through their mother's voice. And suddenly my visit feels like the most natural thing in the world. Once I'm seated on the couch Ginny helps me with my crutches, she kisses me on the mouth and forehead. Before she will allow the kids to open their presents—an art set for Nessa, a battery-powered motorcycle for Ryan—she makes them give me a hug.

"You didn't need to bring anything," says Ginny. "It's enough we get to see you."

She sets out a tray with hot tea and cookies. Nessa is lying tummy-down on the floor, her markers squeaking against the pages of a sketch pad; Ryan is scraping his new toy along the coffee table.

"Well . . ." says Ginny.

She sits in a chair across from me. She brushes invisible crumbs from the front of her shirt, straightens the pleats on her slacks. The skin around her eyes is dark and spokey with lines. Her hair has been pulled away from her face in a messy ponytail—wild, springy pieces bend in every direction like faulty electrical wiring. Settled ominously along the ceiling of my vision, behind Ginny, is a crowded row of condolence cards resting on the fireplace mantel.

"How've you been?" I ask awkwardly, perhaps too soon in the conversation.

"We're surviving. My mother came down from Lexington. That was a big help."

I'm trying to figure an appropriate way to unburden myself. Tell her what I'm thinking. Apologize. But every time I prepare to talk, gathering strength so the words spill out in a stream of sensible emotion, she interrupts me. She wants to know what's happening in *my* life.

"You were terrific on the Kellogg show," she says.

"I saw you!" announces Ryan unexpectedly, looking up from his toy.

"You *did*?"

When we make eye contact he turns shy, cocking his head and thrusting a finger into his mouth. Ginny signals for him to remove it.

"I was watching in my room. I let Ryan come in bed with me; he had a bad dream."

"About foxes," says Ryan.

Ginny shrugs, as if to imply she has no idea where Ryan would've heard such a thing.

"He was a little confused when you appeared," whispers Ginny. "Trip used to tell the kids he took your picture for TV."

Once more, I attempt to offer my thoughts. I let her know how sorry I am. And lonely. But when I begin leading myself toward contrition, she breaks in with a loud call to Nessa. Sustained by purpose, I hadn't noticed the girl scribbling colorful strokes on my leg cast.

"Mom," she says, admiring her handiwork, "you know Kate from my class? She broke her arm. And everyone got to draw things on it."

"That's fine, Ginny." I smile, squeezing Nessa's shoulder. "They're cutting it off in a few hours anyway."

"Can I have it?" asks Nessa.

"I want it," shouts Ryan from the kitchen.

"You don't even know what we're talking about," says Ginny, winking conspiratorially. "And no one gets the cast. It's dirty and smelly. You kids would break that thing into a million crumbly pieces."

When she leans down to retrieve my empty teacup, I mouth the word, "*Smelly?*"

"You should have Kiki draw a picture," says Nessa. "She's

a really great artist. I didn't wash the tattoo on my arm for *three* days."

After another forty minutes, they follow me outside. I take one final pass at my confession. Speaking quickly, as though I'm trying to rid my mouth of a rotten taste, I describe the scene before Trip's death. But Ginny doesn't want the rest. She somehow understands what I've been struggling to say.

"He really liked working with you." She's talking softly, her fingers curled around my wrist. "That's the only thing you need to remember."

I hold her against my chest, afraid if I release her prematurely I may collapse right here in the driveway.

"Stay in touch," she says.

She calls for the kids to wish me goodbye.

As I lower myself in the car, I wave to them. It takes me a few moments to pull away—sliding the crutches into the passenger seat, starting the engine. Through the window I can see the kids tugging on a garden hose. And Ginny's nearby. She's crouched over a flower bed, gathering furry bundles of weeds.

FROM WITHIN THE MURKINESS OF A predawn sky comes the flicker and flash of a strobe. Lightning without sound. I'm standing on my doorstep, dressed in sweatpants and T-shirt to retrieve the morning newspaper. The first thing I think is that a street lamp has expired. When it happens again, I trace the source to a row of decorative hedges across the sidewalk. There's movement, the rustle of an opossum, a

dog. I take three steps forward. A man outfitted with a med-
ley of cameras—one slung across his torso like a beauty contestant's sash, another dangling from his right shoulder and,
lastly, one he's gripping in his hands, aiming in my direction—
separates himself from the shrubbery he's hiding behind.
The flashbulb alights twice more. He's camped out to take pictures of me. I navigate the scored walkway in my bare feet.
Should I feel embarrassed? Angry? I stoop to collect a fistful
of gravel, raising it near my ear in a throwing position. This,
of course, is the worst possible thing. He takes a few more
shots as he backpedals toward a white Pontiac, a rental,
parked down the block. I've given him what he wants, the reason he waited out the empty hours before I arose.

"Get!" I say.

And he does. But not before nodding slightly while
climbing into the car, as though acknowledging the peculiar-
ity of his profession, the situation in which we both find ourselves. Several moments of a shared acceptance that is our
lives. And then a breamy suggestion for what my future holds:
This is how it's going to be, pal. Get used to it.

I watch the tail of his exhaust climb from the pavement
like squiggles of heat. When I look down, my face stares back
at me from the front page of the *Bentleyville Barker*. Though
the photograph was taken yesterday while I was standing
outside WYIP, I don't recall seeing anyone stabbing his camera through the gaps in the wire fencing. The guy probably
snapped it from a great distance, using the telescopic powers
of science. As I make my way back to the apartment, a hand
closes the blousy curtains in the window across the street.

My leg aches. Yesterday Dr. Metzel removed my cast. Because the break was minor, he said it's unlikely I will need extensive therapy. Still, he gave me the name of a physician in New York.

TWIN PLUS SIGNS ARE AIMED UPWARD from the soles of my shoes. They resemble the crossed-out eyes of a cartoon character who's been freshly konked on the head, tweeting birds and blinking stars swirling in a halo. I remember affixing the masking-tape X's to the bottoms of these cap-toes for traction against the slick studio floor. Now the shoes are resting upside down on my taut bedspread, beside my suit-case. I'm trying to decide whether I should remove the tape. I'm fearful I'll be sitting in a network meeting and, as is my custom, I'll pull my right ankle onto my left knee. The last thing I want is for my new colleagues to think they're work-ing with a hayseed. They've probably got skid-free floors in New York. Or a person who's employed to spritz the under-sides of slippery shoes with a light adhesive agent.

I lean against the headboard of the bed, plucking lint from between my toes. I instinctively run my fingers beneath my nose; they smell like grilled cheese.

Though it's early, I can already feel a spider-bite of pain in my lower back. I'm worried about the length of this after-noon's flight. Should it bother me that Yulish hasn't again sent down the private plane? Is this a bad sign?

From the brief glimpse I've had into my new way of life, I can tell the perquisites have intoxicating power. I've already begun to distance myself from my past. Peeling the old masking tape from my shoes, I shudder when I recall the realities of my position at WYIP. No more six-hour car rides, no more box lunches or roadside motor lodges.

I have no idea how long I'll last at the network. I signed a two-year deal. But I presume the novelty of me will have long since worn off by the time my contract expires. Yesterday when I departed from the station, I was nearly overcome by anxiety. Everyone pinning their hopes on me. *Make us proud.* That's a lot of fucking pressure. And the only thing I've done to earn this extravagant promotion is get my ass kicked by a storm.

What if I don't like it there? What if *they* don't like *me*? I have this terrible habit of losing myself in conjecture, allowing the possibilities to turn paralyzing. Lying in bed some nights, I consider the myriad things that can go wrong—from reminding myself to replace the batteries in the handheld microphone to more important stuff, like all that's at stake in my new job.

Years ago, during my first month at Channel 2 in Indiana, I had difficulty sleeping more than four hours a night. I remember carrying around a reporter's notebook in the pocket of my shirt; every time someone made a suggestion—regardless of how small or seemingly insignificant—I'd copy the idea into the pad. But somewhere along the way, I lost sight of my goals. I stopped focusing on trying to please everyone, I stopped focusing on trying to please *anyone.*

Looking back, I know a big part of my ambition disappeared with Flynn. For such a long time it felt as though I had failed at the only thing that truly mattered. And, unlike with work or personal relationships, there was no way to make it right. I fantasize about how my life would look with Flynn around because that's all I can do: pretend.

Walking into the bathroom, I splash cold water on my face. I squeeze a curl of toothpaste against my lip and move it around my mouth. As I prepare to lower myself onto the toilet, I hear a noise at the front door. A short ring, a knock.

Fearful of lingering reporters, I sneak past the window and look through the tiny peephole. It's Kiki. The last time we spoke, she told me she couldn't find anyone to cover her shift. I was planning to stop by the bar on my way to the airport.

"Hey," she says, stepping into the living room.

My refrigerator is nearly empty. I have some Oreos, a jug of mineral water. We split the final root beer.

"What happened?" I ask.

"One of the girls got a babysitter for her kid."

Surely it means something that she's gone to so much trouble to come see me.

"Are you excited?"

"I'm not sure." I take tiny sips from the soda, needing to make it last. I know the bottle is the only thing occupying my hands, keeping me from erupting in a hundred nervous tics. "I guess."

"Come on," she says, slapping her thigh for emphasis. "This is a *dream*."

I nod.

She's wearing a violet blouse, a black knee-length skirt. I think it's the first time I've ever seen her in something besides pants. She walks across the room and examines a weather-systems globe on my bookshelf. She gives it a spin, placing her finger near the bottom and pretending to twirl it like a basketball. Standing over the table, she looks intently at the drawing of me that came in the mail.

"What do you think?" I ask.

"Maybe . . ." She holds down the sides with her fists. "Maybe not."

We both smile.

"Will they give me a ticket for parking on the street?"

She kneels on the couch, pokes her head through the curtains. There's a slit along the pleat of her skirt. Because she's arched in a peculiar way, I can nearly see the skin at her hip. As a child, I remember watching a locomotive in the window of a toy shop. The glass was so crystal-clear I wasn't aware a barrier existed. I reached forward, purposefully, and jammed my wrist.

Similarly, my hand is again operating under its own queer momentum, rising toward Kiki. My fingers make contact with her waist. She seems surprised, but doesn't resist. The two of us spill awkwardly into the arm of the couch. I fumble for space, my elbow nudging a gap along the seam of the backrest. I feel the seat cushion sliding from beneath us. As we sink down, my mouth collides with her chin. We break into laughter. The collar of her shirt is mashed against my nose.

"That was romantic," I say.

Fearing she'll back away, I take her face in my hands. I press my cheek against the cool skin of her neck. I kiss her gently on the mouth. She tastes sweet and citrusy. When my arm brushes innocently across her breast, she moans in a deep, fragile way. It's maybe the most exquisite sound I've ever heard. Her pleasure has everything to do with me, with *us*.

She has threaded her legs between mine. Gazing down, I notice her blouse has come untucked and revealed the smooth slope of her stomach. I run my hand along the inside of her thigh. She breaks into a shallow grin. In the fragmented spears of sunlight, her eyes shimmer like polished stones.

I'm driven by the clean burn of anticipation; I've waited a thousand nights for this. And now, embarrassingly, my erection is tightening the material of my trousers. I'm reminded again of adolescence: I'll need all my powers of concentration—*think* storm fronts; *think* awful, terrible things; *think* of all the people left homeless by the hurricane—to keep from ejaculating a mighty rush of semen. I'm pleading with her telepathically *not* to touch my crotch, even accidentally, or I'm finished.

I catch the zipper of her skirt between my thumb and forefinger. Delicately, as though I'm simply massaging her hip, I ease apart the teeth of the closure. She grabs my arm, pulls it away.

"Whew," she says, fanning herself with her hand. "Let's slow down a little."

I adjust myself so we're facing one another, my back pressed against the base of the couch and hers against the legs of the coffee table. Her blouse is sheer. Sometime during my clumsy movements—petting, tugging, squeezing—Kiki's right breast was sprung free of her brassiere. I can see her areola, a tea stain on the fabric.

I have spent so many evenings watching her body, *this* body, standing beside all those glistening-fang liquor bottles.

Once I remember she wore a western-style shirt with three snaps unfastened. I'd had too much beer. I was also in the midst of an alarming drought of sexual inactivity; my hormones were racing like slot cars. When temptation finally got the better of me, I locked the door of the restroom and masturbated into the sink. I was drunk, light-headed. I was sure the person waiting to take a leak would recognize the smell of bodily fluid—pungent, ammonia-ny. I also worried about what Kiki was thinking.

I kiss her lightly on the eyelids. I roll her into me. We lie silently, her head on my bicep, her buttocks fitted neatly into the well of my waist. We share the same relaxed pattern of breathing. I kiss the back of her neck. I tunnel my hand between her knees, lifting upward in a natural motion until I reach the elastic trim of her underpants. Again, she stops me; she threads her fingers through mine, pulling my wrist against the warm skin of her throat.

We drift in and out of consciousness. Every so often, I glance at a clock mounted near the bookshelf. I'm half hoping we both fall into a hard sleep and I miss my flight. She would rustle me awake, softly calling my name. "Oh, God," she'd say. "It's dark outside." That would be fine. Perfect. We could drive somewhere for dinner. Or bring it home, eat in bed with a bottle of wine.

Instead, she rises and retreats to the bathroom. I stand on the patio, listening to the trees scrub together in a calm breeze—cottonwood, maple, spiky pine. We are both tired. In the kitchen, we hold each other in a metronomic slow dance, shifting our weight on the balls of our feet. Then she watches in amazement as I take several laps around the apartment, double-checking the locks, the appliances.

"You're nuts," she says, shaking her head. "I have *personally* seen you fiddle with the knobs to that oven three times."

"I know, I know. But I can't help myself."

"Sheesh."

We make one stop during our ride to the airport. She waits in the car as I leave the matching halves of my cast behind the screen door at Trip's house. I'm not sure what the kids will do with it. But it's theirs.

Though neither of us says anything about the status of our relationship (acutely defined, as such), it now has a very different feel. I don't sense either of us regrets what just happened. Or what *almost* happened. Except to say I wish we had done this a long time ago. I'm also desperate for a way to erase the physical distance that's about to come between us.

"How soon will you visit?" I ask.

She shrugs.

Until now, I've never been the kind of person to engage in public displays of affection. (Then again, I haven't had that many girlfriends.) But while preparing to board my flight, I bury my hands in the waistband of Kiki's skirt. The two of us kiss, intently. When we're finished, I blink my eyes against the fluorescent lights.

I know people are watching. But I'm not letting it bother me. I'm pretending the attention has nothing to do with who I am; rather, it's simply the regard people would give any pair of lovers preparing to part.

THEY'VE BOOKED ME IN FIRST CLASS. I expose myself as an inexperienced traveler by entering the plane at the absolute worst time: I accept the airline's gracious offer to *pre*board. Thus, I'm seated in the second row, alone, when the remaining passengers shuffle down the aisle. By sheer force of design, it's impossible for an adult of average proportions to move expediently through a commercial jetliner. Every person who pauses in the congestion beside me, awaiting the stowage of carry-ons in overhead compartments, the browsing of bound magazines for in-flight reading and, in certain instances, the painfully slow disrobing and folding of sportcoats, every single one of them turns to face me in slackjawed amazement. The smiling and staring and whispering (I can *hear* you) and gawking become so uncomfortable I surrender to a new pair of welder-style sunglasses given to me by Dr. Metzel for protecting my injured eye. I also shield myself with a newspaper.

At least a half dozen times during the flight passengers wriggle through the red velvet curtain dividing First Class from Coach in order to solicit my signature, most often on the plastic-lined baggie from the front seat-pocket. Not once does the attendant, conceding my frustration, my need for the same degree of privacy afforded other ticket holders—*more*, for chrissakes, I'm in First Class—kindly escort the autograph-seeker back to his seat.

After we've landed, I walk briskly from the arrival gate with the sunglasses perched atop my head; I don't want to miss the Mr. Pibb sign. My driver, Ruben, takes my shoulder bag and together we ride the escalator down to baggage claim. I notice a mark on the toe of my left shoe and try to polish it clean against the calf of my opposite trouser leg. When we reach the bottom I look up . . . and I'm greeted by a scrum of camera-toting (video and photographic) members of the press. Abruptly, reporters, who are also in attendance, start shouting questions; microphones are thrust at me like pikes into a bull.

"Very bad," says Ruben, pressing numbers into his cell phone.

We stand beside the baggage carousel awaiting instruction from whomever Ruben has chosen to call.

When do you start working at N__?

I shrug.

What's the story with you and Tilly Dayton?

I didn't know we had a story.

There are too many of them for me to simply walk away. Ruben has the index finger of his free hand plugged into his other ear. He's nodding. When he's finished, he takes my arm.

"Come."

We reverse our field and jog up the staircase beside the

escalator. They're following us. Our pace increases. When we arrive at security, Ruben reaches into the interior pocket of my suit jacket and presents them with my used ticket.

"He forgot something on the plane," he says. Then, to me, "Wait back at the gate."

I head through the metal detector alone and nearly break into a sprint once I hit the more spacious part of the terminal. When I peer across my shoulder, a flanker welcoming a deep pass, I see the whole group of them standing harmlessly behind the security station. I take a seat, breathless. I wipe perspiration from my forehead with the back of my sleeve. My recently fractured leg is throbbing beneath the stretchy fabric of my sock. Again, people are staring. And much like during my makeout session with Kiki, I'm not certain whether it's because they're trying to place me or because they've just seen a guy without a plane to catch running through the airport.

I wait. For what seems like a long time. (Five autographs.) In truth, only fifteen minutes have elapsed when two men in dark suits and dark neckties bid me to rise. I follow them to one of those mysterious doors in airport terminals that are always locked. This one's not. We descend a staircase and, with the twist of another doorknob, we're on the tarmac surrounded by goddam jets and gasoline trucks and tractors towing stacks of luggage on rollered carts. To our left is a black Lincoln Town Car. I sit in the back as we weave rapidly—faster than I would've expected given our location—through a series of obstacles. It doesn't take long for us to arrive on the bumper of a similar car, in burgundy, parked near the taxi stand with its hazard lights illuminated. My door is suddenly opened. Ruben takes me by the elbow, leads me into the back-seat of the second car. And we're gone.

There's silence except for the thunderous caw of jets rising and sinking—the amplified hacking of a giant oyster of phlegm. We take the Grand Central Parkway to the Triborough Bridge. It's not until we plunge through the tollbooth that I regain my wits.

"Ruben?" I ask, leaning forward. "Who were those men?"

"I don't know, Mr. Lucas." Because I like the way he says my name ("Loo-*Cassss*"), I choose not to correct him. "I was given a number to call if there's trouble."

"Geez," I say, settling again into my seat. "I could get used to having them around."

Ruben smiles uncertainly into the rearview mirror.

Crossing the park at 96th Street, we drive down Columbus until the mid-80s. Arrangements have been made for me to live temporarily in a furnished apartment. Ruben pulls to the curb beside an exclusive-looking building not far from Central Park. The doorman says something to Ruben, then removes my suitcases, magically retrieved, from the trunk. As I prepare to thank Ruben, he reaches into his wallet and withdraws a business card; he underscores his beeper number.

"It won't take me more than twenty minutes to get any-where in the city," he says.

The doorman shows me to my new home, apartment 14K ("K like in king," he says for clarity). He won't accept a gratuity. The place is so immaculate, so pristine, it's difficult to imagine anyone lived here before me. Most impressive is a bank of floor-to-ceiling windows with views of the park. A short terrace outside contains blooming flower boxes, lounge chairs and a wrought-iron patio set.

Anchoring the living room is an L-shaped couch in rust-colored leather. There's also an enormous television (of course) and an antique coffee table with a vase of freshly cut flowers. Awash in muted earth tones, the walls are empty save for a hinged triptych: an artfully blurred black-and-white photograph of the Chrysler Building.

Erupting from the middle of the kitchen floor is a marble island with gas stove, cutting board and auxiliary sink. The brushed-steel refrigerator is the type favored by restaurants. Much of the counter space is occupied—microwave, espresso machine, a row of tinted mason jars filled with coffee beans, lentils and dry pasta. The network must have had someone visit the supermarket, because the cupboards are stocked. (I have booze!) The fridge holds nearly a dozen small plastic containers of prepared foods: lobster salad, marinated asparagus, London broil, globes of mozzarella with fresh basil. Randomly, I check a drawer near the oven and find a cache of sweets. I plug a spear of licorice into the corner of my mouth and wander down the hall.

In what appears to be a broom closet stands a washing machine stacked beneath a dryer. There's also a case of springwater in liter-size bottles. A small second bedroom has been converted into a makeshift office, housing a contemporary-style desk (with shaded lamp), rollered chair and a sleek computer. Against the far wall rests a black-leather love seat.

The master bedroom seems built around a massive bed. I peel back the gray comforter and finger the sheets, new and starchy. A sliding glass door opens onto an extension of the terrace. Hanging from the wall opposite the bed's headboard is another TV—a *screen*—no more than three inches thick. A straight-backed chair sits outside a narrow walk-in closet. The bathroom is bright, high-ceilinged, offering an anticipatory concession to overnight guests with a second sink. Reflected in perpetuity in a mirror-coated wall is a whirlpool bathtub and separate steam-capacity shower with granite bench. I inaugurate the toilet with a long piss, which flushes soundlessly.

A small keypad reminds me of my old neighbor, Hilary. It operates a high-powered ventilation system that rids the atmosphere of unwanted properties such as cigarette smoke and cat hair.

After I methodically unpack my suitcases, aligning shoes, carefully sorting clothing and toiletries because an apartment this spectacular calls for organization and attention to detail, I collapse on the living room couch. The distant sound of sirens and automobile horns serenades me into a restless sleep. When I awaken, the only light I see is the microwave's green digital clock glowing 11:42 p.m.

It takes a few minutes before I master the sequence of remote-control buttons for igniting both the television and cable box. I'm oddly comforted by an image of myself, mid-shrug, standing beside the baggage carousel at La Guardia. The voice-over says something about my arrival in New York to accept a weathercasting position at N__. Over breakfast tomorrow remains the formality of signing my name to a tower of papers. An attorney friend of Gil Vickers has already reviewed my contract.

I watch another hour of TV and eat a container of pasta salad.

BREAKFAST RUNS SMOOTHLY. A GARDEN of suits frames a long mahogany table. There's danish and coffee. When I finish paging through the contract, they make a big show of presenting me with the gold-plated pen I then use to sign my name. The engraving along its barrel reads, WELCOME TO THE N__ FAMILY! In addition, they unveil a life-size poster of me (an artist's rendering) to be hung in the building's lobby amid many of the network's other "high-profile" personalities. I pose with a few executives for a photo op.

Afterward, I'm whisked to a studio for makeup in advance of my interview with Mark Brown. As I'm staring at myself in the mirror, between spheres of intense-wattage lighting designed to show a person in ways he doesn't want to be seen, a woman enters the room and introduces herself as Gitchy Outzen (our first physical contact). She runs through my itinerary for the next few days. The highlights include a meeting with the mayor; brunch with a reporter from *Time* magazine; an introduction to *my* staff; a conversation with a network-employed stylist, who'll begin "building" my TV wardrobe; and a phone call from the White House.

"Gitchy," I say as the makeup artist busies herself with my face. "When you say, 'White House,' I'm assuming you mean *the* White House?"

"That would be correct. Apparently, the First Lady's a big fan."

"Apparently."

Gitchy smiles. Her auburn hair is cut short and stylish, with a pink barrette to hold back her bangs. She has lean eyebrows that warp into right angles during serious moments. Her mouth is small and plump, resembling a pair of sweetly mashed summer cherries; her teeth are endearingly crooked, squeezed together as though transplanted from a larger jaw. She has trim shoulders that mirror the gentle slope of a ketchup bottle.

Having reviewed Mark Brown's questions with a coach, supplied again by the network, I know the "proper" ways in which to respond. Or, more precisely, I know how the viewing audience will *want* me to respond. ("No, no, no," the coach said when I "incorrectly" answered one of the queries during our mock Q&A session. "People don't want to hear that you were *terrified*. [I was.] It's fine to tell them you were afraid. But you're a hero. Don't be *too* afraid.")

Thus, while taping with Mark Brown I convey to viewers that during the storm I was *not* terrified; merely, I was "concerned for my life." Also, when Camera No. 3 is aimed sniper-like across Brown's right shoulder, I reply, in a voice filled both with pathos and confidence, that not a day passes when I don't think about Trip (which is true) and I'm in the process of starting a fund for his family (which *will* be true). Lastly, I tell the people of America—of the *world*—how touched I am by the outpouring of affection and support they've shown in their many cards, letters, e-mails and phone messages.

The following morning I talk to Yulish from the speakerphone in my bathroom. He informs me the overnight ratings for Brown's interview—the "overnights"—were terrific.

"I'm happy for you," I say, rubbing talcum powder across my chest and groin.

Next I dial Kiki, who answers on the fifth ring. She's just returned home from the hardware store; the screen door on the Airstream snapped off its hinges.

"I sat down to study," she says. "The timing was perfect; I finished reading a sentence and—*kabooey!*—the thing somersaults into the dirt."

There's a playful new spirit to our conversations. She's receptive to my flirtations and, sometimes, she gives it right back. But there's still a tiny part of me that doubts her motivation. (Did the distance between us activate my insecurity gland?) I know what she said: It took my death—the *appearance* of my death—to trigger in her these emotions. And I believe that, I really do. I just wonder whether things would be different if she thought I died in, say, a car crash. No storm, no national exposure. No rip-roaring hype machine. Would she feel the same way?

Admittedly, my instincts are dubious when it comes to matters of the heart. Several years after graduate school I worked as a weekend weathercaster in Toledo, Ohio. One Friday, my station manager called me to his office for an assignment: He wanted me to shoot a remote from a local golf club where a young female teaching pro had aced the same parthree twice in five days.

She was trim and pretty, with tan arms that poured down from a sleeveless shirt. Her hair was short, dark. We filmed our interview from a tee box, breaking between questions so I could deliver the coming forecast. She hit balls toward a distant flagstick, the delicate *ting* of her seven-iron reverberating after each shot. But I lacked decorum: I stood behind her, staring at the imprint her panties made against the fabric of her slacks. When it was over—I don't recall the details of our conversation—she revealed a small S-shaped scar on her stomach from a golf-cart accident.

On our second date she took me for a midnight swim in the water hazard on the club's fourteenth hole. As time passed, we seemed to stay together more out of convenience than companionship. We had little in common and for a while I simply figured we'd continue dating until one of us—presumably her—found a better offer. But when I moved to nearby Ebbets to take a job at WEBT Channel 3, a seemingly perfect opportunity for us to separate on pleasant terms, instead, illogically, we got engaged. From start to finish, the whole thing had the temporary feel of two college freshmen thrown together in a lottery of dormitory roommates.

Some nights when I couldn't sleep, I would sit by myself in the darkness of our kitchen. Maybe I would hear her footsteps on the floorboards above me, walking to the bathroom and back to bed. I would shake my head at the absurdity of it all: I'm *married.*

I find that same uncertainty contaminating my relationship with Kiki. I have wanted to be with her for a long time. And now that it seems some of those pieces have fallen into place, I'm filled with doubt.

I know this is *my* problem. I have been alone for many years—even when I was married. I'm attracted to the types of women who don't make sense for me—a golf pro?—or the ones

I can't have; women who are already involved with somebody or, until now, the ones like Kiki who simply are not interested. For the longest time I would leaf through magazines sophomorically and pause over photographs of movie starlets and models; I would imagine what it might be like to sleep with them. Does my sudden celebrity make this fantasy seem more plausible now? Or am I simply raising the stakes of my crush?

I worked my way into Kiki's life, committed myself. I was driven by a belief that we could find a happy rhythm together. This was originally based on little more than cursory observations, a gentle flutter in my stomach. I liked how when she smiled a small, lopsided dimple appeared against her left cheek. I liked the graceful way she moved behind the bar, as though riding on rollers. She's a good talker, quick to laugh. And, before the rest of it, I was attracted to her clean-scrubbed appearance.

But the more time I spent with her, the more I longed for a different intensity to our relationship. We were both alone. (Lonely?) And I couldn't think of a single reason for us not to pursue something else, something with passion. Unfortunately, I also couldn't think of any reason to suggest our romance wouldn't lead to the same dead place I had landed with my ex-wife.

Still, I had to try; I had to know.

I want to trust in us. I need to keep this afloat until I have a better sense of things—the network, the fame, the chasm of real estate between her home and mine. I stare at a food processor on the counter across the room. A store tag is tied to its electrical cord.

RUBEN IS WAITING FOR ME OUTSIDE. He's reading a newspaper against the hood of his car.

"*You*," he announces, holding aloft my picture on the front page of the morning's *Post*. The photograph was taken a few steps into my retreat from the media circus at La Guardia. The accompanying headline reads, *Coming and Going*.

Protruding from the inside windshield of Ruben's car is a notepad attached to glass by a single suction cup. When I lower myself into the backseat, I notice he's scribbled down my itinerary, complete with times and addresses. We fight a brutal river of traffic—it takes twenty minutes to escape the vortex of Columbus Circle.

Since the night of the storm, I haven't done a lick of work for Yulish. Or anyone else. I submit to interviews; I attend cocktail parties, shake hands and pose for photographs. I'm using the breadth of my meteorological training to critique the Weather Channel from my living room.

While heading downtown I tell Ruben to stop at a slick-looking coffee bar; I'm in need of a caffeinated beverage. As I wait for my double latte, I flip through one of New York's countless freebie newspapers. There's a story about a new fitness club and a longer piece on the owner of a hip seafood restaurant too cutely named Soho Koho. After snapping a plastic lid across the mouth of my drink, I turn to leave. But my path to the door is blocked—there's barely room for a single step. I've been here maybe three minutes and, in that time, a small mob of people were inhaled from the street. The group expands to the sidewalk, where a crooked row of faces is pressed against the window of the café.

My heart is racing. *Take a breath*, I tell myself. I glance down at my trembling arm. Steamed milk spurts from a hole in the cup's lid.

An inevitable sense of propriety seizes the crowd. Congratulatory hands collide with my shoulder, my back. A typically strange assortment of items—Styrofoam cups, napkins, a child's plastic fire truck—are surrendered for my pen stroke. In situations like these, I recall hearing Achilles Loeb say it's imperative to establish a momentum that will carry me to my ultimate goal: departure. Each object I accept should draw me closer to the door. (Said Loeb, "*Never* autograph something that sends you in reverse, even if it comes from a teary-eyed orphan kid.")

There's motion to the tangy bodies—armpits, elbows, an innocent hip check. The tops of my shoes are dusty with footprints. "That's the guy from the hurricane," murmurs a random voice. I'm somehow able to contort my way to daylight. An awestruck Ruben pauses momentarily when he sees me, amid the chaos, before plowing forward to take me by the wrist. The crowd backs silently away, forming a large horseshoe around the car. Someone inexplicably asks for the handkerchief sprouting from my breast pocket. Another person pleads for my sunglasses.

Reflexively, I lift the handkerchief from my suitcoat, snapping its wrinkles away against my forearm. I present the tile of cloth to a young woman near the curb. In a calm, measured tone, she asks me to sign it. And I do. The moment my pen clears the fabric, Ruben and I flee—and that's the appropriate term, *flee*. His foot collapses against the gas pedal with such determination, the tires of his car scrub a patch of rubber in front of the great wall of flesh now spilling onto Seventh Avenue.

DURING MY TOUR OF THE NETWORK studios, I'm treated like a visiting dignitary. Several small clusters of people break into spontaneous applause. As we weave our way through a section of newsroom where desks are separated only by chin-high partitions, many of the inhabitants rise to their feet for unimpeded views.

To keep from laughing at all this silly attention—surely some staffers resent my arrival, my Lottolike leap up the network food chain—I stare at Gitchy's cute little ass. The other day I spoke to my friend Vern Morse for the first time since the storm. After we updated each other on our respective lives—mostly mine—he locked on to a single topic.

"Tell me you're not getting laid every night," he said.

"I'm not."

"Puh-*leeeaze*."

"Seriously, Vern. I'm not."

"Well, that's your own goddam fault."

"—"

"Lemme tell you: If I was in your position I'd be nailing everything that moved."

Because of Kiki and the tender nurturing our relationship has required, I haven't given much thought to taking advantage of my new celebrity for the purpose of carnal pleasures. To be sure, I've fantasized about what might be possible: the same testosterone-laden dreams I used to have leafing through fashion magazines. But the whole notion reminds me of the first time my mother let me stay home alone for a weekend. There's a certain way you're *required* to behave: Take the good car out for a spin; drink beer with your buddies; watch as much pornography as your eyes will permit. Eventually, though, you settle back into your normal life. During my conversation with Vern, I get the sense that I have failed him, whiffed on a remarkable opportunity. ("Do it for *me*," I imagine him saying. "Do it for all the guys who'd *kill* to be in your shoes.") What's the best way to tell him I'm looking to bring back a more ordinary rhythm? How can I explain my world when I don't understand it myself?

My office is an orgasm of burnished hardwood: cherry-shelved entertainment center; mahogany desk and circular conference table; rollered cart of split oak supporting rows of videocassette boxes. An illuminated kiosk panel on the corner of my desk allows for the remote-control operation of window shades, hi-fidelity system, TV, video recorder and DVD player. Cognizant of my herniated disc, Yulish demonstrates the manner in which the arm of my new chair rears open on hinges, revealing assorted buttons and knobs that activate a series of massaging motions along the backrest, like lemurs in a sack. There's a great number of weather manuals and meteorology maps artfully arranged on the counter space. When I begin flipping through one of the texts, Yulish raises his arm toward two visitors standing in the doorway.

His words seem half invented, hinged together for effect. Alien and hazardous. They have the impact of a swift-moving locomotive. As I'm left in brief silence to consider what this new information means—the two men who entered the room have been introduced as the "heart" of the network's meteorological department—the blood rushes from my face in a cascade of centrifugal force. I glimpse my reflection in a silver lampshade. I watch myself deflate: My shoulders slump, my chin darts into my clavicle as though magnetized.

I don't know how to respond. My head is purged of extraneous clutter. I permit this concept to tumble through my thoughts, like a phrase repeated on a foreign-language tape. Of significance, it's the two of *them* who're responsible for all weather-related material—forecast, temperature, humidity level, *dew point*—used in network programming.

Sensing my apprehension—or, more appropriately, my panic—Yulish insists they would welcome my participation. (His words dissolve like a sad promise.) He assures me that Ned Shields, the network's longtime weathercaster and my new colleague, takes an active role in forecasting when his schedule permits.

Eventually, I gather the strength to speak. I tell him the whole idea seems unnecessarily deceptive. Why wouldn't they want me to handle my own research? What's the point in hiring me? If they're simply looking for someone to *read* the forecast, I suggest they'd attract more viewers with a blond in a low-cut dress.

A subtle tension fills the room. Yulish smiles, folding his arms against his chest. He tells me to take it easy, relax. In a slow, measured pace, he begins running through the network's reasons for bringing me aboard as though he's marking off boxes on a shopping list. "Viewers can *smell* a phony," he says. It's imperative weathercasters know what they're talking about. Of course, it doesn't hurt that I've got the AMA seal of approval.

Then comes the part I expected: He admits the network is eager to capitalize on my popularity. They expect my presence to provide a residual bump in ratings for their entire roster of programs. "This will make more sense once you get started," he says. "Believe me, you'll have plenty of stuff to fill your time."

I picture myself at schmoozy lunches with sponsors. Fittings for new clothes. (*Mister Prouty's wardrobe provided by . . .*) Traveling for location shoots: to Washington, D.C., for the cherry blossoms; to Churchill Downs for the Kentucky Derby; to Wauwatosa, Wisconsin, for a look at a carousel-size wheel of cheese.

My eyes have turned cathode cloudy. Everything in the room has a muddy blue tint. A smell of burnt almonds comes from a nearby vent. Yulish curls his arm across my shoulder in a chummy, collegial manner. He continues speaking. And I can tell from the rejuvenated motion of the others—Yulish dismissing the pair of meteorologists with his hand, as though scattering mosquitoes—they believe my doubts have been laid suitably to rest.

I escape to my own executive restroom for a few moments alone. I sit on the toilet seat and unwrap a cake of lavender soap, waggling it beneath my nose. (I'm hoping for a scent strong enough to inspire a smelling-salts reaction.) I must root out the terms of this new deal. Are there special laws that govern celebrity?

This final addendum is devastating. They have suggested I swap the *concept* of me for a spectacular job. An apartment. I can trade my name for the best tables at the hippest restaurants, courtside seats to watch the Knicks play at Madison Square Garden. In return, the network will display me like an eight-by-ten photograph mounted above the cash register. They don't care about my work experience, my proficiency in defining various weather fronts. I'm *commodity*. They've leeched themselves to me like those corporations who slap their logos on the hoods of stock cars.

Still unbalanced, I return to my office and sit across the conference table from a pair of network-employed image consultants. They're young, smartly dressed: She's wearing a gray skirt and pale pink blouse with floppy cuffs; he's in a navy suit and candy-striped dress shirt. The woman takes a long swig from a bottle of imported mineral water she stores in a Lycra holster designed to accommodate imported mineral water. Yulish introduces them as publicity sharpshooters who intend to stoke "all things Prouty."

They patronizingly define the term Q-rating, a tool for measuring a celebrity's popularity among his peers. (Unlike, say, the Nielsens, Q-ratings appraise a person's *likability*—the nebulous collection of qualities that make him/her acclaimed.) They inform me, seemingly oblivious to the preposterousness of their statement, that presently the only two people in the U.S. with higher Q-ratings than me are the President and pop singer Courtney Evans.

"And your goal," I say, bubbling with cynicism, "is to move me past the President?"

"Not exactly," says the woman. "But our research shows in the coming months you're likely to lose ground."

"We can only hope."

They don't seem amused. They've built careers out of taking B-list TV personalities and blasting them into public consciousness, wallpapering their faces throughout magazines, newspapers and talk shows until they're *made* recognizable. Human catchphrases. The punch lines to commercials told again and again by your nephew at the family barbecue.

"If I may . . ." says the woman, fanning out several spreadsheets of statistics.

They've conducted a series of tests to determine how the network might benefit from my fame. The words that keep coming, conjoined irritatingly to my surname, are *maximize* and *potential.* Their intention—and the very thought is so frightening I nearly barf out my spleen—is to continue saturating the marketplace with my name, my face, so I become, for all practical purposes, "branded."

"As in Cheerios? Or Budweiser?" I ask.

They smile wistfully.

SITTING ON THE FLOOR, I SPIT OLIVE PITS into an empty plastic container. The rug is littered with wet, mossy stones that missed their mark. My undershirt has scuffs of tomato sauce, hardened squiggles of butterscotch pudding. I take a deep breath, attempting to launch the final olive, uneaten, into the television screen. Instead, it rings off a vase on the coffee table. Reaching over my head, I retrieve a bottle of beer propped between two seat cushions on the couch. I try drinking the rest in a single swallow, but the beer catches funny in my throat. I cough a white shower of foam.

I make no effort to wipe the mess from my lips, my chin. For two days I have remained a prisoner in my apartment. I don't have the strength to answer the phone, letting each call dissolve into voice mail. Though Kiki has tried me a few times, I can't bring myself to tell her about my meeting with Yulish; I'm afraid to reveal the embarrassing details of my new "job."

This is the worst I've felt since being rescued. My self-esteem is brittle, flaking. I look around my apartment, amazed by what it all represents. Most people would be thrilled, goddam bursting with joy. But I can't shake the notion that if my life can change so dramatically, so completely without reason—based on virtually nothing, not a single definable skill—then what's to stop it all from being stolen back in the same speedy fashion?

I need something to occupy my time. Weather maps, radar screens. Storm cells for interpreting. Any monumental change requires a period of adjustment. But the novelty has worn off. My peppermint-sweet intoxication—a blended elixir of praise and wealth—has produced this septic hangover. Now what?

I'm afraid I won't be able to restore my confidence without work, without meaningful connections. I'm drawing into myself. This is the same thing that happened when Flynn died. (Instead of birth announcements we instructed our friends where they could send charitable contributions.) For months, I had trouble holding a conversation. I couldn't bring myself to tell the story, relive the pain.

Similarly, I'm terrified to return Kiki's calls. I don't want to fracture the only true thing I have left. I'm trying to keep her at a reasonable distance until I get my bearings. "Is this fulfilling?" she'll ask, delicately, dangerously. And, of course, she'll already have the answer.

For too long I was convinced I could survive alone. I was scared of reaching out, leaving myself unguarded, vulnerable. But now I feel different. I *do* need the warmth of human contact; I want the weight that comes from sharing my life with another person. Someone to stand beside me, someone to embrace. It sounds painfully obvious—but I've taken such a long time to reach this place. And I don't want to let it go, running through my fingers like a slithery fluid, before I've had the chance to make it work.

I muddle around a little longer. Skimming newspapers, watching TV. When Gitchy arrives, I'm still not dressed. Dark stubble covers my face like an ugly rash. My hair is dirty and limp, resembling thorns of wet fur. I smell stale from perspiration.

"Are you sick?" she asks, waiting for me to wave her inside.

I excuse myself to shower and shave. When I return, she's unpacked some papers for me to sign. She has a splendid mole on her left cheek that looks as though she missed putting the cap back onto an indelible marker. Her neck seems too thin and dainty to accommodate the weight of her head.

She moves with a dancer's studied precision. Leaning across her shoulder to examine the pages, I inhale a whiff of lilac. I decide it's too light for perfume. It could be moisturizing cream or astringent.

I have tuned the TV to a music-video channel for distraction. Oddly, a band called the Five Flannels, comprised of men, nay, *boys*, no older than twenty, is singing *a cappella*-style harmonies. If I close my eyes, the song "Little Angel o' Mine" plays like something from the fifties. I walk into the living room and check the station.

How strange.

Gitchy confirms my sick suspicion: She says the band had been bumbling around small clubs, a gimmicky act, until *my* interest in oldies music sparked what industry experts are calling a doo-wop revival. (Do they *want* me to believe I'm the center of the universe?) Cryptically on cue, the video is replaced by a young woman dressed in a wristband-size dress, who offers that the Five Flannels consider the Teenagers, featuring Frankie Lymon, "one of weatherman Lucas Prouty's favorite bands," their primary influence.

Absurdly, my life resembles a crime scene with grubby-handed interlopers rummaging through my drawers for additional clues. Teams of reporters have been dispatched to Bentleyville and Mill Valley to uncover more—is there more?—of my past. I read recently where one of my grade-school teachers remembers the type of mechanical pencil I favored. And the clerk from a convenience store near my childhood home regaled TV crews with tales of Lyle Teague and I drinking bladder-busting cups of Mountain

Dew and playing Galaga. Even family members have marked their territory: My second cousin Roger, whom I haven't seen since high school, submitted to a six-minute interview on television.

The whorling knots of pain rising through my lower back, prickly and raw, seem as though someone bore a corkscrew into the soft flesh near my love handles. As Gitchy watches, I stretch, I tug. I collapse onto the couch, each tiny movement causing the leather to squeak. This is what it feels like to fall apart. Hairline fissures sprouting along the frail base of a skyscraper until, eventually, determinedly, the negative space overwhelms the positive. Then the whole fucking thing implodes like those controlled demolitions we watch on the six o'clock news.

Stowed in my dop kit is a white-putty cream for the psoriasis on my face; a transparent, toxic-smelling liquid for my scalp; and oblong-shaped pills, powdery to the touch, for back pain. I lie on the Persian rug in the living room; I lift my right knee toward my left rib cage. And so on.

As Gitchy stands over me, reading aloud the details of a party the network's throwing to commemorate my hiring, I stare at her sharp, lean ankles. She has a small butterfly tattoo on the inside of her left calf.

"So, Gitchy," I say, interrupting. "Do you have a little boyfriend?"

"A *little* boyfriend?"

I hadn't meant to sound so condescending.

"Or a big one?"

From the way she contorts the muscles of her face, I

gather she's not interested in talking about her personal life. But she's kind, generous—a real sweetheart. She'd rather proffer the information than risk offending me.

"I'm not sure," she says, breaking into a sly smile. "I mean, I've been dating a guy for almost five weeks. But I've never referred to him as my *boyfriend*."

I can't explain what happens next, other than tendering the obvious: The events of the past few months have damaged my judgment; they've taken their toll. (The other day I had someone from the network's video archives prepare me a tape—"No longer than ninety minutes"—featuring highlights of every Super Bowl. I'm not even a big football fan. After a courier delivered the package, I gave it to my doorman.) As Gitchy informs me reluctantly about her relationship, I turn onto my side. She continues talking, breaking into nervous laughter while providing me with the sketchy details of their last date. But my head is already someplace else. I wonder how she'd react if I crawled across the floor to where she's standing. Maybe my fingers would drum the rug between her feet before rising to caress her calves.

Would she let my hand glide past her knee? I can see us leaning against the coffee table, pressed dangerously together. Would we make it to the kitchen, the bedroom?

More likely, she'd stagger away in shock. She'd probably *trip* over the coffee table. And I'd drown her with apologies. She'd fumble around the room for her briefcase, her purse. I would follow her to the door with even more excuses. I'd call them out during her flustered walk down the hall.

"You were right," I'd say. "I *am* sick."

The elevator doors would seal closed. And I'd listen to the grinding cables, the pulleys, as she descended toward the lobby.

IT SEEMS LIKE A REASONABLE ENOUGH idea. With the phone pressed to my ear, I listen as one ring folds into the next. What would be so wrong with asking Kiki to come *here*?

Her voice is instantaneously comforting. She races through her greeting, anxious to hear where I've been. This must be handled deftly, delicately. The worst thing is to let it all spill from my mouth in a nonsensical stammer. *I'm lonely; alone. I can't even lose myself in the work. (There is no work.) I'm a goddam puppet.*

"I could have another child," I say suddenly, strangely.

"You could."

"I don't mean that the way it sounds." I boost myself onto the kitchen counter. "Not like when a child's pet turtle dies and the parents promise a new one."

"I wasn't thinking that at all."

Then the words tumble out like fallen dominoes, clamoring messily together. It's the exact thing I wanted to avoid. I tell her about my living here, about the network. I admit there's nothing about this life away from Bentleyville—away from *her*—that's how I imagined it.

Still, I can't bring myself to ask her about coming for a visit, for longer. I'm afraid of the truth: She can't simply withdraw from school; she can't leave her friends, her home. It's too soon.

"Let's take it a little slower," she'll say. "Let's give this some time."

I don't think I can wait. Maybe I'm *not* so confused. I need a hand to hold in bed at night.

"I'm not sure this is what I want," I say.

"It doesn't have to be." I hear the *klop-klop* of her boots against the floorboards. "Give yourself a chance."

She has somewhere to go. But she promises to call me tomorrow. I stare at the phone for a long while after we've finished our conversation. It seems like a reasonable enough idea. The two of us. Here or there.

DURING MY FIRST MORNING BACK IN THE office, I watch TV with my feet propped against my desk. I have satisfyingly removed all the green jelly beans from the decorative jar on my windowsill. My broadcast premiere has been delayed until the network feels it's adequately promoted my appearance. Besides running a series of nauseating commercials, they've purchased advertisements in newspapers and magazines. There's even a fifteen-story billboard of me, umbrella in hand, hovering above Times Square. The tag line reads simply, THE WEATHER GUY.

Over the past couple days, I've done my best to elude Gitchy. (I'm embarrassed I even *fantasized* about making a pass at her.) I refuse to answer my phone. Instead, I respond to her messages with awkward voice mails of my own. She's suddenly preoccupied with the details of a senseless party the network insists on throwing to celebrate my arrival. Absurdly, she's in negotiations with the Federal Aviation Administration: She's attempting to "rent" the airspace above a penthouse restaurant, thereby making it criminal for paparazzi to train their lenses from circling helicopters.

My door is closed. My myriad neuroses now include a strict avoidance of the network's *other* weather guy, Ned Shields. I have seen a couple items in tabloid media columns detailing his obvious (and understandable) displeasure with my hiring. One of his assistants refused to acknowledge me as we stood together in the elevator.

I click through a ceaseless jumble of TV channels. Sports highlights, films. Infotainment. The first thing I recognize is a blueberry-pattern throw pillow resting harmlessly beside *Today's Entertainment* anchor Mimi Maxwell. I can feel my sweat glands ignite, running warm and sloppy. The camera pans back to reveal Maxwell's guest, Annie Mobley, a woman who used to be my wife. Years ago, Annie needlepointed the pillow during a cross-country drive we took to her brother's wedding in Yuba City, California.

Even with the salve of time, I can't recall much that was gratifying about our relationship. I enjoyed the sex for a while: She was fit, athletic. Sometimes she'd wear a pair of two-tone golf spikes during lovemaking, digging them into my calves. (Once she broke the skin, causing me to bleed across our bedspread.)

During the lone winter we lived in Ebbets, the water main beneath our block ruptured. For three days our street was a flattened luge run. The police forced everyone to park a quarter mile away. As residents departed for work each morning, I watched them grow more and more frustrated—trudging through the ice-encrusted snow in business suits and loafers, lowering themselves precariously from the curb as not to lose their footing. Naturally, because I was the local weatherman, they somehow blamed me for the inconvenience. I sensed it; I saw them gaze spitefully at our front window as they navigated their way down the sidewalk.

Though I probably imagined most of it, I prayed for warmth. I spent those three days in desperate interpretation of past weather models; I pleaded for a humpbacked front of Gulf Coast air to visit us, returning cars to their respective ports. Maybe Annie felt sorry for me, maybe she only wanted to segregate herself from her meteorologist husband. But on the third morning, a Saturday, she retrieved her old figure skates from the basement. Our neighbors watched as she skated back and forth the length of our block, from Windmere to Murray. Soon, many of them had joined her. The kids constructed makeshift hockey goals from a peach crate and a discarded end table.

I rise from my desk and move to within two feet of the television screen. I'm trying to determine whether it's the lighting or my imagination, but it seems there's a moistness to Annie's eyes. A subtle gloss. My stomach starts to tighten. I've seen this before: It's a popular technique on magazine-style shows where the guest—in this case, Annie—is spoon-fed to recall an emotional moment. She'll fish her fingers into her shirtsleeve for a purposively deposited handkerchief. Or Maxwell will offer a box of Kleenex.

"I swear to God," I say aloud, "if she says a word about Flynn I'll kill her myself."

It's hard to imagine so much distance has passed between us. This woman, my wife. There had been an argument that morning. And, like others before it, I don't remember the cause.

She sat in our kitchen, her hands—awkward, swollen—fumbling with a butter knife and bagel. I was drinking coffee, standing in the doorway to our living room. On TV, a morning news program provided the details of an industrial fire.

Then she said the words that changed our lives, a phrase I have replayed in my head a million times. It took me a moment to decipher her remark; it had come almost in the form of a question.

"You know, Lucas. I don't think I've felt the baby move in a while."

"What do you mean?" I asked, crossing the room to crouch beside her. "How long is *a while*?"

The oxygen left my lungs with urgency. Only a few days earlier, I'd watched a documentary about circus performers. Trapeze artists rely on a protective harness, with cables and pulleys, to keep them from tumbling to earth during training sessions. And that's exactly what we needed in our kitchen: a tethered vest to hold me aloft; a device to support me during this time when my bones and muscles and skin had surrendered to gravity.

"It's still morning," I said, bracing myself against the table. "Maybe you slept through all the baby's movements."

She shrugged. I suddenly noticed her skin was pale and drawn. She had been nervously shredding a paper napkin into thin strips.

"Annie," I said, afraid of what came next. "Do you remember the last time you felt *any* movement?"

She shook her head.

"Yesterday? The day before?"

On our ride to the hospital, it occurred to me that Annie was in shock. She seemed incapable of forming even the most cursory sentences. Pressed to her lap was a stuffed rabbit someone had sent for the baby's room. She continued stroking its white fur vigorously, as if willing it to respond.

Though we had practiced the drive—from our house to the maternity ward—we'd never considered making the trip under these circumstances. The nurse who met us at the door was subdued, professional. She chose her words with caution and economy; she was occupied by process: helping Annie into her gown, preparing for the ultrasound, filling a plastic jug with ice chips.

The tests confirmed what we already knew: Our baby was dead, strangulated by its umbilical cord.

For nearly an hour, Annie pleaded with her physician. She wanted to be anesthetized, have them cut the fetus from her belly like a failed organ. But it was a surgical procedure and, as such, there were associative risks. (It didn't matter, *none* of it mattered. "I hope I die," said Annie, twice.)

What she wanted most was to have the tiny corpse removed from her body. So she finally relented. She allowed them to initiate a "normal" labor. We cried, together and alone. Only a day before, everything was fine—good, even. And now nothing would ever feel the same way again.

In the weeks and months that followed, we did our best to pretend we weren't destroyed, broken into a million pieces. I imagine it's the same when soldiers return from war: They're traumatized. Day after excruciating day we performed simple tasks in a sleepwalker's haze. Every moment, every decision seemed reflexive, as though we were vacant husks powered by a small engine. One morning I dropped three glasses trying to pour myself a drink. I lost count of the times I got into my car and drove around for thirty minutes, an hour, before coming home, empty, having forgotten where I intended on going.

I didn't return to work for twenty-eight days. By then, for all intents and purposes, our marriage had ended—though we lived together for another couple months. We always figured Flynn was going to save us; we believed she would be our tonic, an adhesive.

During my first weeks alone—in a new city, in a new state—I was again overcome by grief. I threw myself into work. At WYIP, I was able to function because they didn't know me yet; I had no history. (Although a great many colleagues wondered why I had made what even charitably couldn't be described as a lateral career move.) But my nights were horrible. Often I would drive the tangled roads outside of town, listening to an oldies station.

I had desperately wanted to be a parent. Surely I had learned from watching my own father's mistakes. I was intent on doing it differently, on being *exceptional* at this one thing. But within a few short months, my life was devastatingly transformed. Reordered. I had gone from being a husband and expectant father to living by myself. I was consumed by guilt: I *must* have done something terribly wrong to lose so much, so soon. For hours I would lie in bed and wonder if maybe I could have prevented this loss. Perhaps the umbilical cord had slithered its way around Flynn's neck when Annie was stooping to retrieve one of my errant shoes. Was it possible this was caused by stress? By our troubled relationship weighing so heavily on Annie's mind?

I continue watching her face flickering from my office television. She wears her hair longer now, cut straight across her shoulders. She looks less severe, softer.

She still hasn't revealed anything of substance. She discusses my eating habits, my fondness for doo-wop music. She even admits respecting my passion for meteorology. As she continues speaking, I focus on a pair of sapphires dangling from her earlobes. In our final days together we got into a nasty fight and Annie removed those earrings, the very ones now winking for the camera, and pressed them into my hand. They'd been a birthday gift. I remember dropping them into a small padded box I use for storing cufflinks and collar stays. The act remains an indelible part of my memory only because I recall looking down and seeing their shallow imprints against my palm. Until now, I have always assumed the earrings were right where I left them. But sometime between the moment I stowed them and the day I moved away, Annie rummaged through my drawers—she never actually saw me hide the earrings—and took them back.

I turn off the television, staring at myself in the smooth black glass. My face looks tired, fleshy. There's no one I can even talk to about Annie's interview. I walk across the room to my desk. The private elements of my life seem anything but private. They're available on TV, in newspapers and websites. The other day my father left me a message, an apology, after speaking to a writer for a national magazine. He admitted it didn't occur to him that he should keep his mouth shut until maybe ten minutes into their discussion. What was his big revelation? He claimed the only time he remembers getting angry with me was when I coated our front steps with maple syrup to attract ants.

In an ironic little two-step, I can't seem to convince Yulish that unlike during my time at WYIP, I'd now *prefer* working in the bowels of the network's meteorology department to being in front of a camera. The suggestion was met with a loud guffaw. "We're looking for *more* ways to get you on TV," he said. "Not less."

His theory on celebrity exposure seems to be that it's better to give the public too much of me than not enough. They're fickle. It won't be long until someone else supplants me as the flavor of the month. Thus, we—I—should take advantage of my popularity. Later, I listen to a business manager named Stuart Blevins describe a host of opportunities for inflating my bank account. He shares a "tremendous" idea for an advertising campaign in which I will shill product while positioned horizontally across a television screen, as though a violent wind has blown me askew. Blevins is so animated, so enthusiastic, I haven't the heart to tell him the biggest hole in his proposal is . . . *there's nothing to sell.* He intends to pitch the *concept* and, presumably, me, to interested sponsors. Snow tires, telephone service providers, honey-baked hams.

"Why not lash a sandwich board across my torso with the words *Your Name Here?*" I ask gloomily.

Other suggestions are equally unnerving. A clothing manufacturer wants me to endorse a line of foul-weather gear. The makers of educational toys are interested in naming a home meteorology kit (ages 8–18) after me. And, most fantastically, the Kaybron Doll Company would like to include a Lucas Prouty action figure in its *RealFolks* collection. "They already make figurines of firefighters, policemen and nurses," says Blevins, trying, preemptively, to reduce my apprehension.

This is a heavy load. I have grown frustrated, dispirited. Most of my time is spent engaged in trivialities. Publicity shots, merchandising. The other day I sat on a soundstage recording a series of voice-overs for local affiliates. The closest I've come to actually forecasting the weather was standing before a chroma-key during the taping of a promotional spot. It seems woefully hypocritical that I used to be the guy who'd make fun of WYIP's anchors for paying more attention to their clothes than to their copy.

I *want* to believe in myself again. To gain back some of my old self-confidence. But I don't know how to make that happen. Sleepless, I lie in bed and wonder what's next. The whole thing reminds me of those vapor maps photographed by satellite cameras. From a place in the heavens, clouds can appear majestic, florid. But pierce them with a weather plane to discover the truth: They're only air, smoky streaks of air.

Most people are satisfied with the illusion. They *count* on it. Yesterday I was listening to a radio discussion about celebrity. (I heard my name six times.) One of the participants, a college professor with an Eastern European accent, said, "The famous live in constant terror. They're afraid of losing whatever unique gifts or talents they possess that turned them into celebrities."

And how about me? I'm only here because of some random act of nature. My "gift," my "talent," never even comes into play. A few days ago, I tried unburdening myself to my mother during a phone conversation. But twice she interrupted to ask me whether I'd speak at a local charity function.

"*Ma*," I responded in disbelief. "I don't have anything to say."

"Nonsense. These folks would pass a kidney stone to hear you."

I need somewhere to turn. I tried Kiki five different times. She will understand. She always knows how to comfort me.

YESTERDAY I SPENT NEARLY AN HOUR IN the drugstore sniffing various shampoos until I found the one Kiki favors. Before going to sleep, I rubbed some into my linens. I played music—Little Anthony, the Crows. I curled into a fetal position, approximating her body by holding pillows between my legs, against my stomach. In the middle of the night I started mumbling; I pleaded with her to move here. The sound of my own voice frightened me awake. After a bowl of cereal, a glass of water, I thought about calling her again.

This afternoon, I'm treating myself to an elaborate lunch. Yet another distraction. I invite Gitchy along as a gesture of goodwill. Earlier in the week, I overheard her complaining to a friend that she needed a new coffee grinder. So I bought her one.

It's not until the end of our meal that Gitchy remembers the envelope. When I read what's inside, I lose the rest of my appetite. (No passion-fruit sorbet, no cheese course.) It seems the handkerchief I gave to that lady on Seventh Avenue is being auctioned on the Internet. More remarkably, the current price is nearly four hundred bucks.

"Tell me that's not the most obscene thing you've ever heard," I challenge Gitchy.

"Pretty close."

Our paths cross by blind (bad) luck. A *Today's Entertainment* film crew waiting outside the restaurant is preparing to tape a segment on chef Chili Hayes. The ugliness arrives with the speed and certainty of a car crash. As Gitchy and I wade through a crowd milling near the doorway, the reporter casts his microphone. I'm tired, dejected. I'm not sure what it means that parts of me are now being sold in cyberspace.

I tell the reporter it's a bad time. But he continues toward me, his arm rising higher, higher. From where I'm standing, it appears the cameraman's already shooting footage. Someone in the crowd screams gleefully to a friend. The next part is fuzzy, muddled. The reporter lurches forward—is he pushed?— and the mic catches me flush on the chin. At nearly the same moment, the camera scrapes me above my injured eye. I should just walk away, hail us a cab. But I'm not feeling very tolerant. (*Today's Entertainment* is the program that dragged my ex-wife into this sideshow.)

Instinctively, I raise my hand for protection. With my palm only inches from the camera's lens, I give a small shove—a fullback's determined stiff-arm. If we leave right now, I'm certain they won't hold me accountable. It was nothing. A safeguard, a gesture.

But I can't seem to make myself move. I'm frozen to the

sidewalk. For weeks I have been lost in chaos: a bitter cock-tail of tumult and sadness. There's also anger, lots of anger. Suddenly my thoughts are superseded by my actions: I'm operating on reflex, on response.

Comes next a displaced momentum that begins at the hinge of my hip. The motion reminds me of those old football drills where linemen deliver a series of quick-hit shivers against a blocking sled. And my forearm strikes the reporter's chest. As with most things now in my life, I have no sense of perspective. Did I hit him hard? (He stumbled back.) Will this seem worse to others?

Almost immediately, I have my answer: The skin on Gitchy's face has gone pale and slack. I feel dizzy, light-headed. "Did you *get* that?" the reporter calls to his camera-man. I'm trying to maintain my balance, keep from pitching face-first into the street. But the only thing available to grab for support is the reporter. And he slaps my hand away because, undoubtedly, he thinks I'm coming for more.

Gitchy and I somehow make it into a cab. I rest my fore-head against the transparent partition between the front seat and back; I dig my fingers into the vinyl upholstery. My scalp starts to tingle. I can feel my sideburns turning damp with perspiration. Neither Gitchy nor I speak for most of the ride. When I press my cheek to the cold window, my breath fogs the glass with wispy clouds—Cirrus, Stratocumulus.

The heel of Gitchy's shoe taps anxiously. She reaches into her purse and removes a Pez candy dispenser. It takes a moment before I realize what she's doing: She holds the toy beside the illuminated photograph of our driver.

"Think they're related?" she asks, trying to make me smile.

Indeed, our driver bears a striking resemblance to cartoon-rooster Foghorn Leghorn.

"That's something," I say.

BY NIGHTFALL, THE VIDEOTAPE OF MY encounter with the TV crew has made its way into heavy rotation. It runs in a slickly edited, Zapruder-like loop that news stations seem fond of displaying thrice, in rapid succession, during each broadcast. Yulish is apoplectic. He meets with network executives, spin doctors.

I'm sent home.

Waiting for me outside my building, they resemble supplicants, their knees pressed against the hard concrete of the sidewalk. Pleading, chanting—their voices loud and strained. *Please*, they call in near unison, shouting my name as I'm spit from Ruben's car. Like a field of locusts comes the reedy buzz of two dozen auto-wind cameras. They're shameless; they will use any kernel of information to gain my attention. ("Lucas, Lucas! Have you spoken to Annie since her interview? Is that what made you so mad?") The lenses and microphones are stacked atop each other, earth to heaven, like a new-age totem.

I push through a typhoon of strobes and mechanical squeals. My apartment is quiet except for the steady purr of the refrigerator. Bereft of the touchstones that once made me whole, I collapse on the couch. Random thoughts enter my head, one after the next, as though I'm peering into the twin eyepieces on a View-Master. Every time the trigger is squeezed, another stamp of film appears. *My home.* (Click.) *A plate of grits, strong coffee.* (Click.) *The neighborhood bar with its softball trophies and dartboard.* (Click.) *And Kiki . . .*

The bathtub is large enough for three adults. I fill it with water, hot as I can stand; I spike a bottle of orange juice with vodka. The steam smells from eucalyptus bathing salts. I sink dangerously deep, permitting the water to rise into the notch of skin beneath my lower lip. The only sounds come from the hall outside my apartment: doors closing, footsteps, the chime of the elevator. When I move, my body causes the great mass of water to slosh and churn. It feels as though a tiny current, an undertow, is tugging me down toward the drain.

Maybe this is a love story, I think. But not the obvious kind. I miss meteorology. I started tracking snowfall records in second grade. I swear to God I have *dreams* about forecasting the weather. I pore through computer printouts I've smuggled from the office: cold-air masses, warm occlusion, pressure gradient forces, stationary fronts. My memo pad at work is filled with meteorology-related doodles. During my lunch with Gitchy, I rambled on about how upper-air patterns affect our climate; I spent twenty minutes describing the differences between a ridge and a trough.

Maybe this is a love story. The *obvious* kind. A boy chasing after a girl. Many nights I have gone to bed spinning imaginary tales of Kiki and me. Picnics on the beach, long drives through the countryside. One week I fantasized about us racing each other in paddleboats. Later, as we stood on the dock at the fairgrounds, her skin turned to vanilla under the moonlight. We shared saucy spare ribs, funnel cakes powdered with confectionery sugar. My favorite part came when I slipped into the same paddleboat behind her, my knees tucked against her thighs.

Three times already I have left soggy footprints in the carpet on my way to retrieve more booze: two vodkas, one scotch. Likewise, the bath has been reheated to welcome each fresh drink. When I lean back to wash the shampoo from my hair, I nearly aspirate a bouquet of soap suds. I surrender to a hacking cough that, consequently, brings tears to my eyes. I grab for a towel, but the tears keep coming. A weeping noise starts in the back of my throat, small and girlish.

By the time I reach the bedroom, I'm crying so furiously I'm short of breath. Naked, wet, I kneel beside the television. My head is clouded by liquor, exhaustion and a gleaning of thoughts from the past few days. I'm filled with an inevitable sense of failure. And I can't make the sadness go away. I flop onto my back. Maybe I'm subconsciously trying to sabotage my career, my relationship with Kiki.

The most fun I've had in years—better than celebrity parties and private plane rides—was the evening Kiki and I spent with Trip's kids. I think about them more than I should. I worry about how they'll get along with only one parent. The other night before I fell asleep a strange notion passed through my head: What if something happens to Ginny? (A car crash, a burst blood vessel in her brain.) But instead of losing myself down another dark hole, I was lifted by the image of Nessa and Ryan coming to live with me. With *us*—Kiki and me.

During our picnic at the drive-in, Ryan climbed onto the hood of my car. We had just finished eating. Kiki and I were packing our things, Nessa was looking at a weather book on my backseat. But Ryan was sitting with his rump pressed against the windshield. He stood the wipers erect, placing his head between the twin T's. Then he shook himself in a controlled rage—it resembled a tiny seizure—and made buzzing noises that sprayed saliva across his outstretched legs. It took a moment before I realized what he was doing. He was pretending the wipers were high-voltage wires; he was electrocuting himself *to life* like a Frankenstein monster. I smiled. It was the kind of thing I might have done as a boy. And it made me long to see what else occurs when he thinks nobody's watching.

Here's what I know: The only thing I truly want I already had. Almost, anyway. A meteorological position where others relied on me; one that required the breadth of my skills. Also, I wasn't far from mining a sweet symbiosis with Kiki. Isn't that enough? Shouldn't there be some way to make a simple thing work?

I'm no longer crying. Instead, I'm staring at swirls of stucco on the ceiling. A starfish, a Buddha. The kind of potbelly stove used for distilling moonshine. The light fixtures have been installed at jagged intervals. From this perspective, it's impossible to find any seams in the drywall. One night last year, my back went out when I grabbed for my wallet at Stinky's. The spasms were so intense I could barely move. Because the floor was filthy, I was permitted to lie on the bar itself. (The place was deserted.) Hanging overhead was a chandelier made from an old wagon wheel. Its spokes, furry with dust, supported a collection of cobwebs. The ceiling was bumpy and blistered. Concentric rings of water damage—rusty, brown—were so abundant they nearly overlapped.

As I pulled my knees gingerly toward my chest, Kiki kept me company. She cleaned the evening's glasses in a sink below my right shoulder. She told me stories about her brother, who was once a rodeo star. And when it turned too late for anything but sleep, she had a cook and busboy carry me to the bed of her pickup. She covered me with a horse quilt and drove me slowly home, careful to avoid potholes and abrupt stops.

Rising to my feet, I strip the bed clean. I remove the triptych from the wall in the living room, tacking the bedsheet on two exposed nail heads. I create more space by sliding the couch against the patio door. Using a black felt-tip marker, I draw a crude outline of the United States; I fill the map's interior with spiked brackets, double-digit numbers, slanted dashes and a clutter of other meteorological symbols. I prop a desk lamp between two phone books, white and yellow. It's now aimed against the droopy sheet. Wearing only a robe and, retrieved from my closet, a sloppily knotted necktie, I stand to one side and begin talking. *Aloud.*

"Today was a beauty," I say. "Unfortunately, we're not likely to have more of this nice weather over the weekend."

I glance over my left shoulder.

"Listen," I say, smiling at a pair of nonexistent news anchors. "I'm only the messenger."

I run my fist across an enlarged parenthesis with nubby teeth.

"This cold front should reach us around midnight." With my fingers spread, I wave my hand in a clockwise motion as though rubbing moisture from my palm. "The drop in temperature will be minimal. Still, the front will bring along some rain."

I push through the remainder of my report: daytime highs and lows, barometric pressure, spore count (for the allergic), moon cycle and five-day forecast. Of course, the information is fabricated. But the data is probably not much different than what Rick Fasco offers on his broadcast six states away.

I wanted to speak the words again, if only to hear how they sounded. I sit on the couch; I stare silently at my wristwatch and wait, exactly nine minutes, for the imaginary anchors to toss the newscast back to me for a final look at tomorrow's weather. On WYIP, I have about five seconds.

"Rain developing after midnight and continuing through most of the weekend. The clouds may start to break on Sunday afternoon."

And I'm done.

Dodging coils of damp towels, I return to the bathroom and drink two glasses of tap water. My face looks bleached, lifeless. Age lines run deep and dark as greasepaint. I brush away a hangnail of flaking skin from between my eyebrows; I scratch my scalp.

Unmoored, I kneel rheumy-eyed before the toilet and empty the contents of my stomach in a sloppy stream. The sickness comes more from anxiety than alcohol. With my cheek pressed against a bale of cold plumbing, I take a deep breath. Another. My nostrils fill with the chemical stink of disinfectant cleanser.

THE ISOLATION IS DEBILITATING. I MISS the camaraderie of my coworkers, the ability to roam the streets without feeling like a curiosity. I'm lonely for human contact. Sitting on the veranda, I turn my chair toward Columbus Avenue. At least I can pretend to belong.

I enjoy watching passersby strolling to dinner, to movies, devoid of their midday haste. They're armed with ice-cream cones and cappuccinos and shopping bags. I squeeze closed my eyes and imagine I'm walking among them, unrecognized. The same as everyone else. I'd buy apples and beef jerky from the Korean market on my corner. Sometimes I even make believe that Kiki has joined me. Our elbows interlocked, we glide to the same pleasant rhythm. Every couple blocks, one of us pauses to look into a store window or listen to a saxophonist playing for change. Later, we split a bottle of wine over dinner, holding hands beneath the restaurant table the entire time.

This is all I have left, my imagination. A dream for a different existence that combines the best of my old life and my new one.

Last night, I finally spoke to Kiki. She sounded as though she surprised herself by answering the phone. She seemed to understand that I needed to talk with somebody, I needed her. She admitted to seeing the video clip of me pushing the reporter; she claimed to hear frustration in the messages I left on her machine. Frustration and despair.

"It's a road bump," she said. "In a couple weeks people won't remember a thing."

Though she tried to offer the same degree of optimism about my job—"Once you're comfortable, I'm sure they'll let you get more involved"—she went quiet when I asked about us. Then she was honest, sincere. Even though we hadn't defined the terms of our relationship, the boundaries, she admitted to feeling confused. What she believes is that I'm interested in the *idea* of her; I'm sold on having a girlfriend in the abstract sense of the word.

"That's not true," I said, watching my chest quiver with each anxious pinch of my heart. It felt like this enormous thing was bounding down a hillside—a sleigh, a rod of smooth timber—and there wasn't any way to slow its velocity. "Would I come to that bar three, four nights a week if I didn't want to be with *you*?"

We waited with our phones pressed against our ears, listening to one another breathe.

"Let's sit with this awhile," she said softly. "See how we feel in a couple weeks."

"I know how I'm going to feel."

And that was it.

Dressed still in my robe and necktie, I'm growing cold. The bedsheet has lost its grip to one of the nails and collapsed into a cotton harpoon. I wrap myself in a blanket, shuffling into the kitchen for warm tea and something sweet. There are cookies, single-serve cups of pudding.

The windows alight behind a chromium sunset. Purple, peach and valentine red. A stack of Altocumulus clouds resemble the rough scales of a fish. I stand before the patio door, blowing into my cup of tea. Clovers of woolly steam kiss the glass. I don't know what I'm looking for. There's a siren, a car horn. The high-pitched scream of a child.

BENTLEYVILLE SETTLES IN MY THOUGHTS. I'm trying to see what I remember. The YIELD sign near the intersection of Dunn and Rawlings that somebody painted with little daisies. Sugar dispensers at Jibby's Diner made from old Coca-Cola bottles. The smell of Prahti's fresh-brewed coffee in the morning. Gentle ocean noises from the park bench where Jefferson Street evaporates into sandy beach.

One summer, WYIP strapped an old photo booth to the back of a flatbed truck. A group of us drove through town, raising money for local charities by posing for pictures. (Five bucks bought you a ribbon of snapshots with your favorite Channel 7 personality.) By day's end, Trip and I couldn't stop giggling; it didn't help that we'd finished a thermos of gin and lemonade. I'm not sure what we found so funny. Everything, I suppose. At one point, I was laughing hard enough to incite a stitch along my left side. I was curled into a ball, slapping my hand against the spare tire. The truck was moving slowly; grinding, burping. As I tried to stand, stretching the cramp away, I tumbled off the back. I could hear Trip roar as I landed in a roadside ditch. I rolled and rolled—the way I'd seen in movies.

It took me a week to realize the spiky pain near my elbow was a thorn of gravel that had lodged itself under my skin during the fall. Within a few days the discomfort was gone; I never had the thing removed. I can still push it around, watch it swim between bone and tendon. I like knowing it's in there, similar to the tip of a broken pencil. Sometimes I'll glance down, unsuspectingly, and it will bring to mind that afternoon with the photo booth. And Trip. If I'm feeling especially nostalgic, like today, it will remind me of home.

NOBODY KNOWS I'M HERE. I HAVE wandered into the forest, camouflaged myself to the human eye. I prop my arm against the trunk of a shiny maple and urinate onto a mound of matted leaves. In the distance, I can hear the *ping-ping* of my rental car's open door.

This morning I took the first flight—the first *series* of flights—into Raleigh-Durham. My brain expands with a modest conceit: I miss my home. Not only my memories of place, but the way it felt to be *in* that place. The rush of adrenaline when I entered the station on a busy day. The earthy smell of fresh-cut peppergrass in the courtyard behind my apartment. I even conjure how the beach looked under a winter's bone-colored sky.

The rest of the ride is easy, uneventful. "Buzz-Buzz-Buzz" by the Hollywood Flames comes on the radio. "Issued as a single for Ebb Records in 1957," I say, calming myself with something familiar. "Bobby (Day) Byrd wrote the song in fifteen minutes."

The car pitches and lisps in the stone driveway. Piled against the house are columns of old newspapers. The porch is crowded with lawn furniture; tatty, worn. A red charcoal grill lies beside a flower bed. In the elongated shadow of the chimney sits a lounge chair with deeply bowed vinyl straps. Several plastic tumblers, once filled with iced tea or lemonade, are capsized in the grass. Slithering lazily from around back is a leaky garden hose.

I peek into a window cut from the front door, but the sun's brilliance makes it difficult to see anything. I knock. I work my way around the side of the house. The yard is empty except for a soccer ball and a large orange Frisbee. Her truck is parked next to the Airstream trailer. From a place above my head, I can hear the squeaking of floorboards in her bedroom.

For a moment, I pretend we live here together. Kiki and me. I'm returning from a long day at work. We'll sit on the lawn out back, split a bottle of beer. She'll remember a funny story from last night at the bar. Then only a chorus of crickets from the dark throat of the woods.

"Hello?" she says.

I take several steps toward the middle of the yard. Against the hard blue sky the house resembles a piece of theatrical scenery. It's as though I could deliver a swift kick and the entire backdrop would crash down around her, stirring a great ring of dust.

"I'm here," I say, waving my arm.

She's leaning out a second-story window. Her hair is smooth and wet, pulled into a tight ponytail. She's wearing a navy V-neck sweater; when she adjusts her elbows against the windowsill, I can see the easy slope of her bosom.

"What're you *doing*?" she asks. We're still in that confusing place where I'm trying to read her emotions. (Is this a good surprise?) As I start to order my response—what *am* I doing?—she raises her index finger. "Hang on; I'm coming down."

I'm not sure what to expect. But when the screen door slaps open, Kiki hurdles the back steps and wraps her arms around my shoulders. The gesture is reflexive, sincere. And it makes the whole burning-long trip from New York seem worthwhile.

As we kiss—short, tender—I can taste the spearmint flavor of her toothpaste. We hold hands, walking to a broken square of sunlight. It occurs to me, thumb rubbing thumb, that this small compulsion—a return home—has erased a dozen uncertain phone calls. Feeling safe is sometimes enough.

My right foot is wriggling with nervous energy. I have punched a divot into the spongy earth; I notice the whine of a faraway chainsaw. I slide my fingers down the back of her neck, gently guiding her head to the warmness of my chest. Our weight shifts easily from one side to the other.

I don't know what comes next.

There's the vinegary scent of an ocean breeze. Her pinkies laced through the loops of my trousers.

"Oh, *look* at him," she says suddenly, chin propped against my arm.

She's staring at a small brown rabbit—probably the same one that's been terrorizing her garden. Slowly, cautiously, Kiki disengages herself from me.

"Don't move," she says.

She takes a tiny step, then another. But when she's nearly upon him, the rabbit leaps away; he races toward the front of the house in a pinball fury. And, less gracefully, Kiki follows.

"Get!" she yells, shaking her fist in mock anger. She once

told me she has her brother's .22 rifle and, if necessary, she'll shoot the damn rabbits—"I'm very protective of my vegetables," she'd said.

When I join her in the driveway, she's out of breath. With her cheek resting against the hood of her truck, she resembles a child napping on a grade school desk. The heel of her boot is hooked to the front bumper. Her lips, moist with saliva, shine like smudged petroleum jelly.

I usher her into the passenger seat. Her keys are dangling from the transmission, fastened to a silver ring that also keeps a penknife and miniature flashlight. The dashboard is cluttered with audiocassettes, notebook paper and a screw-top coffee mug made of rubber and steel. Behind us, she's threaded an old electrical cord across the pegs of a gun rack; clothespins support a greasy ballcap, a hooded sweatshirt. She's wrapped her university identification badge around the rearview mirror.

We drive to a nearby convenience store, filling our basket with beer and snack food—tortilla chips, salsa, glazed donuts and cheese spread that comes packaged in aerosol cans. We lower our windows so we can feel the air against our skin, cool and light and tasting dimly of aluminum.

"This is all rather mysterious," says Kiki, squirting orange cheese the consistency of dish soap into her mouth.

I smile. My middle finger is curled around the neck of a beer bottle. Except for the rush of wind, the truck is quiet as a cathedral. Sometimes you don't need the spectacular to survive, only the ordinary. A simple pleasure that comes from watching someone you care for dribble cheese sauce down her chin.

Even in darkness, these back roads are soothingly familiar. I have order again, purpose. We've been riding for about twenty minutes when we reach a long dirt driveway, hidden by underbrush and a steep canopy of firs. The truck swivels and squeaks on the knobby terrain. The beams from our head-lights resemble a pair of large white antlers.

"Where are we?" asks Kiki.

She has her hands cupped around her eyes to cut the dashboard's glare.

"You'll see . . ."

About a half mile from the road, we reach a chain-link fence; it's crowned with springy coils of razor wire. It takes me a couple tries to remember the combination on the padlock.

"Jesus," says Kiki, following me on foot through the gate. "This is spooky."

There's a small concrete bunker with a corrugated metal roof. Again, I'm slow to recall the numbers necessary to release the door—this lock requires four digits, arranged hori-zontally like the mechanism on a briefcase. When it finally snaps loose, I hit a light switch on the side wall. The room is low and tight. There's an old desk and chair, a computer, a printer, a file cabinet, a small boxy refrigerator and a stack of magazines.

"You know, Lucas, you're starting to worry me."

"It's okay," I say, booting up the computer. "We'll be gone in a few minutes."

Thankfully, I tacked the instructions over the desk dur-ing my first month at Channel 7. I don't think I've been out here more than five or six times. Now that we're both holding still—I'm punching codes into the computer, Kiki's peering over my shoulder—we can hear a steady baritone hum coming from outside. Kiki's eyes have turned wide and expressive. She's crouching down in order to read what I'm typing. After a series of short bleeps, the computer screen goes gray. Then comes a pair of glowing asterisks that push apart to reveal the phrase *Shutting Down for Maintenance.*

As we make our way back outside, I can sense that Kiki is apprehensive. She takes in her surroundings with quick, sweeping glances. I slip my arm around her waist; I kiss her lightly on the neck. But before either of us can speak, the turbulent humming noise starts fading and fading until, finally, it vanishes into a black hole of silence.

Her foot crunches a bank of dried leaves. With my hand resting against the small of her back, I maneuver her up a grassy berm. It's not until we reach the top that we can see the fleecy halo of light.

"Geez," she says.

Rising from the middle of an empty pasture is a steel tower, painted white, supporting a giant incandescent globe. Stenciled in crimson across its side is Channel 7's call letters, WYIP. A small flag fastened to one of the stanchions flaps with the occasional wind gust, like a carp dragged into shallow waters.

"That humming you heard was the radome," I say, pointing toward the pale sphere. "Three hundred *thousand* watts of Doppler power."

We remove our shoes and socks at the concrete base. Though Kiki still seems uncertain—she's moving slowly, her pupils darting nervously into the corners of her eyes—she continues to follow. The crossbars of the ladder are narrow and sharp; they leave indentations on the balls of our feet. In a considered display, I've chosen to scale the tower behind Kiki—presumably, if she stumbles I'll be in position to break her fall. I stare up at her as we near the summit. A sudden mist has crept ashore with the tide, turning Kiki blurry and faint. Our hands squeal against the hollow railing.

A ventilated catwalk encircles the globe like the brim of a tungsten derby. We move carefully to the rear; we sit with our legs dangling over the edge, our arms resting on the lowest rung of a protective fence. I remove two bottles of beer from my back pockets, where they'd been stored neckside down. A tail of foam bends across my knuckles when I twist open the caps.

In the distance, Bentleyville gleams the chronic blue of acetylene. We listen to the slow calls of the season's last katydids. Beside me, Kiki's nibbling on her fingernails.

"You've done this before?" she asks.

"Once," I say, taking a drink. "When I came out here with our technician."

She nods.

I toss back my head against the sky's deep-sea darkness. My limbs are weary, tight. For too long my life has felt illusory. A mighty abstraction. What would make a man embrace so much that wasn't his?

She takes a steady breath, combs her fingers through her hair. From somewhere comes a smell like tangerine. I'm searching for my home among the stipples of light. It seems so far from this place.

There's a permanence to the time between us—the weight of something honest and pure. *Slide closer,* I want to tell her.

12/05- 13 (8/05)